THE EPIC ADVENTURES OF
THE TECHNO WIZARD
PASSAGE TO AVALON

MIKE THAYER

Copyright © 2018 Mike Thayer

All rights reserved, including the right of reproduction in whole or in part in any form.

The characters and events in this book are fictitious. Any similarity to real persons, living or dead, is coincidental and not intended by the author.

ISBN 978-0-9995110-0-8 (Ebook Edition)
ISBN 978-0-9995110-1-5 (Paperback Edition)
ISBN 978-0-9995110-2-2 (Hardback Edition)
ISBN 978-0-9995110-3-9 (Audiobook Edition)

Cover art by Carmine Pucci
Cover design by Deranged Doctor Design
Map art by Renflower Grapx
Editing by Laurie Klaass
Proofreading by Claudette Cruz

Published 2018 by Hooligan Press

Visit www.TheTechnoWizardBooks.com

To my dad

See you tomorrow

PROLOGUE

King Pomeroy of Grahl chewed his thumbnail as he peered out the window at the assembled commoners. The crowd looked calm, but the king was no fool. These days a pleasant smile only served to distract from the knife inching toward your back. It took him and his men nearly a week to extinguish the flames of this little rebellion, but the king knew that underneath the order, underneath the calm, the embers of defiance still burned hot and could reignite with the slightest disturbance.

"Your Majesty," a voice said from behind.

King Pomeroy spun. "What is it *now*?"

"Pardon, sire. Imperial Emissary Larkin has arrived, Sire," the king's steward said, wringing his hands.

The king straightened himself and took an unsteady breath. "Well, don't keep him waiting. Send him in."

The steward hurried away as King Pomeroy paced the room. How was it that the worst news always traveled quickest? The emperor certainly hadn't wasted any time sending one of his imperial goons to check on the state of things. King Pomeroy needed to convince this emissary that everything was under control here in Grahl, even if order hung by a thread. He peeked at the crowd several more times before the emissary appeared at the doorway.

"King Pomeroy," the emissary said, his voice oily smooth. "So good to see you."

"Quit the pretense, Larkin," the king snapped. "We both know why you're here, so let's get it over with."

The emissary flashed a predatory grin as he followed the king out onto the balcony overlooking the crowd. Thousands of pairs of eyes looked up expectantly.

"My loyal subjects," the king addressed the crowd with a well-practiced smile. "We are privileged to be joined this day by an imperial emissary. During his stay in Grahl, he is a representative of the divine emperor, and should be treated with no less respect than we would give the emperor himself." The words tasted like bile in the king's mouth. Lowering himself to the emperor was one thing, but showing deference to this weasel in front of his own people set King Pomeroy's blood to boil.

"Citizens of Grahl." Emissary Larkin walked past the king to the edge of the balcony. "I am pleased to hear that the missing aether tax was at last returned, and that humility and reason have prevailed. The emperor was concerned—"

"The emperor can go to the void!" someone yelled from the crowd. A small knife zipped through the air and embedded itself in the balcony railing, not two yards to Larkin's right. The emissary turned to the king and raised an eyebrow.

"To the void!" more people yelled as bottles, tools, and sharp objects flew at them from the crowd. The king was ready now and held up his hand, blocking the projectiles with an invisible shield of aether. He had enough power to stop the objects, but he wouldn't be able to forcibly calm a mob of thousands. How dare they rebel again? They couldn't win here. What did they have to gain by provoking the emperor's ire?

"Are these the orderly and obedient subjects that I heard so much about," Larkin motioned to the crowd, "or is there another crowd you wish to show me?"

"What would you know of ruling a kingdom?" the king demanded through gritted teeth. "You tell the emperor that my kingdom will be the paragon of imperial order within the week."

"Tell him yourself," Larkin said as he turned and left the balcony.

Confused, the king followed the emissary with his eyes. His blood ran cold. Standing at the entrance to the balcony was the emperor himself. Before the king could drop to a knee, the emperor walked to the balcony's edge, held out his hand, and gestured downward. The entire congregation fell silent as they dropped to their knees, pressed down to the ground by the emperor's unrivaled power.

"Your Eminence, I can explain—" The king's words were cut short as he too fell to the ground, subdued as if he were no more than an aetherless peasant. King Pomeroy tried to push back with his own aether, but only felt his power drain away the moment he used it. The whole city stayed in silence, forced to bow down before their emperor, forced to realize that their ruler would either have their obedience, or he would take it. After what seemed like hours, the emperor released his hold, turned, and walked away without a word. Nobody dared to move. Not even the king.

"As you can probably tell, Your Majesty," Larkin returned to the king's side, leaning close to his ear, "the emperor has just expended a significant amount of power to restore order to your kingdom. Strange things have been known to occur with such a spike in aether usage. Do let us know if you see something... odd, will you?"

1
HAPPY BIRTHDAY

It wasn't every day that Sam carried around a vial of barf-flavored powder in his pocket. But today wasn't any old day at Rock Valley Middle School. Today was the second Thursday of the month. For Sam, Rinni, and Lawrence, today was prank day.

"You sure this is gonna work?" Sam spoke into his earpiece. He glanced at the cracked screen of his smartphone, which he concealed against the face of a library tablet.

"A bit late to be asking that question, don't you think?" Rinni replied over the channel in his mild Indian accent. Sam could hear the whir of the 3-D printers in the background, confirming Rinni was in position on the other side of the library.

"My questions are never late, nor are they early. I ask them precisely when I mean to."

Rinni groaned. "That is the most forced Gandalf quote I have ever heard."

"No such thing," Sam replied. He glanced over his tablet at their unsuspecting target. Mrs. Blaggham, the school librarian, sat at her desk, her long, decorated fingernails prying open a Tupperware container of her usual egg salad.

Sam fingered the glass vial in his pocket and took a deep breath. A good prank was an art form, a well-coordinated dance. One misstep and it could end in disaster.

"Okay, waiting on you, hot shot," Rinni said.

"What are you talking about?" Sam whispered, looking back down at his phone. "I'm waiting on Lawrence. He still isn't in position."

"He's been there for like a minute, dude."

Sam tapped his phone, but the tracking app with Lawrence's location didn't respond. His stomach dropped. "Piece of junk! Phone's frozen again. If this prank goes up in smoke because of this outdated, busted-up phone—"

"Hey, Sam," Rinni's voice cut in.

"What?" Sam hissed back.

"Lawrence is headed your way. I think we've been compromised."

"What do you mean, *headed my way?*" Sam said, looking over his shoulder. "He's supposed to distract Blaggham from over by the touchscreen tables—"

Panic backhanded him across the face like a WWE wrestler. There was Lawrence, standing beside the vice principal, sheepishly pointing in Sam's direction.

"Well…poop."

Sam's mom stared forward as she drove. She wore her navy-colored company polo shirt and still smelled strongly of massage oils. It didn't take Sherlock Holmes to see that she'd left in the middle of a job. Waiting for her to start talking was always torture. Sam called it the "eye of the hurricane." The chaos of getting caught was behind him, the punishment was still to come, but for now he could only suffer in the unnerving silence. The "eye" was the worst.

"Before you do these things, do you ever stop to consider the harmful effects of your decisions?" Sam's mom finally spoke, her jaw tense.

"I guess I'm just an eternal optimist, Mom."

Sam's mom flipped the car into self-drive and slowly turned in his direction with that intense look reserved only for irate mothers and grumpy cat memes. She looked fit to throttle Sam, which was particularly terrifying since her job as a massage therapist gave her the grip strength of Thor. "Is this part of your joke too? Having your mother leave work early, miss out on clients? This is funny to you?"

"Dad liked my pranks," Sam mumbled.

Sam's mother drew in a sharp breath and paused. "What your father *liked* was for you and me to be happy. Do I look happy to you right now? You need to think beyond the punch line of your pranks, mister. You need to think about what effect you have on the people who have to clean up your messes."

"I technically didn't even do anything. The vice principal just has it out for me. He way overreacted."

"I would agree…if this hadn't been the *fourth* time this year. Somehow I doubt that the vomit powder you had in your pocket was for Mrs. Blaggham's benefit." Sam's mom ran her hands through her hair. "I need you to stop, Sam."

Sam sighed and looked at his shoes. He hated seeing that exasperated look on his mom's face. These things had always been easier with his dad. He didn't feel like he had to apologize to his father, let alone lay it on extra thick to speed along the scolding. It was like his dad just…understood. For the last two years, Sam had been missing more than just a parent. He had been missing his greatest ally.

"Sorry, Mom," Sam said, looking out the window.

"I want you to *show* me sorry, not just tell me. Understand?"

Sam nodded. The car rounded the corner and slowed automatically as they entered Sam's neighborhood. Modest, one-story houses flanked the road, separated by low chain-link fences. Their street, usually teaming with activity, was still. He'd lived on Centennial Drive his entire life, but whenever he got sent home early, he couldn't help the weird feeling that, although this was his home, he only belonged here at certain hours of the day and any deviation from that schedule was out of place.

"And Sam."

"Yeah, Mom?"

His mom reached back for her purse and removed a small rectangular box, tossing it on Sam's lap. "Happy birthday."

2

A GEEK, A NERD, AND A DORK

Sam, Rinni, and Lawrence sat in Sam's basement on a worn-out leather couch, chowing down on bowls of vanilla ice cream and warm chocolate brownies. While getting sent home early from school usually didn't end in a party, all punishments for the boys had mercifully been put on hold in honor of Sam's birthday.

"So, what's the big surprise?" Lawrence asked, stuffing his face with a forkful of brownie.

"You guys ready for this?" Sam said, barely able to contain his excitement. He reached into his pocket and withdrew a brand-new phone.

"No way. The Ziptalk Apollo," Rinni said, eyes wide in amazement. There was a hint of jealousy in Rinni's voice, making the moment all the sweeter for Sam. Rinni's dad was a software company executive, which made it almost impossible to get something cool before he did...*almost*.

"Yes way," Sam replied, brandishing his gift. When it came to phones and tablets, the Ziptalk Apollo was in a class all its own. Shatterproof, shockproof, waterproof, and solar-powered. It was closer to a tricorder from Star Trek than it was to a phone. It could be used for anything from playing games while on the toilet to conducting ultrasounds on pregnant women in remote, impoverished countries. There was even one viral video where a guy claimed it could be used as low-grade body armor and shot one with a .22 rifle to prove it. It could have been fake, but it seemed legit. The add-ons, apps, compatible devices, and features offered near endless possibilities.

"Which voice assistant are you going to choose?" Rinni asked, craning his neck to get a better view of the phone.

Sam went into the settings and started scrolling through the hundreds of pre-loaded voice assistant personalities. There was everything from Iron Man's Jarvis to Cortana from the *Halo* games. Rumor was that the Apollo's voice assistants had borderline artificial intelligence and would evolve their behavior over time based on your questions, location, search history, pictures, and videos. Sam didn't know whether to be geeked out or freaked out.

"There are too many awesome ones to choose from," Sam said.

"Just choose one, man," Rinni pressed.

Sam shrugged, flicked his finger across the screen, and tapped on a name at random. "Heinrich Schneider?" Sam paused. "Who in the fart is Heinrich Schneider?"

Rinni shrugged, but Lawrence nodded emphatically before speaking. "Neither of you guys have heard of the Hein? The mastermind detective? He was like the most popular character on German TV from 2020 to 2027."

"Wow," Rinni said. "I think we have a new front runner for 'worthless and obscure information that Lawrence knows.' And that's saying something."

Sam selected his voice assistant and quickly read the instructions.

"Yo Heinrich. This is Sam Shelton, master of this phone. Recognize my voice."

"Guten Tag, Sam Shelton," his phone replied in a slightly

robotic German accent. "Would you like me to reveal the many features of your new phone?"

"I'm good for now, but maybe later."

"You know where to find me," Heinrich replied.

"I've got to hold it. Can I hold it?" Lawrence asked, his expression like a puppy's begging for a treat.

"Lawrence," Sam said, raising an eyebrow.

"Uh, yeah?"

"You seen that video where the guy runs over one of these with a monster truck and it doesn't put a scratch on it?"

"Yeeesss," Lawrence drew out the word.

"I still don't feel safe handing you my phone. Consider it punishment for botching the prank today." Sam leaned over and slugged Lawrence in the arm.

"Oh, come *on*." Lawrence flinched backward and rubbed his shoulder while Rinni laughed at the familiar scene. Shorter than most, rounder than most, and more awkward than most, Lawrence's only real talents were knowing worthless trivia and finding himself at the butt of every joke and the owner of every mishap.

If Sam was being honest, however, it wasn't Lawrence's chronic misfortune that made Sam reluctant to hand over his Apollo. Even though the phone was essentially bulletproof, Sam felt uneasy trusting *anybody* with his present. Not only was it the most expensive thing he'd ever owned, but he had no idea how his mom had ponied up the cash to get it in the first place. It was almost *too* nice of a gift, but maybe that was the point. Like getting an unsolicited favor from some slick-haired mobster, Sam was unwittingly in his mother's debt. Sam's mom: mob boss of the Guilt Mafia.

"So, my friend," Rinni said, greedily rubbing his hands together. "Have you tried the projector or the language translator? Did you get the hologram generator add-on? Tell me you got the hologram generator add-on."

"Whoa there, Rinni." Sam laughed. Life was just one big

computer game to Rinni…literally at times. By the end of last summer, he managed to crack the world leaderboard in the battle strategy game, *Warcraft of Empires*. Most parents would be furious. His actually took him out to celebrate. "Let me send a text from this thing before I jump into the night vision, ultrasonics, and Taser functions, would you?"

"Wait. It has a *Taser* function?" Lawrence asked, looking from Sam to Rinni.

Sam and Rinni both looked at Lawrence with twin flat expressions. "No," they said in unison.

"Sam," Rinni said, taking another bite of brownie and gesturing with his fork, "we need to take this bad boy for a spin. See what it can do."

"What do you have in mind?"

"Let's do what we've always wanted to do," Rinni said, grinning ear to ear.

"Eat a half gallon of ice cream using only Oreos for spoons?" Lawrence asked.

"No." Rinni rolled his eyes. "I'm talking about hitting the vice principal's house."

Sam drew in a breath. It was the ultimate mark. The lair of their archnemesis. They'd tossed around the idea as a possibility for more than a year now, like one would toss around the possibility of asking Tandi Myers to dance, or the possibility of taking Rinni's dad's Porsche for a joyride. The prospect sounded epic, but when it came down to it, no one had the guts.

"Man," Sam said, shifting in his seat. "I don't know."

"What's this?" Rinni said in mock surprise. "The infamous Samwise Shelton is backing down from an adventure?"

Sam hated it when people used his full first name, or at least when they were using it to mock him. It was an absurd name, Sam would readily admit that, but he was proud of his geek heritage. Sam's grandparents actually didn't know a hobbit hole from a wormhole, but Sam's father was a child of the late '90s and when Peter Jackson's *Lord of the Rings* trilogy came out, his life was changed forever. At least Sam's dad had exercised some restraint when it came to naming his son. Sam could've ended up as a Frodo, or Bilbo, or Gandalf. Sam probably had his mom to thank for that. Despite getting teased sometimes, he was proud to have the name. Being a fantasy geek was something that he could always share with his dad, something that he could remember him by.

Sam, Rinni, and Lawrence: the geek, the nerd, and the dork.

"So, what'll it be, Mr. Shelton?" Rinni coaxed.

"Dude, we're all on probation," Sam stressed. "My mom would *kill* me. Your parents would *kill* you. Lawrence's parents would…be glad he got the exercise."

"Hey!"

"Sorry." Sam chuckled. "Look, Rinni. You think my mom's going to let me keep my phone if she finds out I used it to pull a prank on the vice principal…like four hours after she gave it to me? I'd like to hang on to this thing for more than one evening, thank you very much."

"I brought my gear," Rinni said.

Sam was about to take another bite of brownie but stopped short. "Listening."

"And you can use it," Rinni said enticingly.

"How much of it?"

"All of it." Rinni flashed a confident grin.

Sam paused, contemplating. "Probation's overrated," he finally said as he shoved the last of his brownie into his mouth, pocketed his phone, and headed for the door.

3
ON SHAKY GROUND

It was late evening. Sam crouched behind a well-manicured shrub and sifted through Rinni's black tactical backpack. It was like instantly leveling up a character in a video game and gaining access to all the unlockables. Earpieces, nano cameras, listening devices, long-range voice recorders, and more. He had to physically restrain himself from giggling with joy. The bag had a ridiculous amount of pockets and compartments, and not a single one went unused. The thing must have weighed fifty pounds. Sam reached into a side pocket and fished out a hard case that contained his favorite bit of gear: a pair of angular heads-up display goggles that the boys called the "HUD specs."

He snuck a peek through the shrubs at the vice principal's house. Only a few outside lights were on. A faint light flickered through one of the ground-floor windows, the telltale sign of someone watching TV. Sam turned back around and readied the final bits of gear he'd need for the night: a mini drone with quick-release latch, a piece of string with a small pouch, and an egg. He donned the HUD specs and synched them to his phone with a tap of the screen. Numbers and letters popped up in the corners of Sam's field of view, telling him everything from his heartbeat to the exact position of their trio. Sam felt like Iron Man.

Sam tapped his phone again and his earpiece went live.

"Come in Gold Leader, Mundungus, this is Gardener."

"Gardener, this is Gold Leader." Rinni's voice pattern scribbled across the corner of Sam's HUD.

"Mundungus?" Lawrence's voice came over the channel. "Why do I have to be Mundungus?"

"Sorry, man. Already programmed it into my phone. You almost ready with that camera?"

"Give me a second," Lawrence grumbled, obviously not thrilled with Sam's choice of call sign. "Try it now."

Sam looked at his phone and saw a new device icon appear. He pressed the image and a video feed popped into view on his HUD, showing the dimly lit solar-powered battery bank on the side of the vice principal's house. "Sweet."

A moment later, Rinni came into the picture, sneaking up to the battery bank as if it were a sleeping pit bull. With smooth, practiced movements, Rinni reached around the back of the battery bank and disconnected the main power feed to the house. All the lights went out.

Sam touched his goggles and his darkened surroundings came to life, bathed in the fluorescent green lines of night vision. He turned on the drone, and with a mechanical whirr, the mini quadcopter took to the night sky, its egg cargo dangling a foot below. With the drone's video feed patched into the HUD specs, Sam expertly maneuvered the drone into position, some fifty feet above the house battery. He panned the camera down to look directly beneath the quadcopter. He'd only have one shot at this.

The back door burst open and Sam jumped at the noise, almost dropping his phone. He peered through the bushes to see the vice principal, dressed in his pajamas, stalk toward the side of the house with his cell phone flashlight held out in front of him.

"Target coming into position," Rinni whispered.

"Target acquired," Sam replied.

"Camera rolling," Lawrence added.

"Gardener," Rinni said, "release package at will."

Sam eyed the feed from the drone and saw the vice principal come into position at the battery. This was it. No turning back now. With a tap on his phone, Sam watched the egg fall away into the darkness toward its unwitting target. Before it landed, a miracle happened. The kind of miracle that reaffirms one's faith in the prank gods. The vice principal looked up.

With a *splat* and a string of curses, the vice principal wiped frantically at his face. He looked down at his egg-coated hands and froze, his rage approaching critical mass.

"You rotten, pestering, little twerps!" the vice principal bellowed in the night. "I know you're here somewhere."

"Uh-oh." Sam enabled the auto-return on his drone and began packing his gear.

"Guys," Lawrence whispered sharply. "He's headed right for me. I think he sees me."

"Mundungus. Do *not* move!" Rinni commanded. "He can't see you. Just stay put."

"What should I do?" Lawrence's voice grew more panicked.

"I just *told* you what to do," Rinni hissed. "Stay put."

"I'm gonna make a break for it."

"Mother Hubbard," Sam cursed as he saw Lawrence's GPS marker start to move…in *his* direction. Before Sam could run, he heard a deep rumble like the approaching of a far-off thunderstorm. Sam looked to the sky for signs of lightning but saw nothing. Then the ground began to shake. Windows and streetlights rattled as the shaking intensified. Car alarms set off like a street-long firework, blaring into the night air. Sam rocked back and forth as if he were standing on a paddleboard in the middle of a lake before falling to his hands and knees.

"Holy boogers," Sam yelled into his com. "It's an earthquake!"

"What do I do?" screamed Lawrence. Sam could hear his friend's voice from across the yard even without his earpiece. "I'm scared, guys. What do I do?"

"Just get on the ground, man," Rinni called out.

Sam didn't have much of a choice. He curled into a ball and threw his hands over his head. As the rumbling grew louder, an odd sensation washed over him. It was an explosion of chills that started in his gut and radiated out through his organs, muscles, and skin before reversing its course and flowing backward into his core. The wave of chills overtook him again, pulsing outward like an army of a thousand frozen ants escaping from his stomach, only to return a moment later.

"Uh, guys," Sam said, "I feel funny."

"Yeah, it's a farting earthquake." Rinni's voice was hardly audible over the din of the quake.

The weird sensation repeated again and again, quickening with each successive flow. Sam curled in tighter, clutching at his chest. Something was seriously wrong, and it wasn't just the earthquake. His vision faded to black. He tore off his goggles, but still saw nothing. Voices came in over his earpiece, but he couldn't make them out. His heart hammered, his breathing quickened. He didn't feel the shaking anymore. The last thing he remembered was wondering if the earthquake had suddenly stopped.

4
TASTE OF DIRT

Sam didn't like the taste of dirt—not that he knew anyone who actually did. Tasting dirt was a sign that something hadn't gone according to plan: you dropped your food on the ground, you tripped and face-planted, or some bully was rubbing your face in the grass. Sam couldn't recall if any of those applied to his current situation; he just knew that something hadn't gone according to plan, because there he was, tasting dirt.

He turned his head and spit several times before opening his eyes. It was daytime. He was lying on the ground…ground that wasn't moving. He sat up slowly and looked around. A snow-topped mountain range surrounded him on three sides with a forest's edge not far away to his left. The air was crisp and fresh and reminded him of the time he spent with the scouts at Glacier National Park. The scenery was as breathtaking as it was puzzling, since the last thing he remembered was being outside his vice principal's house in Bozeman at night, trying to ride out an earthquake.

He heard voices and turned around to see two figures, some

ten yards away, rooting through Rinni's black tactical backpack. A pair of brown and white horses stood off to the side.

"Hey," Sam yelled out reflexively, coming to his feet. "What do you think you're doing?"

The two men turned in Sam's direction and he immediately wished he was back facedown tasting dirt, although something told him he might get his wish. The men looked like a pair of Renaissance festival peasants, if the peasants had lost their way in the forest for about three months. They flashed humorless smiles with a combined number of teeth that fell well short of a single complete set. Sam's stomach twisted, and he hoped to heavens these guys were just really dedicated cosplayers.

"Uh, scratch that," Sam relented. "Carry on with the, uh, rummaging. I'll just be on my way."

"Be on your way?" one of the men mocked, in what Sam figured was a British accent. The man's voice was squeaky and discordant, as if someone had just strangled a dog toy. Sam suppressed a gasp at the stranger's appearance. One of the man's eyes was bright yellow, with a small vertical pupil, as if he'd stolen the thing from a house cat. Sam thought it might be a trick contact lens, but aside from the wrong color, the eye was also the wrong size. "You can't be leaving already. We've been waiting for you to wake up this whole time, my friend. Haven't had a chance to properly introduce ourselves, you see. I'm Reynold, and my companion here is Gurn."

Sam had never felt so anxious in his entire life; not when Sheriff Tirrell caught him putting a dry ice bomb in the Pineview Park drop toilet, not when he forgot his only line as Mopsy in the school play of *Peter Rabbit*, not even when he mixed up his valentine cards in fourth grade and mistakenly confessed his love to Kami Robertson. Devastating as they were, none of them had carried the underlying threat of mortal danger. This was different. Sam didn't know where he was, who these men were, or what they wanted. All he knew was that they were looking at him like a mountain lion eyes a stray fawn.

Despite his best efforts to stay calm, he felt his legs start to tremble.

"Don't be shy, boy-o," Gurn said, his voice like the deep croak of a bullfrog. "Just want you to explain these curiosities in your bag here, friend."

"Just hold on a second there," Sam said, hands raised and slowly backpedaling toward the tree line. If he needed to make a break for it, the nearby woods would be his best chance of escape. "If this is some kind of prank for getting the vice principal with that egg, I give up. I'll even turn over the video files. They're saved on the drone. I was just streaming them to my specs. I seriously don't care. You got me. Fair and square."

"What's he going on about?" Gurn turned to his partner, confused.

"I'd say he's stalling." Reynold smiled as the two men inched forward, matching Sam's slow retreat.

Gurn reached into Sam's pack and removed a black tactical flashlight. At first, Sam thought the man was wearing one brown glove, but at second glance, Sam could've sworn that the man's fully functional hand looked like it was made of wood.

"So what's this thing do?" Gurn said, shaking the flashlight experimentally.

Sam stopped and cocked an eyebrow. He looked around, half-expecting his friends to pop out from behind cover with cameras live streaming. "Seriously?"

"Don't you get smart with us, boy," Reynold said, squinting his cat eye and jabbing a short club in Sam's general direction.

Sam hadn't seen Reynold pull the club. He swallowed hard, as confused now as he was terrified. "It's a flashlight, guys."

"It's a what?" Gurn croaked, his fat face scrunched.

"Oh, come on," Sam said, his anxiety fading at the absurdity. "You guys are putting me on. Rinni? Lawrence? I don't know where you got these two jokers, but you got your money's worth."

"Jokers?" Reynold squawked. His darkened expression

brought back every ounce of Sam's fear. "You wanna see a joke, you little twit?"

Reynold nodded to Gurn, who starting walking quickly toward Sam. Sam bolted toward the trees, not daring to turn around, not knowing if at any moment he would be seized from behind. He hadn't gone ten steps before he tripped and fell onto his face. Before he could stand back up, he felt a strong hand grab him by the arm and yank him to his feet.

"Where you off to in such a hurry, boy-o?" Gurn asked, breathing heavily.

Sam almost gagged at the rot of the man's breath. He looked down to see Gurn's wooden hand locked around his arm like a vise. Sam panicked. He tried to pull away, but Gurn's grip was unshakable. He had to do something. He had to get away. He didn't know what to do…and then he felt it: a cold tingling where Gurn's wooden hand gripped his arm. It was similar to the sensation he felt before he passed out, if not to a much lesser degree. Was it happening again? He didn't like how it felt and instinctively tried to suppress the sensation. When he did, Gurn screamed and fell backwards. Sam looked down at his arm and saw the bandit's disembodied wooden hand still holding on like the world's most morbid armband. He looked at Gurn, who sat up and stared dumbly at his own right arm, which now ended in a smooth, handless stump.

"This has got to be a dream," Sam whispered to himself. But it didn't feel like a dream. To his mind, yes, but to his senses, no.

"What in Mother Aether happened here?" Reynold asked as he finally caught up to his partner. "Gurn, your blazing hand's gone."

"I know me blazing hand's gone," Gurn wailed as he scrambled away from Sam. "Little whelp must be some kind of drainer or something."

Reynold's cat eye went wide as he looked from his partner to Sam.

"Uh, that's right…I'm a drainer." Sam held out his palm as

threateningly as he could. Sam had no idea what just happened, but he decided to roll with it. "I'll drain you too if you get any closer."

Gurn scrambled to his feet to stand next to Reynold. The two thugs took several steps backward before stopping; their eyes darted to the ground. Sam stole a quick glance and finally noticed what he tripped on. A black knapsack lay in the dirt not a yard in front of him.

Reynold started forward, but Gurn grabbed him with his one remaining hand. "It ain't worth it, mate. You *just* got that eye. Don't wanna lose it like me hand. Leave the knapsack be."

"Don't know what you are, kid," Reynold squinted his contrasting eyes and jabbed a finger in Sam's direction, "but I know some folks who'd be interested to find out. Next time you see us, we'll take *your* hand as payment. Mark my words, you little whelp."

Reynold glared at Sam a moment longer before Gurn pulled him away. Sam stood, dumbfounded, as he watched the thugs mount their horses and make their way down the trail.

Sam bent over, hands on his knees, and took slow, deep breaths. It was all he could do not to faint. He reached over and tried to pry the wooden hand from off his arm, but it wouldn't budge. Several minutes passed before he could stop from shaking.

"At least they're gone now…with Rinni's friggin backpack! Hey, get back here!" Sam yelled, before thinking better of it. Losing the pack was a small price to pay for escaping with his life, although there was a good chance that *Rinni* would murder him when he found out the pack was stolen. Catch twenty-two. There was at least forty grand worth of gear in that pack. Sam was a good friend to Rinni, but not forty grand good. Sam's wallet was also in that pack, although the joke was on the thieves with that one. Seven bucks, a school ID, and an Arby's coupon weren't much of a steal.

Sam patted himself down to see if Reynold and Gurn

hadn't picked him completely clean while he was out cold. He checked his jacket and breathed a sigh of relief when found his phone still in his inside pocket. Sam reached up and plucked out his earpiece. They hadn't taken that either, although he doubted those buffoons would've even noticed. Didn't appear broken, but it definitely didn't have any signal to Rinni or Lawrence. Sam stashed it in his jacket for safekeeping. He bent down and picked up the knapsack that the thugs had left behind. Turnabout being fair play and all, he opened it up and rummaged through its contents. A knife, some old, ratty clothes, a few copper coins he didn't recognize, and a length of rope. Not exactly a stellar tradeoff for forty thousand dollars' worth of tech.

Sam stopped and looked around again at the surrounding mountains. "Where in Merlin's beard am I?" Other questions flooded his mind as he stared blankly at the countryside. *What's a "drainer?" Did that guy really have a cat eye? And where is the nearest Chick-fil-A?* He was starving. Lucky for Sam, most of life's questions could be answered with his phone. All a man needed was his phone. Well…that and free Wi-Fi.

5
WILLOW

Sam took out his phone to check the time. Oct 24, 2032 at 10:30 a.m., the morning after his birthday. Nothing seemed amiss in that regard.

"Yo, Heinrich, where am I?" Sam asked his phone.

"Guten Tag, Sam. I cannot confirm your current location, as I do not have a signal," Sam's phone said in a pleasant German accent.

"No signal? What is this, 2020? What's my last known location, then?"

"Before losing signal at nine twenty-four p.m. last night, you were thirty-one miles northeast of Te Anau, New Zealand."

"New Zealand?" Sam scoffed at the news. "Cutting-edge tech my stinky socks. Must've glitched out during the earthquake."

Sam shook his phone—his universal first attempt at fixing anything electronic. His phone probably didn't know what to do with itself without a signal. The double-edged sword of getting something too advanced was that it typically relied on other advancements for it to actually work. "Gone are the days where you could just pop in a video game and start playing the blasted thing," Sam's father used to lament every time a new game required some terabyte update prior to playing.

New Zealand was on the other side of the *planet*. Even if he hadn't spent his entire night blacked out for who knows what reason, he couldn't have gotten to New Zealand this quickly. And yet, the impressive landscape did look rather...New Zealandy.

Sam needed to get a signal so he could find out where he was and call for help. Sitting on this valley floor probably wasn't helping much. He'd have to gain some elevation. He also needed to get out of the open. Reynold and Gurn could come back, or, heaven forbid, someone worse could come along. Sam slung the knapsack over his shoulder and made for the nearby woods.

There was no trail where he entered the forest, just tall moss-covered trees and spongy earth. He set a brisk pace, checking over his shoulder every few minutes. He pried at the creepy wooden hand as he walked, but made no progress in loosening its grip. Several times, he stopped and listened closely after hearing what he could swear were footsteps. He'd spent enough time in the outdoors, though, to know that even a seemingly quiet forest was full of moving creatures. There was always something on the prowl.

After an hour, he stopped and pulled out his phone.

"Yo, Heinrich, you get any signal yet?"

"I have not received a signal since we last spoke, Sam."

Sam kicked a nearby tree. "Gal dang it! Worthless thing."

"Are you referring to *me*, Sam?" Heinrich asked. "Please do not judge my value on my ability to access a non-existent network."

"Well, you're not exactly much help at the moment," Sam replied, finding it a bit ridiculous to argue with his phone. "Can you at least point me in the right direction from where I last had signal? Which direction is home?"

"From where you last had signal, home would be to the

northeast."

Sam looked up through a break in the trees to orient himself with the sun. He turned slightly to the left and continued walking. The direction was as good as any and it was still uphill, which was the important part. Apparently, he still needed to get higher to get a signal.

"Don't go that way," a voice said from behind.

Sam spun around. "Who's there? Who said that?"

"Don't ever go that way." The voice was close, but Sam still couldn't see anyone among the trees. It sounded like a young girl, but had a stilted cadence and accent that Sam had never heard before.

Sam pocketed his phone and nervously turned from side to side. "Come out nice and slow."

There was a playful giggle and movement to his right. Sam blinked hard as a small human-shaped silhouette peeled itself away from the forest, solidifying into a person…or at least, kind of a person. Standing not five feet in front of him was what looked to be a nine-year-old girl, if nine-year-old girls had textured tree bark skin, braided vine hair, leaf clothing, and eyes of pure amber.

"Holy boogers!" Sam stumbled backward and tripped over a large rock. He rummaged around on the forest floor for a weapon before grabbing a discarded tree branch. He waved it back and forth—leaves rustling—in a comic display of self-defense. Sam shook his head and blinked hard several times. This all felt too real to be a dream. And yet, what else could it be? The clash between senses and logic made his head spin.

The strange tree girl laughed again. "I am sorry to scare you."

"Stay back. I'm warning you." Sam scrambled to his feet and shook the branch again.

"You are funny," the tree girl said as she walked forward and playfully tapped on the branch with her finger. At her touch, the branch came to life, writhing in Sam's hand like a python.

Sam yelled and dropped the branch. "What do you want from me?"

The girl smiled wide, her amber eyes squinting. "I would like to be your friend."

Sam stopped. "You what now?"

The tree girl's face fell, and she jutted out her bottom wooden lip. "You don't want to be my friend?"

Sam had no idea how to respond. This girl, this creature, had been completely camouflaged. If she meant Sam harm, she could've easily done it. "No, no. I didn't say that. We can be friends."

The girl's smile immediately returned. "Oh, that is good news. I have waited for the right friend for so long."

"And, uh, what exactly...sorry, *who* exactly are you?"

The tree girl playfully cocked her head to one side. "Why, I am a Nartareen, of course."

"A Nartareen," Sam repeated.

The Nartareen nodded her head enthusiastically.

"Alright," Sam drew out the word, "and do you have a name?"

"Yes, it is a most beautiful name in my language."

"Let's hear it."

The tree girl made a croaking groan that sounded like a mash-up of an angry crow and an overstressed two-by-four.

Sam raised an eyebrow. "Not exactly Elvish."

"In your language, it means 'skin of the tree,' or tree bark."

Sam scrunched his face. "I'm not calling you Tree Bark."

"You will give me a name, then?" the tree girl asked, her amber eyes wide.

"Why not?" Sam wasn't sure why he was humoring her, but she seemed friendly and he was in short supply of friends at the moment. "I'm Sam, and how about we call you...I don't know...something to do with trees. Twig, Leaf, Oak, Willow."

"Willow," the tree girl said emphatically, clasping her hands together with a wooden *CLACK*. "Oh, thank you, friend Sam. I have never had a human friend before."

"And I have never had a...tree friend before." Sam had so many questions, he hardly even knew where to begin. With how nonsensical the day had started, it was only logical that he might start getting answers by talking to a sentient tree. "Now that we're friends, I was wondering if you could help me."

Willow nodded her head eagerly.

"You said you knew where we were."

"Yes."

"Can you tell me?"

"Yes."

Sam rolled his eyes. "Willow, where are we?"

"Vale of the Edgemont," she said with a satisfied grin.

"And where is that?"

"The northern border of the Sea Peaks."

"And where's *that*?"

"In the south isle of Avalon."

"Did you say Avalon?"

"Yes, friend Sam. The south isle of Avalon."

"Avalon, like the resting place of King Arthur? The place where Merlin got Excalibur? That Avalon?"

Willow stared blankly back at Sam. "These are strange names. I know of no Merblin."

"It's Merlin," Sam corrected. Willow just continued to stare back at Sam. "You know what, never mind. How about those men who took my bag? Did you at least see them?"

"Oh yes. I see all the men that come this way. Travelers, traders, hunters, thieves, bandits. I have seen them all," Willow leaned in close to whisper, "but they have never seen me."

"So you saw what happened, then?" Sam asked, tapping on the wooden hand attached to his arm.

"I most certainly did. I have never seen someone drain the aether out of a grafted hand before. It was a delightful plan." Willow smiled and gently clapped her hands together.

"Plan?"

"Oh yes, I saw what you did, friend Sam. Very sneaky to trick the men to grab you so that you could drain their aether." Willow nodded and gave a mechanical wink.

"Willow, I'll be honest with you," Sam shook his head, "I didn't have a plan. I don't really know what's going on. One moment I was at home with my friends, and the next thing I know, I wake up in a mountain valley facing off against two magic-wielding thugs…and now I'm friends with a tree. I don't know where I am or what a drainer is, and I want to either wake up or go home. *And* I have this creepy wooden hand stuck on my arm to top it off."

Willow stood there a moment, as still as the trees that surrounded her. "That is a very odd story, friend Sam."

Sam sighed. This was going nowhere. He pulled out his phone and checked for signal. Nothing.

"You need to get a better oracle, friend Sam," Willow said, pointing at his phone.

"A what?"

"Your oracle, Heinrich. I saw you ask him a question and he gave you wrong knowledge. You do not want to go in the direction you were going. A very nasty place is in that direction."

"Oh, this is just my phone, Willow," Sam said. Willow stared back blankly. "It's my phone. My pho—never mind. Yes, it's my oracle. Heinrich is an all-knowing, techno-magic oracle."

"He does not seem all-knowing."

Sam held his phone above his head and started walking in an erratic pattern. "He's taking a nap, Willow."

"Friend Sam," Willow said, looking on.

"What?" Sam replied, staring at his phone as he continued walking.

"What are you doing?"

"I'm looking for a signal."

"What does it look like? I will help look for this signal."

"You can't see this kind of signal, Willow."

Willow paused. "That is a very odd kind of signal."

Sam stopped, put his phone down, and stared at Willow. How could this be real? How could *any* of this be real? He needed to do something. He couldn't just stand here all day talking to a tree. If only he had his stupid backpack. Well, technically it was Rinni's stupid backpack, but whatever. There were still at least two nano drones in that thing. He could've sent them off to scout the area and find out where he was and what direction he needed to go. There were countless other gadgets in that bag that would come in handy in a pinch, and by the looks of it, he was in one epic pinch. He needed to get that backpack back.

"Willow, did you say you saw which direction those two men ran? You don't happen to know what town they might be headed toward, would you?"

"Oh, yes. I think I do."

"Well?"

"You do not want to go that way, either. In fact, I suggest that we actually run in the other direction."

"And why is that, Willow?"

"Friend Sam, you drained the fat man of so much aether that he lost his grafted hand. That is a very rare thing. Word will spread of this. The emperor will come. The emperor will want to meet you."

"The *emperor?*" Sam asked.

"The one who rules the race of men. He will want you dead."

"What?" Sam shook his head. "I thought you just said he wanted to *meet* me."

"He will want to meet you so he can make you dead, friend Sam."

"Willow, I need to get my bag back." Sam didn't know how much to believe this strange Nartareen, but he did know how badly he needed to retrieve Rinni's pack.

"Oh no. You have little time. We must go to Ogland. I see

much, hear much, you see? I know secrets," Willow drew in close to Sam and whispered. "Some people fight against the emperor. Some of them gather in Ogland, in secret. They are the Mavericks. They will help you."

Could he really just abandon the pack and follow the advice of this strange tree girl? However odd she was, Sam was in an unfamiliar place and she was the only help he had. And what would happen if he went after his pack and actually found it? He was lucky to get away with his life the last time. Sam needed to find another human, preferably one that wasn't trying to rob him or kill him. If Willow could help Sam with that, then following her might be worth it. He just wished he knew for sure that he could trust her.

"Willow, why are you even helping me?"

Willow's wooden lips widened into a smile. "Because like all young Nartareen, I have been tasked to watch these woods for strange things, and you are the strangest thing I have ever seen. The other Nartareen will be jealous that I have found a drainer like you. I have seen nasty Reynold and foul Gurn many times, and they almost always get their way, but not today. I also think that you are cute."

"There's that word again...wait, what?" Sam blushed. He hadn't had a lot of experience with compliments from girls, especially one with tree bark for skin. Sam quickly changed the subject. "So, what's this aether you keep mentioning...and what's a drainer supposed to be, anyway?"

Willow stared blankly back at Sam. "Friend Sam, unless you have been hibernating since you were a baby—like the screeching bark beetle—then I do not know how you do not know these things. There is much I do not know, but I know that you are not a screeching bark beetle." Willow turned on her rooty-toes and walked south. "I will explain on the way to Ogland."

6
THE ORACLE

Willow followed no path as she led the way through an endless forest of moss-covered trees. The ground was soft and without much undergrowth, which made for easy walking, except for the persistent incline. Sam's legs were on fire. Tree people, as Sam soon found out, didn't really get tired. Willow didn't move quickly—although Sam didn't doubt that she could—she simply kept the same steady rhythm, step after step. Sam's stomach grumbled and he checked his phone: 1:47 p.m. They had been walking for the better part of three hours. Sam strained to remember the last time he'd walked for three *minutes*. Scouts maybe...back when his dad was around.

Just like inexplicably waking up in a strange world of mountains, magical thugs, and tree people, two years ago, Sam had gone to sleep one night and unexpectedly woken up in a very changed world. His father had also fallen asleep that night; he just never woke back up. That tends to happen when you're driving eighty miles per hour on a Montana highway. However odd the reasoning, maybe his father's death was why Sam took his current predicament in stride. He was used to living in a world that didn't make sense, in a world where he was very much alone.

Sam trudged forward, following Willow through the forest as the trees became thicker and thicker.

"You sure this is the right way?" Sam asked, crouching under a low-lying branch.

"This is the right way," Willow said, reaching out a finger and tapping a branch that blocked her path. When she did, the branch magically curled back, opening the way forward.

"Okay, you need to explain to me how you're doing that." He had tried asking Willow several questions on the way, but she had always claimed to be busy "talking to the trees" which, apparently, she did by placing her hand on a tree every so often and meditating for ten seconds. "Willow, you need to understand that I'm not from here. Back where I come from, we don't have drainers and aether, and we don't have talking trees. You gotta help me understand what's going on here."

"I don't know how you would get here if you were not from here, but I will explain all the same, as if you were a dumb sapling child. Aether, you see, is the breath of life. All living things collect and consume it; non-living things can become a living thing with it." She tapped another thin branch and it curled back like the first.

Sam walked up to the branch. "And that's what you did just now?"

"Yes, friend Sam. I gave life to the tree branch. I gave it aether. It is mine now, or at least until someone else makes it theirs."

"And how do they do *that?*"

"First they have to use some of their aether to get rid of my aether. That returns the thing to normal."

Sam examined the bent branch, mesmerized by the seemingly simple and yet utterly impossible act. *This has to be a dream.* The thought echoed again and again in his mind, but he knew it wasn't true. His muscles wouldn't ache and his clothes wouldn't be drenched in sweat if this were all a dream.

"Cool," Sam said, tentatively reaching out and touching the branch with a finger. As soon as he did, the branch whipped forward and smacked Sam across the face. "Ow!"

"Or if someone drains it," Willow added, looking on. "Draining removes the aether quite well."

"Thanks," Sam said, rubbing his nose. He apparently didn't have complete control of his draining powers yet. Things worked differently here, and if he ever wanted to make it back to his precious Montana, he got the feeling that he'd better figure out just how those things worked.

"After an object is drained of its aether, it only takes a little to control it." Willow reached over and tapped Gurn's wooden hand. When she did, the curled fingers straightened and the hand fell to the ground.

"Hey," Sam said, rubbing his arm where the hand had been.

"Oh, I am sorry, friend Sam. Do want me to put it back on?"

"No, I don't want you to put it back on. You could've done that this entire time?"

"I thought you might be wearing it as a symbol of your victory." Willow shrugged.

Sam rolled his eyes. "So, why can't I do that? Why can't I make tree branches move and wooden hands creepily come to life?"

"Aether works differently for different beings, friend Sam. The Nartareen can use it differently than humans and humans differently from others. Those with much aether can do even more things, sometimes strange things. There are very few that cannot hold aether and aether cannot hold them. It runs from their touch."

"People like me. So, are there others?" Sam picked up the wooden hand for inspection.

"I hear men tell many stories. Stories of the League of

Cowboys, or even the Musketeer Guild from long ago. But even these men do not repel aether like you do."

Cowboys and musketeers? Maybe Sam wasn't so far from home after all. He *had* to get to the nearest town or get cell signal and figure out just where on Earth he was and what was going on.

"So, why am I like this, Willow? What makes me different from you...uh, other than not being a tree and all?"

Willow scrunched her wooden features. "I am very smart, friend Sam, but I do not know this. Someone in Ogland may know."

"And that's why you say this emperor guy will be coming after me? Because I'm a special drainer? Why would he care so much?"

"Because aether is *all* he cares about. He will kill for aether. He forces all the people of Avalon to give him most of their aether. He does not like drainers. His great power does not work on them, you see? They could also drain him of his power. You are a threat to him."

A threat? Sam was hardly a threat to the vice principal of a middle school when he was trying his darnedest, how could he be a threat to a wizard-*emperor*?

"You know, Willow, I would be more than happy to just simply make my way back home. No need for anyone to hunt me down or anything. Speaking of which," Sam said, glancing around, "should we be worried about this emperor guy finding us here in the woods?"

"My friends have covered our trail for now," Willow said, gently patting a tree. "But I do believe that the emperor will not stop until he finds you, friend Sam."

"So I've been told. How far is it to this Ogland?" He appreciated what Willow was doing, but he was looking forward to talking with another human to see if he couldn't give the Nartareen's claims a bit of context.

"With your soft human legs," Willow said, sizing him up, "we will not arrive before the sun reaches its peak tomorrow."

Sam groaned. He didn't know if he was more put off by being told he had soft legs, or the realization that he was going to have to spend a night out in the woods with nothing but the clothes on his back. Sam's stomach growled.

"You don't have anything to eat, do you? I mean, for a human, that is. Last time I ate was brownies and ice cream in my basement."

Before Sam could finish his sentence, Willow's hand was extended, offering him what looked to be a dozen or so brightly mottled raspberries. "Eat."

Sam warily took the handful of berries and examined them. "What are they?"

"These are opal berries," Willow said, as if expecting him to recognize the food now that she said the name. When Sam's expression didn't change, she continued. "They can be hard to find for humans, but everyone knows of them. Very rich in aether, which is wasted on you, but they are still good food."

Sam popped the berries into his mouth. "Not bad." They were surprisingly tasty, like a mix of raspberry, strawberry, and blueberry.

"Is your oracle hungry as well?"

"My what? Oh, no," Sam said, taking his phone out of his pocket. "I've got him on a very strict 'sunlight only' diet. No berries today."

"Oh," Willow said, her wooden eyebrows rising. "You are a very harsh taskmaster, friend Sam."

"If there's one thing I'm *not*, it's a…" Sam trailed off as he checked the time on his phone.

"What is it?" Willow asked. "Did your oracle wake up?"

"You could say that," Sam said, staring at his screen. He had twenty-one unread text messages.

7
TEXTS

"Did you find the signal, friend Sam?" Willow asked.

"Dadgumit. When did I get these?" Sam held his cell in the air. "No, Willow, I don't have the signal."

"Then what is it?"

"Just a few messages from my techno-oracle," Sam said, thumbing through his texts. Most of them were from his mom.

Sam, where are you?

Sam, where are you? Need to know if you're OK.

Thanks for checking up on your mother after an EARTHQUAKE. I'm fine, BTW. NOW would be a good time to get back to your mother.

Call me immediately. This is a very very very bad time to be pulling one of your pranks.

Sam, I'm getting worried. Are you injured somewhere? I spoke with Rinni's parents. Rinni says he doesn't know where you or Lawrence are. What is going on?

This isn't funny. You call me right now, Samwise!

I'm not mad. I just want you home. The town is in chaos. Please come home.

Lawrence's parents have called the police. Sam, what is going on?

Her other messages were a similar mix of threats and pleas. Sam's stomach twisted into a knot of guilt. He had nothing to do with being transported to Avalon, but he *had* been outside when the quake hit. If he'd never gone out to pull his prank, this might not have happened. His mom did have a tendency to overreact, but in this case, her worry was justified. Her son was missing after an earthquake, and now the police were involved. Sam had only ever had his mischief escalate to "police level" twice before. Untangling that knot was always an order of magnitude more difficult than a simple trip to the principal's office. *What is this about Lawrence being gone as well? Is he in this weird place, too?* Sam's stomach wrung even tighter. This place was dangerous. There were thugs and tree people and supposedly an evil emperor. Lawrence couldn't last an afternoon in Scout camp, let alone whatever this place was.

"Willow," Sam asked, trying to hide his growing anxiety. "You sure you only saw one kid like me in the last little while? Your fellow Nartareens didn't happen to see anybody else? Not a, uh, rounder kid than me? Blond hair, that hangs over his eyes?"

Willow looked quizzically back at Sam. "No, friend Sam. I have not."

"Any of your…friends see him, by chance?" Sam asked, gesturing to the surrounding trees. Sam wasn't sure if that was how it even worked, but he was getting desperate.

"I have not heard of anyone else," Willow confirmed. "Is there someone else like you here?"

"Maybe," Sam mumbled, looking down at his other messages. Most of the rest were from Rinni.

Dude, you OK? That was CRAZY!

Who knew there were even earthquakes in Montana?! I mean, I did, but that's because I'm a genius.

Dude, where are you? Rushing home to check on my parents. They'll be looking for us so I'm skipping the post-prank meeting place.

Sam, What The Fart! You and Lawrence never came back?! UR killing me! R U with Lawrence? I just woke up and had to cover for the fact that we were out last night. Lawrence hasn't texted me back either. I don't like lying, man.

Stupid time to make your mom worry, man. Now I'm getting worried.

I just checked my master tracker. Says my gear is in flippin New Zealand??? I've been searching online to see if your new phone even has the power to mess with my GPS like that. Not funny, man.

So Lawrence was definitely gone as well, and it wasn't just some malfunction in Sam's phone that caused it to show him as being in New Zealand. Rinni's GPS master tracker had independently tracked his gear to the same spot. The odds were very slim that both Sam's phone and Rinni's tracker would both be wrong together. Of course, the odds that Sam could get knocked unconscious in Montana and wake up in New Zealand the next morning were…well, zero. None of this made sense.

"Are you okay?" Willow asked. "You appear troubled."

"Just confused, is all," Sam said, massaging his temples. "Yo, Heinrich. When did I get these messages?"

"Guten Tag, Sam. You received these messages one hour

and seventeen minutes ago, after acquiring a one-bar signal for three seconds."

Sam was an idiot. He still had his phone on silent from when he was running the prank last night. He hadn't even bothered turning on the volume. "Yo, Heinrich, set an alarm to play next time I get a signal of any kind. And make sure I know when I get another text, please."

"As you wish. If you don't have any preference for an alarm, I will choose a tone based on my research of your preferences."

"Knock yourself out."

This whole thing just kept getting worse and worse. He desperately needed to get a hold of his mom and Rinni. Perhaps even more urgently, he needed to find Lawrence. The folks back at home would be worried, but at least they weren't in any danger. Sam needed to get a signal, and he needed to talk to anybody that may have seen Lawrence, neither of which would be found sitting here in the woods.

"Alright, Willow. Time to get my soft legs moving," Sam said, stretching.

"I am happy to hear that. We Nartareen have a saying: 'What stays in one place will one day grow roots.'"

Sam raised an eyebrow. "Are you trying to say that my breaks are too long?"

"Oh yes, friend Sam." Willow nodded. "I am certain that is how your legs have become so soft."

Sam looked up the mountainous incline and took a deep breath. "A *tree* is telling me I don't get enough exercise. Even considering everything that has recently happened, that is still a very low moment."

"You are funny." Willow giggled. "Come, come."

8
OGLAND

As Willow predicted, it was just after noon the following day when Ogland came into view, visible through a break in the forest. Sam had never seen anything quite like it, at least not in person. He looked down at the town, nestled at the edge of a long lake, and felt like he'd been transported back in time a thousand years. Any expectation of finding a paved road, cell phone tower, or even just electricity, was hopelessly dashed. From what he could see, it was a moderate-sized, medieval-era town, complete with meandering narrow streets, a high turreted stone wall, several watchtowers, and sprawling surrounding farmland.

"Huh," Sam managed, rubbing his forehead.

"Are you not happy to see Ogland? I would have thought from your heavy breathing and slowed pace that you would be more excited."

If Sam had the energy, he would've protested the comment. "It's just not quite what I expected."

"What were you expecting?"

Sam looked over at Willow, reminding himself for the hundredth time that he was talking to a tree. "I have no idea."

"You have strange thoughts, friend Sam," Willow said, resuming her steady pace.

They made their way toward town, staying just inside the tree line as they passed acre after acre of farmland. Although Willow had revealed herself to Sam, she had explained it would be wise to steer clear of other humans. From her observations, most humans wouldn't take to her appearance nearly as well as Sam. Most folks' knowledge of the Nartareen started and finished with "they're the reason you avoid the forests." Her sudden appearance would at best draw attention, and right now their survival—if Willow was to be believed—relied heavily on them staying hidden.

As they walked, Sam peered through the breaks in the trees, catching glimpses of laboring farmers. Hacking away at the earth and loading their spoils onto large horse-drawn carts, the men and women worked barefoot and wore threadbare clothing. It wasn't until Sam spotted a cart near the tree line that he noticed these farmers weren't harvesting food, but what looked to be softly luminescent crystals about the size of a bread loaf. Like robots in an assembly line, the farmers methodically placed crystal after crystal onto the cart in neat stacks.

Sam jogged up to Willow and tapped her on the shoulder. "Hey, what are those people doing?"

Willow stopped and peeked through the trees. "They are farming, friend Sam."

"Yeah, but *what* are they farming? What are those crystal things?"

"Aether ingots. There are many aether springs in the Nartareen forests, but few humans dare to come inside. The soil is rich and pure at the forest's edge, so they plant the Capture Crystals to harvest the aether."

"Wait." Sam scratched his head, squinting at the faintly fluorescent blue crystals. "How do the crystals get the aether?"

Willow stopped a moment and looked around. She walked

further into the woods before coming to a stop next to a small stream. "Do you see this stream?"

"Sure do."

"What directions do streams always go?" Willow asked.

Sam didn't know if this was some kind of riddle or not, but decided to answer the question straight. "They flow downhill, Willow."

Willow smiled and tapped Sam on the forehead twice with her wooden finger. "Very good, friend Sam. Aether is like the water. Capture Crystals are like the bottom of the hill."

"Ah," Sam said, not sure he entirely understood her meaning. "So, these farmers gather the aether up and then do what with it, exactly?"

Willow turned and put a hand on Sam's arm. Her amber eyes stared intently into his, as if she was preparing him to receive grave news. "They send it away."

"Send it away?" Sam was surprised. "Send it where? Why don't they keep it?"

"I do not know, friend Sam. I know only what I see and what I hear from my place in the trees, which can be much or can be little. I watch the aether springs and spy on aether mines. That is where most towns and villages are built. I do not know much of what happens to the aether, only that the workers keep very, very little of what they pull from the ground."

Sam looked back through the trees and saw two men digging in the dirt with their hands. Some fifty yards behind them stood a pair of armored guards lazily keeping watch. Sam was probably close enough that the farmers could see him now, if they ever bothered to lift their heads and look around. But something told Sam that he could be standing five feet away and they wouldn't notice him. It was the way they hunched, seemingly focused on nothing beyond their own two calloused hands. It was their empty, efficient motions. They weren't farmers. They were slaves.

By late afternoon, Willow and Sam had reached the forest's edge nearest Ogland. Sam swapped his black tactical clothes for the ill-fitting spare clothes he found in Gurn's pack and stared at the city's front gate not a hundred yards away from the shade of the trees. His stomach tied itself in a double knot.

"Are you sure about this?" Sam asked, popping his knuckles one by one.

"I am sure about what I heard, friend Sam. The Mavericks always meet in a place called 'The Cup of Rosemary.' They were looking for a man called Cornelius Thompson the Fourth."

Sam thought for the last day how great it was going to be to talk to other humans and try to figure out what was going on, but now that it came time to leave the forest, he stood frozen as nose hairs in a Montana winter. What if there were more thugs like Gurn and Reynold? He didn't understand this place. He really didn't even understand what he was doing. He woke up, got robbed, met a talking tree, ran from a wizard-emperor, and now he was about to go into a bizarre medieval town and ask a complete stranger for information and protection.

He checked his cell phone one final time. Nothing. Before he put his phone away, he stared at the background picture. It was Rinni, Lawrence, and himself all dressed up in their spy duds. What was he thinking? He could do this. He was Samwise flippin' Shelton, Drone-flyer, Egg-tosser, Flaming-paper-bag-placer. He *lived* for this kind of stuff. He breathed deeply a few times and started mumbling in the different voices and accents he commonly used for prank calls. He settled on what he figured was his best low-class British accent. His friends told him it sounded like a mix between Alfred, the butler in *The Dark Knight*, and Tiny Tim from *A Christmas Carol*.

"I will wait for you here…with my friends," Willow said, gesturing to the trees. "Are you okay?"

"Never better," Sam responded with an accent, before walking out of the woods toward the front gate.

With each step his nervousness waned. He observed the steady flow of people making their way in and out of the city and instinctively adjusted his posture and gait. He dropped his shoulders slightly, shuffled his feet a bit more. By the time he reached the main entrance, his own mother couldn't have picked him out of the crowd.

He entered the city gates and felt like he'd walked onto the most authentic medieval village movie set ever made. There was one detail above all others, however, that reassured him that he wasn't in a movie: the stench. Sure, Hollywood would try to film a movie with as much realism as possible, but no sane individual would've recreated the abominable smell that filled Sam's lungs. The extras would've bathed in the last decade, the pigs and livestock would've been computer animated, and the random piles of garbage would've probably contained less animal waste. Not since Thorne Crabson locked him in the outhouse at fifth-grade camp had Sam smelled something so repulsive.

Sam braced himself against the reek and pressed forward, approaching the first person he saw who looked like they didn't want to rob him blind and throw his body down a well. In this case, it was a moon-faced man with a large gray mustache standing in front of a clothing shop.

"Excuse me, sir," Sam said, laying the accent on thick.

The man looked down at Sam. If he was surprised at Sam's appearance or dubious of his accent, he didn't show it. "What's that, lad?"

"Looking for me father. Told he'd be at The Cup of Rosemary," Sam said, scratching the back of his neck something fierce. He figured lice would be about as common here as frost in January.

The man raised both eyebrows at the mention of the name. "If your father told you to meet him there, he isn't much of a father, if you ask me."

"Please, sir. I've got to meet him. He'll be awful cross if I'm late."

The man shook his head and gave a deep sigh. "Look lad, go down this road, left at Hoffman's Apothecary, follow that road to the church and take another left. Go a bit further and you can't miss it, but I strongly suggest you do. You understand me, boy?"

"Thank you, sir. Yes, sir," Sam said, nodding profusely as he scuttled down the street. It wasn't until he passed the church that he began to see why the man was so concerned. The road narrowed, and Sam got the distinct feeling that his surroundings were slowly closing in around him. The crowds of people previously busying about the streets were reduced to the odd figure here and there hanging about the shadows, or else tottering down the middle of the road in a conspicuous drunken waltz. By the time he saw the dimly lit wooden sign for The Cup of Rosemary, it took everything Sam had not to break into a dead sprint. As he got closer, he could see slivers of light shining through the shuttered and boarded-up windows. Muffled music and loud laughter came from within.

Sam walked to the front entrance and swallowed his growing apprehension. "I'm Samwise flippin' Shelton," he whispered to himself, and pushed the door open.

CUP OF ROSEMARY

The Cup of Rosemary—despite exterior first impressions—wasn't quite as bad as Sam had anticipated. He had prepared himself for a "den of medieval scumbag thieves and malefactors," but in reality, it was more like a "low-end tavern establishment for drunkards and card sharks." The words of warning from the moon-faced man still echoed in the back of Sam's mind, but he breathed a sigh of relief...a *small* sigh of relief. It was kind of like stepping in what you thought was dog poo, but finding out it was only mud. Sure, you still might track mud through the house, but it was much more manageable than the alternative.

Sam glanced around the tavern. There was no way to know who he was looking for. The tavern's fifteen or so tables were each occupied with half a dozen people who were either drinking, eating, playing cards, or doing all three. A few people danced in an open space near the bar and kitchen to Sam's left as three musicians plucked and drummed a set of instruments that he had never seen or heard before. Sam was relieved to see a few kids, roughly his age, bussing tables. He was worried a thirteen-year-old would stick out like a dwarf at elf prom, but no one gave him a second look from what he could tell.

Sam didn't know exactly how to play this. He thought it probably wouldn't be prudent to walk around the place asking if anyone had seen "Cornelius, leader of the Mavericks, secret resistance against the all-powerful and oppressive emperor." Sam was a stranger here. No one could vouch for him, no one would be coming in after him if something went wrong. He was playing at a game with no extra lives and no continues. He needed to be subtle. He'd only have one chance at this.

A crash sounded to Sam's right and he spun to see one of the busboys standing over a mess of broken ceramic pieces and spilt drinks. The kid ran both his hands through his shaggy brown hair, his face screwing up in an expression like he just smelled the streets of Ogland for the first time. Sam knew that look. He'd seen it on Lawrence a hundred times before. It was the look of one who couldn't afford to get in trouble again. A smile tugged at the corner of Sam's mouth as an idea materialized.

As Sam approached the scene, a door burst open over by the kitchen and a squat, middle-aged woman stormed out toward the mortified busboy.

"What in the blooming blazes is going on here?" the woman screeched, her voice like the caw of a crow. It was so loud that Sam had to consciously restrain himself from covering his ears. Despite the woman's piercing voice, the activity in the tavern went on uninterrupted. This apparently was not a rare occurrence.

"I...I'm sorry, ma'am," the boy said, not meeting the woman's gaze. "I'll...I'll clean it up straight away, ma'am."

"That'll be the *least* of what you'll do, you blundering little whelp. You think those plates just spring into being from all my spare aether? You'll work extra time and get half meals until you've paid off them plates. You hear me?"

"Yes, ma'am. I'm sor—"

"Excuse me, ma'am," Sam said, raising a finger. The woman and boy stopped talking and slowly turned in Sam's direction. "I'm sorry, your worker here is just being a good chap, my good lady. It was I who broke your plates."

"You did what?" the lady crowed, turning her thick head from Sam to the boy and back.

Sam cleared his throat. "Yes, it was me, ma'am. My utmost apologies. I don't have much money, but I can work off the plates."

The lady stood there, unsure how best to direct her wrath. "One week. You start tonight," she squawked, and stomped back toward the kitchen.

The busboy stood there, more stunned than when he first broke the plates. He slowly worked his mouth open, but no words came out.

"Well, that was a close one, wouldn't you say?" Sam asked, patting the kid on the shoulder.

"Why'd do you that?" the kid finally managed, looking up from the ground.

"Chaps like us got to stick together; am I right?" Sam replied, not sure if he was pouring on his cockney chimney sweep accent a bit too thick.

"Well, thank you. I mean, really. Thank you. I'm not so sure I could have survived another round of half meals. Look, I don't have much, but anything you need, just ask."

"Actually," Sam said, trying to stay casual, "I was wondering if you knew where I might find a Cornelius Thompson the Fourth?"

The kid stopped short at the mention of the name. "Who's asking?"

"The kid who's owed a favor." Sam leveled a knowing gaze.

The boy nervously darted his gaze around the tables before stopping on Sam. He leaned in close. "Three tables back, wide-brimmed hat, pipe in his mouth. We're even. We're *more* than even."

Sam nodded in thanks and then turned and left the busboy to clean up. He weaved his way through the crowded tables before getting a good view of his mark. Cornelius Thompson IV tipped back on two chair legs, a spread of playing cards in one hand, a drink in the other, and a large pipe hanging from his mouth. His frayed poncho, large mustache, and wide-brimmed hat made him look much more cowboy than medieval peasant. Sam neared the table as Cornelius rocked forward and triumphantly laid his five cards face up on the table. A chorus of groans and complaints erupted from the other four at the table as they discarded their hands. Cornelius chuckled and reached out to collect a pile of coins from the middle of the table.

"Pleasure doing business with y'all," Cornelius said, his voice deepened from too many years at the pipe. His accent made Sam stop in his tracks. This man sounded like he was pulled straight from an old Western movie. This place was different, stuck in the Middle Ages with peasants and magic and odd creatures, but nowhere in that narrative had Sam made room for a medieval cowboy. Gathering himself, Sam took a deep breath and inched his way to Cornelius's table.

"Another dragon tongue, my good sir," Cornelius said, holding up his empty glass. Sam stopped and looked around. "C'mon, kid. Wouldn't want to run the risk of me sobering up now."

Sam stood there confused until Cornelius turned and looked straight at him. Sam's stomach lurched. "Sir?" Sam managed.

"You got cotton in your ears, kid?"

Finally realizing that Cornelius had mistaken him for a busboy, Sam reached out and took the proffered glass.

"Are you Cornelius Thompson the Fourth?" Sam asked in a low voice.

"Last I checked," Cornelius said, staring at his coins as he arranged them into neat stacks.

Sam swallowed hard. "I'm looking for the Mavericks."

"Go ask your mother for a bedtime story, then." If the question surprised Cornelius, he betrayed nothing.

Sam looked around to make sure no one was listening and continued. "I'm told you could help me find the Mavericks. I'm in need of—"

Sam's heart hammered to a stop. Three tables away, with a tray of used cups and plates balanced on one hand, stood the most beautiful girl he had ever seen. Her blonde hair ran along the sides of her head in small tight braids before opening into a golden waterfall down her shoulders and back. Her eyes were large and of such a piercing green that he could see the color from where he stood. Light freckles graced her nose and cheeks. She was a Viking princess, a fairy goddess.

"What you're in *need* of is a cold shower, kid," Cornelius chuckled.

"Huh," Sam said, looking back to Cornelius, who followed his gaze. Sam flushed and tried to regain his bearings. What was he doing again? Sam looked at the glass in his hand. The Mavericks. Lawrence. The emperor. He couldn't afford to get blown off. He needed answers. "Cornelius, I *need* to talk to you. I met a Nartareen that said you could help me."

"A Nartareen?" Cornelius tipped up the front of his hat and turned in his seat to get a better look at Sam, a look of genuine amusement on his face. "Well, I'll be a goose's uncle, I was just talking to a pile of dirt the other day and he told *me* to tell you that if you don't go get my drink that I should feed you this deck of playing cards."

This was not going well. Cornelius looked more likely to bury Sam in a shallow grave than help protect him. He felt his opportunity slipping. He *needed* this to work. What was it his mother was always saying, honesty was the best policy? He dropped his fake accent and went for broke. "Listen, I'm a pure drainer. I don't know where I am. Two days ago, I was back home in Montana with my buddies and the next thing I know I'm here. I had two thugs try and attack me. I drained their power; they took my pack. I met a tree girl. She said the emperor would want me and that the Mavericks would protect me. I need your help."

"Montana, huh?" Cornelius raised an eyebrow while inspecting his freshly dealt hand of cards.

"Yes, that's where I'm from…" Sam trailed off as he noticed the whole tavern grow silent. No music, no banter. Just the squeaking of some chairs and a few coughs. Sam saw Cornelius's gaze lift from his cards to the front door. Sam turned to see a band of half a dozen soldiers standing at the entrance of the tavern. They were lightly armored and sported a sheathed sword on one hip and a coiled chain whip on the other. There was no way they were here for him. Sam had taken a short cut through the woods. They didn't even know which direction he'd gone, or that he'd even come to Ogland, or come to *this* tavern. He tried to still his nerves. They weren't here for him.

"We are looking," the head soldier announced with the voice of one used to talking to large crowds, "for a young boy, by the name of Samwise Shelton."

"Oh, poop," Sam breathed. How did they know his name? How could they *possibly* know his name? Then it came to him. His wallet was in his pack. It had his school ID. He blanched and felt like he was going to faint just as Cornelius grabbed him by the arm.

"Steady there, partner," Cornelius mumbled. "Get your wits, kid. Don't move until I tell ya."

The soldiers made their way through the crowd, asking questions to and intimidating those they passed. A pair went into the kitchen and returned with four busboys. Before the soldiers could begin questioning the boys, the squat, squawking lady from before came bursting out in a rage.

"What is the meaning of this?" she yelled, jabbing one of the soldiers in the chest with a wooden ladle.

Cornelius squeezed Sam's arm. "She's setting a distraction.

Move slowly now. Move quietly. Long as we don't get noticed, we're golden."

Sam took a deep breath and turned to go. Before he could take his first step, however, he heard a sound that in any other moment would've been great news. From his pocket burst the theme song from *The Legend of Zelda*, Heinrich's apparent selection for alerting Sam that he just acquired a phone signal. All the heads in the tavern slowly turned in Sam's direction.

10

DAMSEL IN DISTRESS

The Ziptalk Apollo, among its many impressive features, sported what had to be the world's loudest cell phone speaker. The stirring *Legend of Zelda* anthem blaring from Sam's pants might as well have been a gigantic neon sign hovering above his head with the words "I'm the moron you're looking for." Trying his best to play it off, Sam looked around the room as if he too was trying to figure out where the music was coming from. He slyly reached down and squeezed the outside of his pocket to silence his phone.

Three of the soldiers pushed their way through the rest of the crowd, chain whips jingling like a cowboy's spurs, to stand directly in front of Sam and Cornelius.

"What's your name, boy?" the lead soldier asked, conspicuously placing his hand on the pommel of the sword sheathed at his waist.

"Who? Me?" Sam finally replied, as if the question was so absurd he couldn't believe they were asking it.

"Name," the soldier repeated.

"Philbert McGibbons, my good man. At your service," Sam

said with a slight bow. *It's just like talking your way out of trouble with the cops. It's just like talking to cops,* Sam repeated in his mind.

"And who are you supposed to be?" the soldier demanded, nodding toward Cornelius. "You fancy yourself from the League of Cowboys, do you? Looky here, everyone. We're blessed to be in the presence of one of the few Cowboys left in all of Avalon." The two soldiers laughed at the suggestion.

"Something like that," Cornelius responded.

"And where do Mr. Philbert and his cowboy companion come from?" the soldier asked mockingly.

"I...came from under the hill."

The soldier looked at Sam with a funny expression before turning to the soldier next to him. "What's he saying?"

"I think," the other soldier said, leaning in close to Sam, "that he's being smart. What was all that noise you was making, smart boy?"

"Noise?" Sam feigned confusion. "From me? I think your—"

The Zelda treasure chest sound effect chimed from his phone, signifying a text had come through. Before he could even think of reaching for his cell, it played again, and again, each time driving another nail into Sam's coffin.

Sam pursed his lips and drummed his fingers against his chest, avoiding eye contact with any of the soldiers while he waited out the barrage of message notifications. "So...you were saying?"

"Get down," Cornelius yelled as he yanked Sam to the floor. Sam looked up to see Cornelius flip a table into the two guards, knocking them to the ground. The whole tavern, as if on cue, erupted into chaos. It was an instant war zone of flying bottles, glasses, and chairs. Men and women sprang from their tables to wrestle soldiers to the ground while those without a soldier to attack simply threw a punch at the man closest to them.

"We need to vamoose!" Cornelius shouted at Sam.

Sam got to his feet and hunched down at Cornelius's side. "Where are we supposed to go?"

"This way!"

Sam stayed close behind Cornelius as he wove his way through the bedlam. The cowboy seemed to have a sixth sense for incoming projectiles, casually ducking and dodging everything thrown his direction. Twice he caught hold of someone in his way and inexplicably tossed them end over end through the air as if they weighed no more than a sack of potatoes. At last, they came to a door at the back of the tavern.

"Through this door; down to the cellar. There's a way out from there," Cornelius said.

Sam nodded and stole a glance back at the chaos. He froze. On the other side of the tavern, near the kitchen, he spotted the pretty blonde girl. Broken chair leg in one hand, bottle in the other, she was slowly getting backed into a corner by a pair of meat-headed thugs.

"What you waiting on, kid? Gotta move!" Cornelius insisted, before following Sam's gaze. "Gal darn it, kid."

Before Cornelius could stop him, Sam was already halfway across the tavern. He did his best to zigzag through the madness, fueled by the invincible mix of adrenaline and hormones. He jumped over a broken chair and was almost to his mystery girl when a soldier and two men stumbled in front him. The soldier held his chain above his head where it magically writhed in the air like a thin metallic snake. The chain struck out and wrapped itself around the neck of one of the men. Without thinking, Sam ran forward, grabbed the chain, and pushed down on the cold sensation of aether he felt on his palm. The chain went limp as a cooked spaghetti noodle. The stunned soldier looked at his chain, then at Sam, then at the two men who started to charge.

Sam danced forward out of the way, ready to save his damsel in distress. The men were almost on her when, in apparent desperation, she cocked back both hands and threw the bottle and chair leg. It was the absolute *worst* throw Sam had ever seen, as both objects went well wide of their targets.

Talk about throwing like a gir—before Sam could finish his thought, he watched the bottle and chair leg spin back around, returning with a boomerang-like vengeance. The objects smashed against the back of the two men's heads and they toppled to the floor.

Sam stood in awe. He wasn't sure if he believed in love at first sight, but this stunning, magic-wielding bargirl was making a strong case for it. She retrieved the chair leg and looked up at Sam. Her eyes went wide as she threw the chair leg again, this time at no one in particular. Sam heard a *crack* followed by a loud *thump* and spun around to see a soldier on the ground not three feet behind him.

"Sam, Roanna, this way," Cornelius said, breaking free of the crowd.

Roanna, Sam mused. It was a beautiful name.

"You don't plan to tuck tail and run, surely?" Roanna said in what sounded vaguely like a Scottish accent. She locked eyes with Cornelius. "We need to stay here and fight, cowboy."

After watching Roanna up close, Sam quickly abandoned any notions that this girl had a single damsel bone in her body that was in distress. She was definitely more the Viking princess type, which was all the more alluring.

"What I plan on doing is living, and with every second we stay here, the odds of that drop faster than a featherless prairie chicken. Look, Roh, you see that lawman take off out the front door?" Cornelius asked, pointing back toward the entrance. "Well, he saw *you* just as you brained that other lawman with a chair leg. You think there are a lot of pretty little blonde girls running around this place? They'll know who did it. You're a wanted woman, little miss."

"What was I supposed to do, let the soldier get the lad?" Roanna asked, pointing to Sam.

Lad? Sam thought. This girl couldn't have been more than a year or two older than Sam. "I appreciate the help, but you don't need to worry about me. I can handle myself." Sam's best attempt at looking confident was met with a confused look from Roanna.

"What kind of accent has this one got?" Roanna asked, turning from Sam to Cornelius.

"Look, we can chat half the day about how goofy this kid sounds, but them lawmen come back with reinforcements and we're gonna need more than a broken chair leg. We need to skedaddle, little miss," Cornelius urged, hand extended.

"Fine," she said, holding up her pointer finger as if it were a knife. "But don't you ever call me 'little miss' again."

With that, Cornelius turned and led the way back to the door. The fighting had almost entirely subsided, leaving the tavern a wreckage of overturned furniture, unconscious bodies, and broken glass. Sam followed Cornelius and Roanna through the back door and down a dark stairwell. Instinctively, Sam pulled out his phone and turned on his flashlight. Cornelius and Roanna spun, muscles tensed and fists at the ready. Sam jumped backward and almost dropped his phone.

"Whoa there, folks. Just a flashlight, not some kind of futuristic death ray," Sam said, holding his hands up in placation.

"What is this magic?" Roanna asked, squinting at the light. "That's too bright to be a day stone."

"Look, you want me to turn it off? I can turn it off," Sam said, tapping his phone and sending the stairway back into darkness.

There was a pause before Roanna spoke. "You were the one the guards were looking for, weren't you?" Sam didn't know if a "yes" to the question would be good or bad, but this girl was already connecting the pieces together. As if Sam wasn't already intimidated enough by her looks or the fact that *she* had rescued *him*, now he had to contend with her being Sherlock Holmes. Sam was awkward at best around the opposite sex. This Roanna was Sam's favorite dream and worst nightmare wrapped all into one.

"Come on, you two. We'll have plenty of time to play interrogation later," Cornelius said from the bottom of the stairs. Sam could hear the cowboy rummaging around in the darkness. A few seconds later, a soft blue light appeared from the cellar below. Sam descended the rest of the stairs to find Cornelius holding what amounted to a glow stick the size of a Pringles can. How it worked, Sam had no idea.

Cornelius handed the glow stick to Roanna and made his way to a wall of large wooden barrels stacked three high at the far side of the room. The old cowboy grabbed the barrels and placed them to the side as if they were made of cardboard, again displaying a strength that defied all reason. After moving a column of barrels, he placed his hand against the now exposed wall. Sam heard a muffled *CLICK* as Cornelius pushed against the wall, which swung inward, revealing a secret passageway.

"After you," Cornelius gestured as renewed shouting echoed from upstairs. Sam followed Roanna through the opening while Cornelius quickly restacked the barrels. The cowboy grabbed the side of the heavy stone door and pushed it shut behind them.

Roanna held up her glow stick, the soft blue light only illuminating the next few yards in front of them. "Looks like there's no going back."

"No," Cornelius said, stepping forward into the darkness, "there's not."

11

MONTANA TERRITORY

Cornelius led the way through the circuitous network of tunnels. At every intersection he bent down to the floor, examining different patterns etched into the stone surface, before choosing a direction. After what seemed like an hour of this, the passageway finally came to a dead end. A wooden ladder, reaching all the way to the ceiling, stood propped against the wall.

"Now what?" Sam asked, not seeing the way out.

"I'm assuming we climb." Roanna leaned over and whispered into Sam's ear as if revealing some long-kept secret. The feeling of her breath on his cheek sent shivers down his back.

Cornelius scaled the ladder, placed his hands against the ceiling and pushed. "Consarn it," he cursed. "Looks like I'm dumfungled."

"Looks like you're *what?*" asked Sam.

"He's out of aether," Roanna said, although her response was more a rebuke to Cornelius than it was an answer to Sam. Cornelius climbed down off the ladder, allowing Roanna to climb to the top. She gently placed her hand on the same spot Cornelius had tried. For a moment nothing happened, then

Sam heard the scrape of stone on stone as a round section of the ceiling broke free and was pushed away, allowing the evening light to spill into the tunnel. Sam followed Roanna and Cornelius out of the tunnel and was surprised to see they were in the middle of the forest. There was no sign of the city. Sam looked around and noticed that the bit of ceiling Roanna had levitated out of the way was actually a large, flat rock that was placed over the entrance to the tunnel.

"Are we alone?" Roanna asked Cornelius as she pulled up the ladder and magically lifted the rock back into place, resealing the hole in the ground.

The cowboy looked around before slumping down against a fallen tree trunk. "I don't reckon we should be lighting a fire or anything this evening, but yeah, we're alone."

"In that case," Roanna said, straightening herself and turning to Sam, "who in all the fracture are you and what are you doing here?"

Although Roanna's voice gave Sam butterflies, and the look in her eye electrocuted those butterflies, he was glad to finally have a captive audience. "My name is Sam Shelton, and I'm from Bozeman, Montana. Two days ago, I was pulling a prank on my vice principal, started feeling funny, and passed out. When I woke up, I was…here. Two thugs stole my backpack, I met a Nartareen named Willow and she said I could find Cornelius in Ogland, that he was the leader of the Mavericks and that they would help me. I've never seen aether in my *life*. I can't use it and people can't use it on me, apparently."

Instead of responding, Roanna picked up a rock, levitated it, and sent it hurling towards Sam's head.

"Are you crazy?" Sam yelled, flinching backward. The rock fell to the earth just before hitting Sam. "What the heck was *that* for?"

"*That*," Roanna said, stepping back to consider Sam with new eyes, "was to see if *you're* crazy. You were either telling the truth and you'd prove it, or you're telling us lies and deserve to get cracked in the head. Cornelius, what do you make of this? Is he some long-lost cowboy's lad or something?"

"I highly doubt it. Never seen no cowboy drain a stone without touching it. All us cowboys is Leeches. We can drain, but not like that we can't. This kid's something different, I reckon," Cornelius said before tipping his hat down over his face like he was about to take a nap.

Roanna took several steps backward, her gaze fixed on Sam.

"What are you looking at me like that for? You'd think I had the plague or something."

"Plague or not, you keep your distance for now until we figure what you are exactly," Roanna said, holding up a hand. "I don't want you bumping into me and draining my aether. You understand me?"

"I don't think it works like that," Sam said, wary about another magical stone being hurled his way. He actually wasn't sure *how* it worked, but he knew he didn't just drain everything he brushed up against. Up until now, his draining had required some level of thought. The stone must've triggered a defensive reflex. "Look, I'm sorry for the mess at the tavern, but I'm not some freak. I hiked through the blasted forest for the better part of two days to make sure I wasn't followed. I have no idea how they could've found me so quickly."

"They found ya," Cornelius said from under his hat, "because they was looking for ya."

"I don't understand," Sam said.

"Emperor's been on the move laying down the rebellion in Grahl. Rumor has it he'll be paying the Peaklands a bit of a visit on his way back north. Lots of aether getting tossed around these parts. Strange things happen when you fumble around with that much aether, and the emperor knows it."

"What are you saying there, cowboy?" Roanna asked.

"Sam here," Cornelius pointed a thumb at Sam, "is a strange thing."

"So wait," Sam interjected. "The emperor's *aether* brought me here? But why me? Why not someone else?"

"Tarnation, kid, I don't know," Cornelius said. "I look like an aetherologist to you? What were you up to when you came over?"

"Nothing out of the ordinary," Sam said. "I was just sitting there minding my own business trying to ride out the earthqua…" Sam trailed off.

"Trying to do what now?"

"There was an earthquake," Sam said distantly. He didn't know how the pieces of this puzzle fit together, but he knew that he'd just discovered a big piece. "They hardly ever happen in Montana, and never that big. Could that have caused it?"

"Look, kid," Cornelius said, tipping up his hat to spit on the ground. "I don't know. All I know is I'd bet the emperor was expecting something might happen and he'd have all of Avalon with its ear to the ground. I reckon lookouts saw you walk out of the woods and into the city. Who knows, though? All I know is that we should avoid the open road for a while."

"How long is a while?" Roanna asked, her face growing darker.

"A few months should do it."

"Out here, in these woods, for a few months?" Roanna shook her head. "I think I'll take my chances back in Ogland."

"You know you can't go back to Ogland, Roh," Cornelius said.

"And *you* know I've got no issue being openly at odds with the emperor's men, but I wanted it to be on *my* terms." Roanna pointed sharply at her chest.

Cornelius laughed. "Your terms, huh? You let me know when that happens. You deal with lawmen long enough and you'll learn it ain't got nothing to do with your terms or who did what or how something started. In the end, we're all left holding each other's bag. No two ways about it."

Sam's stomach twisted. He had had pranks go wrong in the

past, but getting into a brawl with the authorities was a bit beyond throwing a few rolls of toilet paper over old man Tennyson's trees. Sam was beginning to think that taking Willow's advice to go to Ogland had been a very big mistake. But where else could he have gone? He felt like he was a passenger on a runaway train, being propelled forward from one situation to the next with no control over where he was going. And worse yet, none of this seemed to be helping him figure out how he was going to get back home.

"Now that you mention it," Roanna said, looking from Sam to Cornelius, "how *did* this whole sticky mess start, anyhow?"

"The kid mentioned he was from Montana," Cornelius replied.

"That's it? He's from Montana. Never even heard of it," Roanna said.

"Exactly. Not many folk have. Story goes that the League of Cowboys all started from my great-great-granddad. He also came over from a strange place. Said to have had some pretty impressive draining powers as well."

"And he was from Montana too?" Sam asked, his interest piquing.

"Don't know where he was from. Mysterious fella he was. I'm told he kept a journal, but it went missing before my time. I do have his old pipe, however, and on the back of it you'll find engraved none other than *Montana Territory Smoke Shop*. You can see it right here."

Cornelius patted down his poncho and then his pants, before his eyes went wide with terror. "Dadgumit! I lost my pipe in the scuffle. I lost my dadburned pipe. We got to go back."

"Go back? Have you lost your mind?" Roanna shot back. "You *just* told me we *couldn't* go back. Now we're going to risk it all for some gross, old, chewed-up pipe?"

"It is a family relic of both personal and historical significance," Cornelius said as he triple-checked his pockets.

"It's a pipe," Roanna said blandly.

Sam didn't know what the relationship was between these two, but it was an odd one, he knew that much. He thought about what Cornelius said about his great-great-granddad. Sam had just studied Montana State history and however much he tried not to learn, he did remember a few things. Montana became a state in 1889, and twenty-five years before that it became a territory. If the pipe was from the Montana Territory, then that suggested that the cowboy's ancestor arrived in Avalon somewhere around the 1870s. Sam's stomach dropped to his shoes. If Cornelius was still here one hundred and fifty years later, then it probably meant that his ancestor had never found his way back home.

12

THE FELLOWSHIP

After a few minutes of rummaging around in the forest, Cornelius brushed the dirt from the top of a buried wooden barrel. The threat of having to leave Ogland in a pinch was obviously something the cowboy anticipated. There weren't many supplies, but the dried meats, packs, blankets, and simple tools were better than nothing, especially if they needed to stay out of sight for a while. The one impressive item that Cornelius withdrew from the barrel was what looked like a cross between a pickaxe and a sledgehammer, which the cowboy slung across his back.

"We need to take the fight to *them*," Roanna said, picking up a small knife from the barrel and shaking it. "We can't sit around this cursed forest for half the year. If Sam is a Void, then he's the weapon we've been waiting for. He could finally tip the balance. If the emperor is so determined to get him, that should tell you something."

"It tells *me* that we should get this kid back home and forget that we ever saw him," Cornelius said, fastening a rolled-up blanket to the top of his pack. "No offense, kid."

"Uh...none taken," Sam said, not sure what Cornelius was getting at.

"Forget we ever saw him?" Roanna said in disbelief. "This is the opportunity of a lifetime, of many lifetimes. You said yourself the emperor is on his way to the Peaklands. That means we know where he's going. That means we can set a trap. All Sam has to do is shake the man's hand and it's all over. This is the opportunity the Mavericks have dreamt about for two hundred years."

"Just cause a chicken's got wings don't mean it can fly, Roh."

"And what do you mean by that?" Roanna asked.

"Look, I seen my fair share of rebellions, thank you kindly," Cornelius said. "Having a Void is a tempting weapon to wield, yes, but we'd impale ourselves on our own sword. I agree the concept is simple enough: get a Void close enough to touch the emperor. Way I see it, it's a bit like gator wrestling. Just gotta get close enough to hold their mouth shut. But go count the fingers on your average gator wrestler and then come back and tell me that the execution of the matter is that dadgum simple. That's why I came to South Avalon. Heard folks down here at least had more common sense than God gave a goose. Reckon I was mistaken."

"Wait a second," Sam interjected. "Aren't you supposed to be *leading* the Mavericks against the emperor?"

"What, because a walking tree told you so?" Cornelius chuckled. "Kid, I don't lead anything. I'm a road sign. I point the right people in the right direction and the wrong people in the wrong direction."

"But what about all the rest of the people at the Cup of Rosemary?" Sam asked. "The whole tavern rose up against those soldiers."

"Kid, those weren't Mavericks." Cornelius shook his head. "Those were drunkards and thieves who predictably took advantage of an opportunity to punch someone in the face, and if that someone had a badge then all the better. Who do you think those two deadbeats were that tried to attack Roanna? The world is full of opportunists, Sam."

"So, all the Mavericks in Ogland are..." Sam trailed off.

"Presently gathered," Cornelius said, nodding to Roanna, who leaned against a tree with one hand on her hip.

"So now what?" Sam asked. He didn't like this talk about being used as part of some grand plan by the Mavericks. He hadn't played this thing right. He ran from one group that wanted to kill him into the arms of another group that wanted to use him as a weapon, when all *he* wanted to do was go home and be left alone. At least Cornelius was on his side. Sam had no stake in the struggles of Avalon, and he sure wasn't in the mood to get sacrificed for their cause. He had to stick with Cornelius until he could find somebody who knew more about how he got here and how he could leave.

"Well," Cornelius said, getting to his feet, "seems like we're stuck with each other for a bit. We can't go back to Ogland. I know a few folks who might know more about how ya got here, but they ain't exactly close by and we can't travel out in the open. We got to figure out how to get you—all discrete like—to someone who can help ya. Then I can wipe my hands of ya. No offense, kid."

"And how are we going to do that?" Roanna asked.

"We can go through the forest," Sam said, as if it was the most obvious answer in the world.

Cornelius glared at Sam, both eyebrows raised. "I'd rather go knock on the emperor's front door."

"Oh come on. We can go straight through these woods," Sam said. "I've got the perfect guide."

"And who might that be?" Cornelius asked.

"Just wait. She'll be here," Sam said, looking around, as if half expecting to see Willow standing camouflaged somewhere close by.

"She'll *be* here?" Roanna asked, confused. "No one even

knows we're here. In fact, I'm not even sure I know where we are."

"If we're in the woods, she'll find us," Sam said. As if on cue, a strange warbling howl echoed in the distance. Sam's eye went wide. "What was that?"

Cornelius panned his head from side to side. "Let's hope she's the only thing that finds us."

With every passing minute, Sam grew more nervous that Willow wouldn't show. He paced back and forth between two trees, scoring a path in the dirt and chewing his fingernails to stubs. Cornelius looked to be asleep against a tree, while Roanna sat on the ground playing with an odd spinning top that magically twirled in the air above her palm.

More strange howls sounded in the distance, making Sam's blood run cold. He didn't know how much longer he could wait. In desperation, he walked over to a nearby tree and placed his hand on the trunk. He had no idea how Willow's communication with the trees actually worked, but he was quickly running out of both time and options. "Uh, Willow?" Sam whispered, not wanting the others to know what he was doing.

"Yes, friend Sam," Willow said, appearing from her forest camouflage not ten feet from where Sam was standing.

Sam's heart seized in his chest as he flinched backward. "Willow?"

"Dadburn it," Cornelius cursed at the sudden sight of the Nartareen. He scrambled to his feet and pulled his pick-hammer from his back. "Keep your distance, you dadgum tree demon."

"Oh, I am sorry, friend Sam," Willow said, her amber eyes growing wide. "I did not mean to scare you and rugged Cornelius and pretty Roanna. I am here to help."

"How long have you been standing there?" Sam asked, breathing as if he'd just run a mile.

"I have seen you pace between the trees ninety-four times." Willow nodded.

"Ninety-four...why didn't you say something?" Sam asked.

"I did not want to surprise you. I was waiting for you to call my name. Did you find out where your friend is, friend Sam?"

"Friend?" Roanna asked, raising an eyebrow. "What friend is this? You said you appeared here just the other day."

"It's nobody," Sam said, trying his best to brush it off.

"Do you not remember your friend?" Willow asked, her wooden features bunching up. "You spoke of him often. He came over here with you, but you cannot find him. You were worried that the emperor might catch him, because he would be a pure drainer like you, but he is a stupid person, so he would get caught."

Sam groaned and put his palm to his forehead. "Ah yes, Willow. *That* friend. Of course. Thank you."

"Oh, you are welcome."

"Kid, I would *highly* recommend that you shoot straight with us," Cornelius said, still holding his pick-hammer at the ready.

Sam looked over at Roanna, whose glare told him all he needed to know. He hadn't wanted to talk about Lawrence unless he absolutely had to, and unless it was with someone he could absolutely trust. He could try fibbing his way through, but something told him that pulling the wool over Roanna and Cornelius's eyes wouldn't be quite as easy as bending the truth to a schoolteacher.

"Willow's right," Sam admitted. "I found out that my friend came through too. I'm worried about him. That was one of the main reasons I came looking for the Mavericks. I've got to find him. If he's here, he's in danger."

"Maybe he transported somewhere nice and safe," Cornelius said.

"That kid would be in danger if he was covered in bubble wrap at a pillow factory."

"He'd be what now?" Cornelius asked.

"He's in danger," Sam said flatly. "Look, I have to find him. Please, that's all I'll ask of you two. Just help me find my friend."

"He could be another Void..." Roanna mused. "Cowboy, you might not want to get involved in another rebellion, but if the emperor has a drainer of his own, you might not have a choice. We need to find this friend before the emperor does."

Sam was shocked. Of all the things to get Roanna suddenly on his side, it was *Lawrence*. He knew her being agreeable had nothing to do with himself and everything to do with the prospect of two Void drainers to fight the emperor, but Sam wasn't about to shun this turn of good fortune. This was progress.

"I return to our original conundrum, my young friends," Cornelius said, still glaring at Willow and finally returning his pick-hammer to his back. "How we gonna look for this friend, when the emperor is looking for *us*?"

"The Eldest Tree can help us," Willow said.

"The who?" Sam asked.

"The Eldest Tree, friend Sam. She is the oldest of the Nartareen, connected to all the forest. I speak with a few trees of my forest, she speaks to them all. One of them will have seen your friend. Bring the Eldest Tree your stories and your problems and she can grant miracles."

"I ain't going into no devil woods, led by no devil sprite, to speak to no oldest of the devil trees," Cornelius said, making the sign of the cross.

"What kind of miracles?" Roanna asked, ignoring Cornelius.

"Oh, pretty Roanna, the Eldest Tree can grant great miracles or no miracles at all," Willow explained. "She has all the aether of our forest. She hears those that make their way to her and decides if they are worthy of a miracle."

Sam didn't know what angle Roanna was playing, but he knew what angle *he* was playing: this was his ticket home. If what Cornelius said was true and mass amounts of aether were responsible for bringing Sam here, then maybe a mass amount of aether was the only way to get back home...and find Lawrence, of course. For the first time since he arrived in Avalon, Sam felt a glimmer of hope.

"C'mon, cowboy," Roanna said, walking over to Cornelius and slugging him in the arm, "we'll need your help."

"Oh yes," Willow began, "we will certainly need rugged Cornelius. The forest is dangerous. If you want to arrive at the Eldest Tree and not be dead, we will need much help."

"Uh...what?" Sam asked. "Aren't you sort of like *part* of the forest? How could we be in danger?"

"Silly friend Sam," Willow laughed, "*I* would not be hurt. It is you three who may be horribly hurt and eaten. The forest is peaceful and is my home, but the Eldest Tree has made it home to many other creatures. With the law of the wild in place, only the worthiest reach the Eldest Tree. Shall we go?"

13
TECHNO MAGIC

The bizarre howls kept Sam awake for most of the first night. Even without the eerie animal calls, Sam doubted he would have slept much. Between the night chill, Cornelius's snores, and Sam's grumbling stomach, there was plenty to lose sleep over. His ration of dried meats tasted like blanket and the thin blankets smelled like meat, but before Sam could complain too much, a phrase popped into his head: "better where there's none." It was one of his dad's many catch phrases. Sam had heard the line his entire life, but only recently understood what it meant: Before you complain about what you have, realize that it would be a whole lot more appreciated if you had nothing in the first place.

Despite all the good memories of his father—the time they spent playing video games together, cracking jokes, or watching old sci-fi movies—it was the catch phrases which most often came to his mind, which most often guided his life. It was as if his dad was somehow still there, whispering words of fatherly advice. Better where there's none. A phrase from his father that Sam never really truly understood until he had no father.

In the morning, Sam marched on through the forest, despite his sickening anxiety of who pursued him from behind and who or what lay in wait up ahead. He tried to be thankful for the reluctant medieval cowboy, the headstrong bargirl, and the peculiar talking tree who accompanied him. However unlikely their alliance or diverse their motives, he was infinitely better off with them than without them.

As before, the pace that Willow set through the forest wasn't fast, but it *was* relentless. Sam could've set his watch to the steady, constant footsteps of their Nartareen guide. Both Roanna and Cornelius seemed much more suited to handle the hike through the mountainous forest than Sam was, although Sam didn't set that particular bar all that high. On the third day, the group took their midday rest at a small clearing. The warm afternoon sun was a welcomed treat. For Sam, every step through the heavy, shadowed woods caused the world to close in more tightly. He sat on the grass, closed his eyes, and tilted his head back. Reflexively, he took out his phone and laid it beside him to charge in the sun. It had been several days since he last charged it, and its batteries were running low.

On their walk through the forest, Sam read and reread the text messages he'd received back in the tavern. For the most part, the messages were just more of the same.

Where are you?

Please come back.

I hope you're safe.

You're still showing up in New Zealand, but you've moved slightly.

The only interesting bit of information came from Rinni, who said that the disappearance made the local news, and that they were so desperate, they contacted the New Zealand authorities to investigate Sam's last known coordinates. They found nothing, of course.

Rinni even sent a few satellite images of the landscape in Sam's supposed location. The pictures were an exact match to what Sam saw around him. He was in New Zealand and yet he was not. None of this information was useful, of course, other than to make his heart feel heavy. He went stretches without thinking about his family and friends back home, but when he finally did, the dread, the homesickness, and confusion all came crashing back.

Sam didn't know how everyone would react when they got his reply messages, complete with several selfies of Ogland, the mountainous panorama, and Willow. He compiled messages for Rinni, Lawrence, and his mom. Heinrich was instructed to release the messages the moment he got signal. When Sam checked last night, the messages appeared to have gone through. His next batch of replies would be interesting, to say the least.

"What *is* that thing?" Roanna's voice jarred Sam from his thoughts.

Sam opened his eyes to see Roanna standing next to him, pointing to the phone. They had spent the last two and a half days on the run, hiking through the forest, and sleeping on the ground, and yet this girl still managed to look more attractive than anyone he'd ever met. It wasn't a kempt or flawless beauty. She was dirty, some of her braids were coming out, and her dress was torn in several places. It was natural beauty, like that of the surrounding mountains, with the weathering from their time on the road only working in her favor. These were new feelings for Sam. A couple of years ago and he couldn't have cared less how beautiful she was; yet now it held every bit of his attention hostage. Had she not addressed him directly, he doubted he'd ever work up the nerve to so much as look her in the eye.

"What, this?" Sam said, holding up his phone. "It's just a gift from my mom back home."

"But what *is* it?" she pressed.

Sam took a deep breath. He had no idea how to explain this stuff to these people. He could explain that smartphones were commonplace from where he came from, but that wouldn't make him look very cool. He didn't feel like he was in the best standing with Roanna, so perhaps he could use this to his advantage. He knew a golden opportunity when he saw one.

"It's my personal techno-oracle."

Roanna cocked an eyebrow. "Am I going to have to ask my question a third time?"

"Look, believe it or not, we don't have aether where I come from. We have a very different form of magic. Where I come from, we discovered the secrets of creating the techno-oracle," Sam said, getting to his feet. "Given only to those who have proven themselves worthy, it is a being of near limitless knowledge. It obeys every command, feeds off sunlight, predicts the weather, sees in the dark, detects hidden objects, solves complex problems, and that's just the beginning."

Sam couldn't tell if he was impressing Roanna or just confusing her further.

"When we were in the cellar, it created light," Roanna said, inching her face closer to the phone.

Of all the cool features to be interested in... "Yes, we call it a flashlight."

"How does it work?"

"Well, I guess you could say that it stores some of the sun's light and I can summon it back up whenever I want. It's harmless," Sam said, tapping the phone several times to toggle the light on and off.

"And you *made* this?" Roanna asked, reaching out to lightly touch the screen.

"I contributed..." Sam said, swallowing with some difficulty.

He never was one for telling a flat-out lie. That would be dishonest. Bending the truth, on the other hand, was a valuable art form of which Sam was a ninja. Had he worked in the cell phone factory? No. Had he set up his profile, chosen his AI and loaded the apps? Yes. Yes, he had.

"Can you make us more?" Roanna asked.

"Not exactly," Sam deflected. "You guys don't…uh…have the right materials here. I do have a bunch more stuff in my pack, though. If we could get that back, I'd really show you what this techno-oracle could do."

"Pack? What pack is this? You never said anything about a pack."

Sam told her about his run-in with Gurn and Reynold, as well as Willow's advice to keep his distance. When Sam was finished, he got the distinct impression he knew where this was going. Roanna wasn't trying to get to know him at all. All she really wanted to know about was the phone and whatever services Sam could provide in the Mavericks' fight against the emperor. Sam didn't like being played, and in all honesty, given the choice, he'd steer clear of this "Maverick versus emperor" conflict altogether. This wasn't his fight. His concern was getting Lawrence and getting back home. His alliance with the Mavericks was a means to an end, nothing more, but if they could be convinced to help him get his pack back, it might be a mutually beneficial endeavor.

"So, I've answered your questions. You gotta answer mine now," Sam said.

"Fair enough," Roanna responded. "What would you like to know?"

"What's that weird top thing I keep seeing you playing with?"

Roanna reached into her pocket and took out the odd trinket. "It's just a twiddler. Most folks don't have the patience for them, honestly. They take a bit of practice to get them to do much, but once you get the hang of it, they can do all sorts of tricks."

Sam watched as the top-like object floated off her palm and started spinning. As it picked up speed, the twiddler changed shape, morphing from round to square.

"It's like an aether fidget spinner," Sam said, leaning closer.

"A what?" Roanna asked.

"Oh, nothing. Just these little spinning things that were really popular back when my dad was a kid. So, since you're so good at the twiddler, does that mean you're some kind of super powerful aether person or something?"

"Me?" Roanna laughed, pocketing the twiddler. Her laugh was surprisingly un-feminine. It wasn't an unpleasant laugh, just a bit more robust than Sam was expecting. "I'm a lowly Sparker just like most everyone else I know. I just have a bit more… finesse than most, I reckon."

"Friend Sam," Willow interrupted, materializing out of nowhere. "I believe it is time to leave."

"Gal dang it, Willow." Sam startled, placing his hand over his heart. "Can you stop sneaking up on me like that? Is our break already over?"

"No," Willow said, looking past Sam's shoulder at the tree line. "There is just a very angry equine-ape that is making its way very quickly in this direction. I would advise running for your life."

"Come again?" Sam asked, confused by Willow's nonchalance.

"From what direction?" Roanna pressed. Sam had no idea what an "equine-ape" was, but from the look on Roanna's face, he was certain he didn't want to find out.

"There." Willow pointed due east.

"You have any more of those opal berries?" Roanna thrust out her hand, which shook slightly. Willow reached into her side satchel and withdrew a handful of the multicolored berries. Roanna took them and jammed them into her mouth. Roanna's eyes went wide with intensity from what Sam figured was a shock of aether. "Where's the cowboy?"

As if on cue, Cornelius sprinted into the clearing from the north, holding on to his hat with one hand. "We got company. Time to vamoose!"

14

GORILLA-HORSE

A terrifying guttural roar sounded from the forest to Sam's left. His fear would've frozen him in place if Roanna hadn't grabbed his arm. They ran toward Cornelius as the sound of snapping branches and a thumping gallop grew closer and closer. Just as they reached the northern tree line, the beast burst into the clearing, announcing its arrival with another deafening roar. Sam couldn't help but turn and catch a glance of the monster. An equine-ape was apparently the rhino-sized mash-up of a gorilla and a horse, if that creature was later adopted and raised by Satan himself.

The beast had fierce gorilla-like facial features and long, thick arms that ended in meaty, clawed hands. The whole thing was covered in wild, black, shaggy fur. It looked around the clearing before locking its cold, dark eyes on Sam. Sam stared back, mesmerized by the monstrosity, before it launched into a dead sprint directly toward him.

Sam didn't know what to do. He stood petrified for a moment before his instincts took over. He turned and ran into the woods, yelling to Cornelius and Roanna, who were running some ten yards ahead.

"I don't think we're going to outrun this thing!" Sam yelled.

Cornelius and Roanna stopped and spun around. Without hesitation, Roanna extended her arm to Cornelius, who reached out and grabbed it for a few seconds before letting go. Roanna jetted off to the left while Cornelius launched into a dead sprint back toward Sam. The cowboy readied his weapons mid-run, slipping a hand into his poncho to don a pair of spiked brass knuckles before reaching over his shoulder to unsheathe his pick-hammer.

"Wait, where are you going?" Sam called after Cornelius as he raced past.

"Just keep running the other dadburned direction!"

However much that made sense to Sam, there was something about a hammer-wielding, brass-knuckled, medieval cowboy sprinting toward a crazed gorilla-horse that simply demanded his attention. His curiosity outweighing his fear, Sam turned and went back as far as the clearing's edge. He hid behind a tree and did what any other kid would do in his shoes: he pulled out his cell phone and started recording.

Cornelius broke into the clearing, making a reckless dash straight for the angered beast. The gorilla-horse was ready for him, or at least it thought that it was. Cornelius covered the last ten strides in a flash, as if someone pressed the fast-forward button on the cowboy remote. Pick-hammer in hand, the cowboy cracked the gorilla-horse on the right leg and dodged away, narrowly avoiding the animal's massive fist that clubbed the ground with the force of a wrecking ball. The beast hardly seemed affected, its thick feral hair a natural armor. Cornelius tried again and again, each time racing in with inhuman speed to strike a blow, and each time coming away with little to show for his efforts.

Out of some mix of desperation and frustration, Cornelius attacked again, ducking underneath the monster's giant arm to leap up and plunge the spike of his hammer into the monster's ribs. The beast bellowed in rage while it thrashed about.

Cornelius whipped around as he still hung to the hilt of his weapon. Undeterred, the gorilla-horse rose on its hind legs and snatched Cornelius from the end of his pick-hammer.

Holding the cowboy in its gigantic hand, the beast yawned open its mouth of fanged white teeth. Sam didn't know if he could watch. He felt petrified with fear and sick with guilt for not helping, yet he couldn't manage to do anything but keep recording. Just as Cornelius was about to be devoured, the cowboy wrestled free an arm, reared back his brass-knuckled fist, and cracked the monster straight in the jaw. A huge white tooth shot from the monster's mouth and soared across the clearing. The enraged beast hurled Cornelius through the air straight into an unforgiving tree trunk.

Sam screamed; the sight of the cowboy's body smashing into the tree and dropping limply to the ground was simply too much. The beast turned its gaze once again to Sam, blood oozing from its lips and down its black fur in a dark slick. Sam swallowed hard and slowly put away his phone. This was it. This beast would run him down and kill him right here. There was nothing he could do. This was how it would all end for Samwise Shelton, adventurer and prankster extraordinaire: devoured by a gorilla-horse.

A small object zipped in from the trees and tagged the beast directly in the eye. The monster reared backward just as a huge net of vines flew across the clearing, entangling the gorilla-horse and toppling it back against the trees. Sam couldn't believe his eyes when branches from the adjacent trees slowly closed in to wrap the monster in a wooden embrace.

"Now, Sam!" he heard Roanna yell from the other side of the clearing.

"Now, *what?*" he yelled back, not sure what *he* was supposed to do.

"Go drain the blooming thing of its aether! The net won't hold him long."

"You want me to go *touch* it?" Sam yelled back again, hoping he heard wrong.

"Stop being a coward and just do it already!" Roanna screamed across the clearing.

Sam still didn't even know how his draining worked. What if he got over there and nothing happened? He'd be torn to shreds. And what would draining it do, anyway? The thing didn't need aether to eat him alive. Sam looked to Roanna. She wasn't messing around. He hated moments like these. Like cliff diving at the quarry. You climbed up and the only way down was jumping. So, just like running to the cliff's edge, Sam sprinted across the clearing toward the trapped monster. There was no turning back now. He lowered his head, steeled his courage, and threw himself onto the gorilla-horse. Sam latched onto the beast's thick fur and willed himself to drain whatever power was there. He felt a cold pressure wash over him like a brain freeze from a dozen slushies. The gorilla-horse went limp, as sure as if someone had just flipped an off-switch.

Sam rolled off the beast and breathed a sigh of relief, his heart still pounding against his ribs. He turned to see Roanna and Willow running to his side.

"Thank the gods," Roanna said, looking at the now inert creature.

"Are you all right, friend Sam?" Willow asked, placing her hand on his shoulder.

"I'm fine. I think," Sam said, getting to his feet. The creature's chest rose and fell in a steady rhythm, but made no other effort to move. "So, what did I just do?"

"You drained the creature of its aether," Roanna said, experimentally nudging the gorilla-horse with her foot. "For humans and the other main races, aether is a power. For most animals, however, it's a bit like their will. Take that away and it sort of just…stops."

"Huh," Sam said, scratching his head. "Now what do we do?"

"I reckon we skin the dodgasted beast and sell its hide to a gravedigger to clothe rotting corpses."

Sam turned to see Cornelius stumble over to the group, one hand on his head, the other supporting his back. "Cornelius, are you okay?"

"Takes more than a goofy-looking goose like that to put ol' Cornelius Thompson the Fourth in the ground. Apologies for missing the end bit. Trees in this forest don't have a lot of give, it would seem. Thanks for checking on me, by the way."

Sam didn't know how it was possible that he'd forgotten about Cornelius. Nothing like one's own peril to make one forget about someone else's. Sam did feel bad. The cowboy ran headlong at the monster, throwing himself at danger so Sam could escape, and Sam didn't even have the decency to just take off like he was told.

"Thank you, Cornelius, for running out there. How are you even walking, honestly? I saw what happened. There's just no way," Sam said, shaking his head.

"Cornelius is a Leech," Roanna said.

"He's a what, now?"

"A Leech," Roanna repeated. "He's a bit unique in that he can drain aether and use it on himself. He can't fill other objects, however, like most everybody else can."

"You use it to make yourself faster and stronger," Sam said, connecting the dots. "That's why you can have bursts of speed, strength, and healing. You're using aether. That's also why you grabbed Roanna's arm before you charged. You drained some of *her* aether, right? That's awesome."

"Something like that, kid," Cornelius said, twisting from side to side and popping his spine into alignment.

"But wait," Sam said, holding up a finger, "what makes you a Leech and everyone else not?"

"My fifth-generation cowboy heritage, I reckon. As I said, some think my great-great-granddad was a bit like you. I'd guess the draining power fades with each generation."

"So are there any other Leeches out there? Anyone other than this League of Cowboys?" Sam asked.

"Not that I know of anymore. The Musketeer Guild had a pretty good run a few hundred years back, but their line is even older than the Cowboys' and their draining power is all but gone."

This was the second time that Sam had heard of the Musketeer Guild. There was no doubt in his mind that people, or groups of people, had been transported over to Avalon for centuries, maybe even millennia. The strange thing was, Sam had never heard or read about a single account of anyone magically showing up back on Earth, wondering how to get back to Avalon. Sam hoped he was wrong, but it seemed like this interdimensional door only swung one way.

15

PLACIDATION

Roanna walked around the unconscious equine-ape and looked it up and down like she was sizing up a truck at a used-car lot. "We should take control of the beast."

"Take control of the ape?" Cornelius questioned with a humorless laugh. "Unless you're storing aether in a hollow leg, I don't think you got it in you, little miss. Plus, I'd only take control of the thing if we planned to walk it off a thousand-foot cliff."

"Just to get us through this forest," Roanna said, giving Cornelius a look that told him 'I thought I told you not to call me little miss.' "Willow, do you have enough opal berries to get me to a Blazer tier? I can't infuse my aether into an animal as a Sparker. I need more aether."

"The Nartareen do not support placidating animals." Willow folded her arms and shook her head.

"Placidating?" Sam asked. There was so much about this world he didn't know.

"Just like putting aether into a rock or stick allows you to control it, putting aether into a fully drained animal allows you that same control," Roanna explained. "Having an equine-ape placidated would be incredibly useful."

Willow stamped her foot. "I do not like that humans placidate what is meant to choose for itself."

"I don't like letting live what is meant to be dead," Cornelius countered. "We don't placidate it, then I'm taking its meat and its hide."

"Rugged Cornelius!" Willow exclaimed, as if she was a mother who had just heard her child say a swear word. She looked back and forth between Roanna and Cornelius. After a pause, she huffed and put her hand in her satchel, withdrawing what looked like a small, multi-colored stone.

Roanna's green eyes went large. "A mottled truffle," she said in amazement, reverently taking the small object. "You're just going to give it to me?"

"Nartareen do not hoard aether," Willow replied. "We use what we need and return the rest to the Eldest Tree. You need this for your task, so it is yours."

"But what is it?" Sam asked, a bit lost in all this aether talk.

"A mottled truffle," Roanna said, still in awe of what she held in her hand, "is extraordinarily rare. I'd heard to buy one you need a diamond of equal size. A find like this could change a family's life. It'd change you from a peasant to a knight or minor lord. Eating this should get me *well* into the Blazer tier."

"Level up. Sweet," Sam said. The three others stared at Sam, uncomprehending. "It's like she's leveling up. Getting new powers and abilities...never mind. So what does this mean?"

"I'm no aetherologist. I just know the rumors, really," Roanna said. "I should be able to infuse aether into animals, among other things. Since you drained the equine-ape, any amount of aether should allow me to control it as long as I'm Blazer tier."

"Take small bites, pretty Roanna," Willow begrudgingly offered.

Roanna nodded and took a nibble from the strange rock-like truffle. She closed her eyes. Her whole body shivered as if she had a wicked case of the chills. She shook her head and then smiled. She repeated the process several more times until the truffle was gone; each time the side effects seemed to lessen.

"How do you feel there, partner?" Cornelius asked, extending a hand.

"Different," Roanna said slowly, as if still processing her emotions. "I think I passed the tier on my second bite. This is incredible!"

Cornelius, Roanna, and Sam helped untangle the dormant beast from the net of thick vines, while Willow worked on "telling the trees" to retract their branches. Sam noticed large stones were woven into the ends of the net, which is most likely what Roanna used her aether on to magically throw the whole thing across the clearing. This girl was as crafty as she was beautiful. She was also as beautiful as she was indifferent to Sam…so that stunk.

After they got the gorilla-horse completely untangled and the pick-hammer removed from its chest, Roanna took a deep breath and moved to place her hand on the creature's leg.

"Wait," Sam interjected, pulling out his phone and walking to the head of the gorilla-horse.

"What now?" Roanna demanded, obviously annoyed at the interruption.

"Gotta take a selfie with this thing." Sam cautiously prodded the creature a few times before leaning in close, holding his arm out and snapping a few pictures.

"Does that further weaken the beast?" Willow asked.

"No," Sam said checking out the photos, "but it will eventually increase my social media power. Very important stuff. Carry on."

Roanna rolled her eyes and moved forward to place her hand on the gorilla-horse. The giant animal stirred, letting out a deep groan as it rolled over onto its feet. It was the same creature, yet it was not. The relaxation of facial muscles and temperament turned it from a raging behemoth to a gentle giant. Sam had to convince himself it was the same creature that tried to bite Cornelius in half not five minutes prior.

The beast slowly crouched down, then pressed its belly to the ground. Roanna scrambled up its side and onto its back. "There's plenty of room for everyone," she said, patting the black fur behind her.

"The only way I'd be riding with that monster is if the tarnal beast had eaten me and I was inside its stomach," Cornelius said, folding his arms.

"Sam?" Roanna asked, extending her hand.

"One second," Sam said, running off into the clearing. He bent over and began searching through the grass.

"What in tarnation are you doing?" Cornelius asked.

"It's got to be here somewhere...ah ha!" Sam returned to the group with the gorilla-horse's knocked-out tooth in his hand. "Never know when a big ol' monster tooth will come in handy. Way too cool to just leave behind."

Roanna rolled her eyes and turned to Willow. "Which way to the Eldest Tree?"

Willow pointed north, and the gorilla-horse responded in an easy gait. The others followed close behind.

"Hey, Willow," Sam said.

"Yes, friend Sam?"

"Why didn't you give the truffle to Roanna earlier?"

"Adjusting to a new level of aether under stress can be dangerous. The opal berries were enough," Willow said.

"No, I mean, *before* the gorilla-horse. Why didn't you give her the truffle days ago?"

"I didn't have it, friend Sam."

"Well, where did you find it?"

"Outside of an equine-ape's nest."

"Willowwww," Sam drew the name out. "Was this before or after the gorilla-horse came charging for us?"

"It was before, friend Sam...just a moment before."

16
THE ELDEST TREE

The next few days went smoothly, thanks largely in part to the gorilla-horse, which, after Willow explained was a female, Roanna decided to call Milla, after her late aunt. The woman was, as Roanna explained, an absolute terror until she became ill late in life. The change in temperament was thought similar to the gorilla-horse's. Even after the explanation, Sam still found it an odd way to immortalize one's aunt.

It wasn't that they hadn't seen any other creatures while in the forest; it was just that those creatures decided to keep their distance from Milla and her crew of four. Like periodically honking the horn to ward off roadside wildlife, Roanna would have Milla give the occasional intimidating roar to keep any curious creatures at bay. Willow warned that they still needed to be careful, however, since the top of the forest food chain was more of a rotating position than it was a permanently held seat.

On the dawn of the sixth day since entering the woods, they had at last arrived at the home of the Nartareen. Sam had little doubt that without Willow as their guide, and Milla as their escort, there would've been a zero-percent chance of finding this place. In fact, even with Willow announcing their arrival, it wasn't even all that obvious that they'd actually arrived. From what Willow said, the Nartareen didn't survive by intimidating and overpowering their enemies; they survived by misdirecting and confusing them, by keeping their powers, their whereabouts, and themselves shrouded in secrecy.

There was no discrete entrance to the Nartareen kingdom, no door or gateway to announce they'd crossed any threshold. At a certain point, Willow instructed Roanna to leave Milla parked by a particularly large tree, as the Nartareen wouldn't take kindly to someone walking into their kingdom on top of a placidated animal. Shortly after they left Milla, Sam noticed that the spacing and alignment of the trees slowly became more ordered. Plants and tree branches formed increasingly organized patterns and symbols. It was subtle at first, but before long Sam found himself walking down a tree-lined path ornately decorated in complex natural designs. Other Nartareen could be seen walking along and across the trail, paying little or no attention to the foreign group who now walked among them.

Sam looked at Willow and back to the other Nartareen. They were all as different to her as she was to him. They were roughly humanoid in form, but not to the precise dimensions of Willow. Gnarled branches grew haphazardly and twisted together to form the shapes of limbs. They had no distinct necks or rounded heads, and small twigs sprouted from the surfaces of their bodies. If Willow was a woodland sprite, these were more like woodland trolls. They weren't scary, per se, but Sam could finally see where the townsfolk got their wives' tales of the forest demons.

"Willow," Sam said, looking around at the other Nartareen. "You don't look like the others."

"No, I do not, friend Sam."

Sam sighed. By now, he should've known he needed to ask more direct questions with Willow. "*Why* do you look different?"

For the first time that Sam could remember, he thought he detected a bit of unease from Willow. She shifted ever so slightly and cast her amber eyes from side to side. "I like humans, friend Sam. I always have."

Sam could've asked any number of follow-up questions, but Willow was obviously a bit uncomfortable talking about the subject, so he let it be. Plus, he could most likely already fill in the narrative. She mentioned multiple times before that she'd basically spent her whole life spying on humans. Sam bet she had a bit of a Pinocchio complex going on. She wanted to be a human girl, or at the very least was fascinated enough with them that she emulated their looks.

"Willow," Roanna said, casting her eyes around the surrounding forest, "where does everyone live?"

Now that Roanna mentioned it, Sam did find it odd that he hadn't seen any buildings of any kind.

"They live here, pretty Roanna," Willow responded, as if the answer was obvious.

"No, I mean where are their homes? Where is *your* home? Where do you keep your belongings?"

Willow looked at Roanna with that blank, immobile stare that only a Nartareen could give. "Roanna, *this* is our home. *This* is my home. *These* are my belongings." She gestured around at the forest.

"You know," Sam chimed in, "it actually kind of makes sense. What's a tree going to use a house for anyway? Our indoors are their outdoors...or maybe it's the other way around."

"That doesn't make any sense," Roanna responded blandly.

"You just need to open your mind, Roanna," Sam said. "What do you think, cowboy?"

Sam looked over to see Cornelius giving a wide berth to every Nartareen that walked by. He could hear the cowboy muttering a string of nonsensical cowboy curse words and something about needing his "pipe at a time like this."

After another half an hour or so, they arrived at the very center of the Nartareen civilization: the Eldest Tree. The ancient being stood alone in the center of a vast clearing populated with the most colorful and magnificent flowers Sam had ever seen. Some petals bloomed open, revealing wildly fluorescent centers, while others spiraled and twisted in complex patterns. Every flower seemed its own uniquely exotic creation.

From a distance, the Eldest Tree seemed just that: a gnarled and ancient tree standing in stark contrast to the vibrant flowers that surrounded it. But as Sam grew closer, he could tell that this tree was more Nartareen than tree, or at least it used to be. The Eldest Tree stood firmly planted in the earth, its legs twisting off in a wide network of meandering roots. Its arms were cocked at odd angles and sprouted off in a dozen or so branches. Sam could make out the faint lines of a face in the trunk of the tree, but just barely, kind of like when people claimed to see the image of Mary in a cinnamon roll.

There were no escorts or guards; no one was even watching. Sam figured if one got this far in the forest, they'd probably passed enough security checkpoints. Willow slowly approached the Eldest Tree, following a small path through the flowers. Sam and the others lagged behind, unsure of the protocol. Willow knelt down, bowed her head, and placed her hand reverently on one of the numerous exposed roots. No words were spoken.

After a minute or so, Sam heard a groaning noise so deep that he wasn't even sure he'd heard it at first. The sound grew louder, changing pitches slightly, followed by the unmistakable creaking and snapping of wood. A mouth and a pair of amber eyes strained open on the body of the tree, breaking apart a skin of bark that had grown over the top. Sam guessed that the Eldest Tree didn't have too many visitors. It was all he could do to not take out his phone and start recording.

The mouth moved rigidly as more strange noises emanated from the ancient being. Willow—her eyes still closed—began to speak.

"Welcome, brave travelers," she translated. "Why has your party sought the Eldest Tree?"

The question was perhaps the simplest that the eldest Nartareen could ask, yet Roanna, Cornelius, and Sam exchanged hesitant glances. They had all come for different reasons, all seeking different things. Sam had come to find Lawrence and get back home, but he wasn't sure if he was supposed to speak on behalf of everyone.

"I come to seek the means to rid this land of its tyrannical emperor." Roanna stepped forward, posture straight, voice resolute.

"Look inside you; look around you," Willow responded after a short pause. "You already have it. Don't lose it."

Roanna's confidence popped like a bubble. She opened her mouth to speak again, but struggled to find any words. She stepped back in line with Sam and Cornelius, a pensive look on her face.

Willow turned to Cornelius, her eyes still closed.

"Oh," Cornelius said, looking around, "I didn't realize we were all here to take turns with a tree genie. Well, in that case, all I want is my peace."

Instead of answering straight away, Willow held out an open hand to Cornelius. The cowboy hesitated a moment, before walking up and grabbing the offered hand. There was a pause before Willow spoke. "Keep another from what robbed you of your peace, and you shall have yours back."

Cornelius nodded his head and released Willow's hand. The words made little sense to Sam, but the sober look on Cornelius's face made Sam think the cowboy knew exactly what the Eldest Tree intended.

"I am here to find my friend, and find a way back home," Sam said, clearing his throat. "I don't know why I'm here or how I got here, but I just want to go home." There was an even longer pause this time, so long that Sam was about to repeat himself when the Eldest Tree finally spoke again.

"Much aether was required to pull you here," Willow began, "and much more is required to send you back."

"But *can* you send me back?" Sam blurted, not waiting for the tree to continue. As far as he knew, this was his *only* chance to get back home, and he was luckier than snot to even make it this far. He felt like he was in court waiting for the judge to declare whether he would have life in prison or was free to walk. *This had to work.*

"Rescue your old friend, help your new ones, and prove yourself worthy of the miracle you seek."

Sam waited for more this time, but more didn't come. His heart pounded. "So does that mean you can send me back? Prove myself worthy and you'll send me back?"

Willow lifted her hand from the root and stood up as the Eldest Tree closed its eyes and mouth. "Oh, friend Sam, you do not look so well."

"Well…what was *that*?" Sam grappled for the right words. "I thought this thing was supposed to grant miracles. It just gave us some advice. That's not a miracle. It's not a miracle if I could get the same thing out of a conversation with my grandpa. We've gotten nowhere. We didn't get any help. I *know* I need to rescue my old friend. That's what I just *told* the thing. It could've at least told us where we should *start* looking—"

Sam's rant was abruptly cut short by the unlikeliest of sounds. It was the ominous music of "Shelob's Lair," song number eleven on *The Return of the King* soundtrack. Sam's mother was calling.

17
VIDEO CHAT

All eyes were on Sam as he quickly reached for his pocket, grabbed his phone, and answered the call. The group huddled around as an image of Sam's mother appeared on the screen.

"Sam?" his mother asked, her eyes wide with shock. Sam had only been gone a week or two, but his mother looked older somehow. Her hair was uncharacteristically frazzled, her eyes lined with heavy bags. "Sam!"

"Mom?" Sam had to fight back tears.

"Sam, are you okay, honey? Are you safe?"

Sam didn't exactly know how to answer that question. He wasn't okay and he definitely wasn't safe, or at least once he stepped beyond the Nartareen village he wouldn't be. "I'm okay, Mom. I'm safe."

Sam's mom took a shuddering breath and wiped her eyes. "I thought I'd lost you. I didn't know what I was going to do."

"I know, Mom," Sam swallowed a lump in his throat.

There was a long pause before his mother finally continued. "Your messages finally came through. I don't understand what's going on, sweetie. Where did you go? What happened?"

This was going to be even harder to explain to his mom than Earth technology was to Willow. "I guess a picture is worth a thousand words," Sam said, tapping his screen and switching to the 360-degree camera. Sam slowly panned the area, making sure to get a good shot of the Eldest Tree and Willow. "Say hi to my mom, everyone."

Cornelius and Roanna stared at the screen with expressions that were one part confused, the other part amazed. Willow gave an enthusiastic wave.

"Is this some kind of trick, Sam?" his mother challenged. "Is this some weird new app on your new phone or something?"

"No, Mom," Sam laughed. "It's not some new weird app. I know this is…impossible to understand, but somehow or another I blacked out in Montana and woke up here. I'm not sure how, but I think it has something to do with the earthquake. This is a strange place with strange things, Mom. I can't explain it. I met some good folks who have helped me out. I'm trying to find a way back home."

"Who's that older gentleman? He looks responsible."

"Cornelius Thompson the Fourth, ma'am," Cornelius said, tipping his hat.

"He's our cowboy in shining armor."

"Well, he is rather handsome," Sam's mom whispered.

"Wait, what?" Sam shook his head. "How does *that* make a difference?"

"I don't know," Sam's mom said defensively. "It just *does*. And what's this about Rinni saying that the GPS shows you're in New Zealand? How is that possible, Sam?"

"I don't know, Mom. Rinni sent me pics of New Zealand at my exact coordinates and the landscapes match. It's like I'm in New Zealand, but I'm not, not our world's version of it anyway. I've only had flashes of signal until now, which is why I haven't called. I think whatever inter-dimensional rift brought me over here must have some small gaps that allow cell signal every now and again. It doesn't make any sense, Mom, but trust me when I tell you that this is actually happening."

"Inter-dimensional rift," Sam's mom repeated slowly. She let out a long breath before continuing. "So, what do we do now?"

Sam looked at the Eldest Tree, then at Roanna. "I think I've met somebody that can help me get back home."

"Now? Can you come home now?" Sam's mom said, perking up at the news.

"It looks like I need to do a few things first."

"Well, what kinds of things? How long will that take?"

Again, Sam didn't know the best way to handle this question. He couldn't exactly tell his mom that an ancient tree has tasked him with being the primary weapon for a group of freedom fighters in their attempt to overthrow a tyrannical wizard-emperor. "Some folks need help and I'm—apparently—uniquely qualified to provide it. I don't know how long it will take, but it could be a while."

They talked a while longer, with Sam doing his best to answer his mom's questions without revealing any detail that would cause her to worry any more than she already was. Sam tried to imagine what his mom was going through. Her son disappears one day only to show up a couple weeks later on a video chat trying to convince her that he was transported to another world. How was she going to explain this to anybody without sounding absolutely insane?

"I almost forgot," Sam's mom said, sensing the conversation was nearing its end. "Have you seen Lawrence? Is he there with you? His parents are worse off than me."

"No." Sam cleared his throat. "That's one of the things I have to do…find Lawrence before I can come back home."

"Well, do you know where he is?"

"I need to talk to Rinni for that, Mom. I'm hoping he might have a way of tracking him. I'm short on supplies here. Although I must say, wicked good timing on the new phone, solar-powered and all. That's the only reason I can still even talk to you."

"I'm glad you like it." Sam's mom gave a weak smile. "Okay, well, you should call Rinni then."

Now that Sam's mom was finally able to talk to him, he could tell she didn't want to let him go. A part of Sam also wanted to keep talking to his mom, but he didn't know how long the signal would last and he desperately needed to talk to Rinni.

"I'm so glad you're safe, sweetie. I can't even tell you how glad I am. I love you."

"I love you too, Mom. I'll call as soon as I can. If not, just keep sending messages and I will too. They'll get through eventually."

Sam hung up the phone. He was no closer to accomplishing any of his goals, but he still felt a titanic weight lift off his shoulders. His mother knew he was okay, or at least that he was still alive.

"Yo, Heinrich, call Rinni."

"Calling Rinni," Heinrich said, followed by a ringtone.

After a few rings, Rinni answered. He stared at his web camera as if he was watching a video of Sam's reanimated corpse.

"Holy crud, it's *actually* you, man!" Rinni screamed. "You're alive! What is going on? I was convinced the ground swallowed you up or something."

"It might as well have. You won't believe what I've been up to." Sam told Rinni everything, starting from the moment he passed out in the vice principal's yard to his conversation with the Eldest Tree. It was the exact opposite conversation he just had with his mother. If anything, Sam *played up* the dangerous parts. After talking for close to ten minutes straight, it was finally Rinni's turn to speak.

"Dude," Rinni drew out the word, "I can't believe you *lost* my flipping backpack!"

"What?" Sam defended. "I fend off two magical thugs,

escape from an emperor's goons, help topple a gorilla-horse, and talk to an ancient miracle-giving tree and *that's* the first thing you say? Plus, the backpack getting stolen is not the same as losing it; just want to draw that distinction."

"Okay, okay. Sorry, this is just a lot to take in, you know? Dude," Rinni whispered, "is that Roanna?" The Apollo's 360-degree camera allowed Rinni to scroll around and look at whatever he wanted in the area without Sam having to pan the camera around.

"No, it's some other random girl in the middle of the forest," Sam hissed, turning his back to Roanna.

"Man, she's gorgeous."

"A lot of thorns on that particular rose, my friend. A lot of thorns. In fact, possibly *all* thorns. Regardless, have you been able to track Lawrence at all? I'll be honest with you. I'm worried, like *really* worried. The emperor's men found me in like a day, and I even got lucky with meeting Willow and everything. My only hope is that he got transported right into friendly hands."

Rinni chewed at his bottom lip. "His phone is dead by now and I never got a signal from it anyway. He could be on the other side of the world from you for all we know."

"So, we got no way of tracking him?" Sam asked.

"I didn't say that. There is a way, but it would require you getting my backpack back." Rinni glared at Sam.

"You're not going to help me unless I get your backpack back? Are you serious?"

"Are *you* serious?" Rinni countered. "Genius, I *can't* help you unless you get the backpack back. I have a pretty powerful auxiliary tracker in my pack, so I've been able to see its location from here whenever I get signal. It also links to my peripheral gear."

"Like Lawrence's earpiece," Sam said, seeing where Rinni was going.

"Precisely. I can tell you where the backpack is, and the backpack should be able to tell you where Lawrence's earpiece is. He might not still have it on him, but it would at least point you in the right direction. Once you get the backpack, the tracker is in an inside pocket in the main compartment. Turn it on and—voila! As long as his earpiece is within like a hundred miles, it should pick it up."

Sam took a deep breath. Most of the time he had to put Lawrence from his mind. Sam knew the odds, and thinking about them just gave him anxiety. The Eldest Tree may not have told Sam where Lawrence was, but if the ancient Nartareen was to be believed, it had at least let him know that Lawrence was still alive. Dead people typically didn't need rescuing. After talking with Rinni, Sam at least now had a plan: backpack, Lawrence, help Roanna overthrow an all-powerful emperor, back to the Eldest Tree, and then home. Just like a really intense episode of *Dora the Explorer*. Simple.

"Okay, so you're my eyes in the sky. Where do I go for the backpack?"

"Stand by," Rinni said, his eyes shifting to a secondary screen. "I'm texting you the GPS pin right now. Looks like it's just north of Lake Wakatipu near a place called Glenorchy. Not too far off from where you are now, actually. It's pretty mountainous where you're at, so it might take a bit."

"Oh, it's mountainous here? Any other pearls of wisdom you wish to bestow?"

"Actually, yes. I almost forgot to tell you, you're famous, man. '#QuakeBoy' is like one of the hottest trending hashtags on the Internet right now."

"Quake boy?" Sam replied in disgust.

"Yeah, man. Montana boy disappeared during Bozeman earthquake sends cryptic messages ten days later, claiming he was transported to another world, complete with pictures of elaborate movie-style creatures." Rinni spoke the sentence in his best news reporter imitation. "The whole Internet thinks you're nuts."

Sam rolled his eyes. "What do *you* think?"

"I don't think you're nuts," Rinni said. "I *know* you're nuts, but I knew that before you got transported to a different world. Don't worry, though; I've been recording this conversation. The Internet is going to *freak* when they see Quake Boy with a tree person."

"Her name is Willow, and she's a Nartareen, not a 'tree person.'"

"Whatever you say, Quake Boy."

"Hey, Rinni, looks like I'm out of time, man," Sam said, noticing his signal bars fading. "It's been good talking to you. Really good."

Rinni nodded his head and then looked at Sam, his face growing serious. "Find him, Sam. I don't know how you're going to do it, but find Lawrence. His parents are a mess. Your mom's a tough bird, Sam. His parents aren't."

"I just got your GPS marker for the backpack. Don't worry. I'll find him," Sam said, hoping he sounded a lot more confident than he actually was.

18
SELFIES

According to Google Maps, -44.8488, 168.3861 marked the location of Glenorchy, a charming little town at the very northern tip of Lake Wakatipu. In Avalon, the location was slightly different. The stunning mountainous panorama was the same, but the quaint lakeside village was replaced with Hagzarad, home to the largest black market south of the Peaklands.

This was both good news and bad news, or so Cornelius explained. The good news was that most of the folks that frequented Hagzarad did so to avoid the long arm of the law, so there was a much lower risk of running into the emperor's men. The bad news was that without law enforcement, the place had degenerated into a crime-infested trading slum that made the wrong side of Ogland look like a five-star beach resort.

Sam, Willow, Roanna, and Milla made camp in the woods outside of Hagzarad. Cornelius had left for town early in the morning to visit a few old acquaintances and see if he could find out anything that would point them in the right direction.

The backpack could be anywhere. All they knew was that it was in Hagzarad about four days ago when the signal had last gone through to Rinni's computer. Until Cornelius returned, their only instructions were to stay hidden in the woods, keep out of sight, and keep out of trouble.

Sam sat against a tree and looked at his phone, thumbing through a few screenshots he took during his conversation with his mom. The Eldest Tree had done something to open up the rift between the two worlds and allow Sam temporary cell reception. If Sam had to guess, he'd say it was some side effect of using aether. If a lot could open up a gateway between worlds, then maybe a little could open up enough of a gap to let cell phone signal through. The Eldest Tree must've used some aether for a "minor miracle" to allow Sam to call home. More than a miracle, Sam felt it was a promise. If Sam upheld his end of the bargain, the Eldest Tree would uphold hers.

"So, is that your mum?" Roanna asked, peering over Sam's shoulder.

"Huh? Uh, yeah. That's her." Sam tapped his screen and pocketed his phone.

"How does it do that? How does it have your mother's reflection?"

Sam had decided he wouldn't go out of his way to show off his phone to Roanna anymore, since trying to impress her never ended well. He wasn't about to pass up on opportunity when *she* brought it up, though. He pulled out his phone and held it up.

"Here, I'll show you. Make a silly face or say something funny."

"I really don't see how that is going to help me understand your oracle," Roanna said, hands on her hips.

"That'll do," Sam said, finishing his recording. He flipped the phone around and tapped the screen, playing back the five-second video of Roanna.

Roanna gasped and threw her hands over her mouth. "What is this? Do I really look like that?"

"That," Sam said, thumbing to the video of Cornelius

fighting Milla, "is called a video, and it's only the beginning of what I can do with this…er, with my oracle."

She finished watching the video and looked up at Sam, her eyes wide with wonder. "I want to know everything there is to know about your oracle."

A hurricane of butterflies swirled in Sam's chest. He might actually be making progress here. He cleared his throat. "Well, uh, the most basic of all techniques is the 'selfie,' of course."

"This is what you did when Milla was drained, am I right?"

"Good memory," Sam said, thinking back. If Sam was going to keep up the whole techno-oracle shtick, then keeping track of all of his lightly spurious claims was going to be a challenge. "Here, we can take a selfie of us. You just gotta kinda squeeze in close here and when I say 'three,' you say 'cheese.'"

Roanna lifted an eyebrow at the nonsensical request, but acquiesced. Sam held out his arm, counted to three, and snapped a photo. "See, here we are." Sam turned the phone around and showed Roanna.

"And this will also increase your social media power?"

"Without a doubt," Sam said, looking at the photo again and tagging it to upload to his accounts once he got signal.

"Help me!" a distant voice yelled. The words were barely discernible, but the urgency in the voice was clear.

"Did you hear that, friend Sam?" Willow asked, materializing at Sam's side.

"Dog blast it, Willow!" Sam yelped, throwing his hand over his heart. "For the love of…would you please stop doing that?"

"I heard it, Willow," Roanna said, struggling to contain a grin. The happiest Sam had ever seen the girl was when Willow startled him. He kept company with some twisted women.

"I will go look," Willow said.

"Willow, our only instructions from Cornelius were to stay in the woods and stay out of sight," Roanna said. "That sounded like it came from over by the main road. You heard what

Cornelius said about this area. Lots of people traveling to and from Hagzarad. Could be a trap for all we know."

The cry for help sounded again and the three exchanged glances.

"I will stay in the woods and stay out of sight, pretty Roanna. No one has ever seen me that I did not want to see me."

"I've got absolutely no doubts there," Sam muttered. "But I'm coming with."

"You are not," Roanna countered. "*Milla* moves through the woods more silently than you do."

"Awesome, then make sure she trails right behind me, because if someone is in trouble, we might need the backup."

19

THE TRAVELER

Sam and Roanna peered through the trees at a tall, skinny traveler. He wore a long leather coat, skullcap, and a ridiculously overloaded backpack. A pair of strange metal goggles sat on top of his head over his cap. Where his gear wouldn't fit in his pack, it dangled off the side, fastened with bits of twine and rope. Facing down the odd traveler was a group of four thugs, looking every bit like clones of Reynold and Gurn.

"Now just hold on—help—a minute there—help!" the traveler periodically yelled, trying his best to ward off the group with a long staff topped with what looked to be a shard of obsidian. "I told you, all I gots here are trinkets and gimcrackery. Bunch of tawdry bits and bobs this is. Going to hawk me wares in town to the doltish royalty and such. Fine, street-shrewd gentlemen like yerselves wouldn't be diddled by this rubbish."

Sam turned to Roanna and whispered, "What's he saying?" It wasn't that he couldn't hear him; it was that he didn't understand a darn word that came out of the guy's mouth.

"He's trying to convince them his stuff is worthless," Roanna replied.

"Right." Sam nodded.

The four men closed in tighter and one of them spoke. "If your stuff is such rubbish, shouldn't be a problem to just hand it over then, would it?"

The traveler recoiled at the words, as if the man had physically made a grab for his belongings. "Hand it over? This here's all I got. But take heed. My valuation isn't in what's on me back, but in the services I can provide. I can locate the oddest of objects, the rarest of rarities, the most precious of prizes. Merely ask it of me and I shall acquire."

"We're asking you for your pack, old traveler," one of the men said, ignoring the traveler's offer. "And if you don't give it up, then we'll have to...I don't know...tear your ears off."

"You wouldn't slay the milking cow for her meat, no doubt?" The traveler laughed uneasily.

"Roanna, we need to do something," Sam hissed.

"What we need to do is stay hidden," Roanna replied. "What would we do anyway?"

"We storm out there with Milla, and scare them all away," Sam said, pointing back into the forest where Milla hid.

"Scare them away?" Roanna echoed. "So they can go tell everyone in Hagzarad that they saw a strange boy and girl burst from the trees with their pet equine-ape? This is unfortunate, but this traveler should know better than to parade down the road, alone, this close to Hagzarad. How he's lasted this long, I'll never know. We can't protect the world's imbeciles from themselves."

"I'm not asking you to protect the world's imbeciles, I'm asking you to help protect *this* one." Sam locked eyes with Roanna. He had spent most of his youth lying in wait, watching some prank victim fall into a trap, but this was different. In a prank, Sam meticulously planned, set up, and controlled the stakes. The person might get upset, but no one was ever truly harmed. What Sam was watching here was a perversion of what he stood for. Pranks were to take a shot at those who most deserved it, someone who assumed they were untouchable; *this* was preying on someone who least deserved it. "Just send out Milla by herself, or maybe Willow could do something."

By the time Sam and Roanna had finished their argument and looked back at the traveler, it was too late. The men rushed in, but before they could reach the traveler, he flipped down his goggles and swung the tip of his staff at the dirt, shattering the obsidian-like crystal. A bubble of blackness radiated outward, enveloping the entire group in a dome of perfect dark. The men shouted, first in confusion, then in pain. There was no way to tell what was going on. One of the thugs emerged from the bubble holding his eyes, only to receive a crack to the head as the traveler's whirling staff briefly reached out from the darkness. After the sound of several more *THWACKS*, the black bubble burst, returning the spot in the road to normal. Four men lay unconscious on the ground.

"Holy boogers," Sam said, gesturing to the traveler with his thumb. "Did you see that?"

"Of course I saw that," Roanna said, her face scrunched in thought. "I'm just not exactly sure *what* I saw."

"We need this guy."

"What do you mean, 'we need him'?" Roanna responded, making sure to stay hidden. "We don't even know whose side he's on. Did you see what he did to those thugs?"

"Didn't I just ask *you* if you saw that?" Sam replied, throwing his hands up. "Look, he's exactly what we need. He just said that he specializes in finding rare stuff. If anyone has heard about or could track down a backpack full of my gear, it's this dude."

Roanna pressed her lips together. At least she was reconsidering. "And what if he decides to turn us in, or spread the word of who he saw? What then?"

"You wanted me in your fight against the emperor, yeah? Well, this is who I am. I roll the dice. There is no way we'll be able to take down a tyrant by playing it safe."

"I know," Roanna hissed back, "we do it by not being *stupid*."

"This is risky, but it's also more…rewardy. Roll the dice with me, Roanna."

Sam didn't know if he could trust the strange traveler, or who the man would tell, but Sam *did* know that opportunities like this weren't to be squandered. It was too serendipitous to be ignored. Perhaps the Eldest Tree had guided them here. The circumstance fit too well to be a coincidence. They needed to find something a bit out of the ordinary and here they found someone who did just that for a living. They could follow the man, but eventually they'd lose him since they had to stay close by for when Cornelius returned.

Sam stared into Roanna's hard, green eyes. Sam knew this was a risk, but in a struggle between your gut and your brain, always go with the gut. "You can do the logical with the brain, but it takes your gut to do the improbable." It was another one of his dad's phrases that had guided his life…maybe a bit too much for his mom's liking. She was quite content for her only son to just stick with doing logical things.

"You want to do improbable things, Roanna? This is how improbable things get done."

She stared at Sam for a long minute before slightly nodding her head. Sam smiled and nodded in return.

"Be ready with Milla," Sam whispered. He took a deep breath, stood up, and began making his way loudly through the woods. The last thing he wanted was to startle a man who had just knocked out four armed men. Sam casually exited the trees onto the road, making a show of surprise as he walked onto the scene. He looked up at the traveler, eyes wide.

"Goodness me, what happened here?" Sam asked, turning on his poor British kid accent.

"Now who, pray tell, are you?" the traveler said, gripping his staff a bit tighter. Sam realized that the man was probably trying to figure out whether Sam was with the unconscious men or not.

"Me?" Sam pointed to himself. "Why, I'm Philbert McGibbons, my good sir. And who do I have the pleasure of meeting on this trail, if you don't mind me being so forward?"

"Name's Gideon Vanduker," the man said, nodding slightly. "And what sort of errands would have a young boy like yerself wandering about them woods? You best be giving them a wide berth, you hear? Treacherous by half, they are. Treacherous even for a wizened traveler like meself."

"Oh, Mr. Gideon, don't worry about ol' Philbert here. I've been in and out of these parts most of me life. Amazing all the unusual things one finds out here in the forest, if one knows where to look, of course."

"Of course." Gideon raised an interested eyebrow. "And what oddities does a stripling like yerself speak about?"

"Are you hinting at a trade of some sort, Mr. Gideon?" Sam asked, eyeing the traveler's bag. "I see you have a pack full of odd items. The natural treasures I can find easy enough, but the man-made ones are hard for me to come by."

"Little boy—"

"Philbert," Sam corrected.

"Philbert," Gideon started again, "a traveler is always amenable to a barter, but I have on me person the finest of me wares. I'm not sure you'll have much that interests me, me boy."

Sam shrugged his shoulders and gave a disinterested frown. "On the contrary, Mr. Gideon, I believe I have something you want, but it is you who does not, as yet, have what I desire."

Gideon let out a long laugh. "I am truly amused and bemused, my young Philbert. Please divulge what it is that I desire and you desire?"

"I have a black bag—or at least I *used* to have a black bag—itself of unique design, filled with objects even more unique. I have reason to believe that my bag has found its way to Hagzarad."

"Your description leaves a lot to the imagination, young Philbert." Gideon stroked his stubbled chin.

"You will know it when you see it. Trust me."

"Alright," Gideon chuckled, "suppose that I will. Now, what is it that I would desire in return?"

"The tooth of an equine-ape," Sam said, pulling out a large white fang from his pocket.

Gideon gave a look of genuine surprise. "Now *that* is a curious object indeed. But how am I to know that you aren't spinning a yarn here, me boy?"

"Milla," Sam yelled over his shoulder. After a moment, heavy footsteps crunched through the forest behind him, until the monstrous gorilla-horse pushed through the trees and walked onto the road, Roanna on her back.

Gideon scrambled backwards, staff held at the ready in both hands. "Jabbering jilleroo, what is going on here?"

Sam casually walked up to the beast and gave it a pat. "Give us a smile, girl."

20

CAMP

Before Cornelius left, the old cowboy had instructed Sam and Roanna to "stay put and make camp," but with no fire, no tent, no marshmallows, and no hotdogs; this was unlike any "camp" Sam had ever been a part of. "Camping" apparently boiled down to eating whatever berries and edible bits Willow could rummage, and finding a spot on the ground to sleep. Sam guessed it could've been worse. At least in Avalon the forest floor was soft and spongy. He supposed he could've been magically transported to a land of volcanoes or jagged rocks.

Sam lay in his spot among a group of large twisting roots. After padding it with some nearby foliage, it felt like he was resting in a human-sized nest. Pale beams of moonlight shone down through breaks in the forest canopy, giving the area its only light. Roanna was no less than ten yards away, nestled in her own spot, while Willow was who knows where. From what he knew of the Nartareen, she was probably about a foot from Sam's face, waiting to appear out of thin air. Gideon had the only thing that Sam would consider an actual shelter, having retired to his small canvas tent about an hour prior.

"Roanna, you awake?" Sam whispered into the darkness. He

felt like he'd made a bit of progress with her today, and with Cornelius gone, he had several burning questions to ask. When she didn't reply, he spoke louder. "Roanna, you awake?"

"I am now," she replied.

"Sorry. Well, now that you're up, I wanted to say thanks for trusting me today. I know I screwed things up for you in Ogland. I'm sorry about that."

Silence hung in the night air for a while before Roanna responded. "Thank you for acknowledging that."

"Uh, you're welcome." Sam had hoped more for forgiveness than simple acknowledgment, but beggars couldn't be choosers, so he decided to roll with it. "Hey, so what's the deal with Cornelius, anyway?"

"What do you mean?" Roanna asked.

"Like what's he doing down here? He said he used to be up north, that he's seen his fair share of rebellions. What's his story?"

"Well," Roanna said, sounding like she was weighing what or exactly how much to say. "From what I can piece together, he made quite the name for himself up in the Greenlands, the uppermost kingdom of the North Isle. You'll find people that have a wee bit of cowboy heritage, but Cornelius is practically purebred. From what I know, someone with his abilities is extremely rare. He partnered up with a powerful Scorcher and eventually got the attention of the king. They made a fortune as the king's favorite enforcers, but something happened and they got crossways with the Greenlands royalty."

"I'm guessing it didn't end well."

"Sam, he watched the king murder his best friend."

"I…didn't know." The comment was a stupid one, but it meant more than the obvious. Sam knew that the cowboy had seen battle, which likely meant he'd seen death. But this was different, or at least made Sam understand things differently. Was Cornelius banished or on the run? Was he plotting his revenge from afar—biding his time—or had he retreated down south in defeat? There was much more to this cowboy than just playing cards and drinking grog.

"There aren't many down here that do know about him, which is why I assume he's here. I don't claim to know his thoughts, but his talent and power are utterly wasted in Ogland. He keeps to himself and runs away when he should be storming forward."

"So how did *you* get to know Cornelius?" Sam asked. "He like a distant relative or something?"

"No, he's not a distant relative," Roanna laughed quietly, "but—for all his shortcomings—I do owe him. He'll tell you he first saw me four years ago at the Harvest Festival during the aether showcase. I took first place for the ten-and-unders. Had myself a promising future."

"What happened?"

"By midday, I stood on the town square dais being handed my trophy by the Count of Ogland. Before the sun had set, I watched that same count, on that very same dais, kick the stools out from underneath my parents' feet where they were 'hanged until dead for treason against the emperor.' They'd been squirreling away aether in an ingot they'd stolen so I could use it to get more practice. I had no idea. They thought maybe I had enough talent to go to one of the universities, leave the Sparker life behind. I found the twiddler in my dad's pocket when they unstrung him. I had seen it on a vendor stall and wouldn't shut up about it. He said we didn't have the money. It was going to be a surprise, I guess. I have no other family. Cornelius took me to the Rosemary. Made sure I was looked after."

There was a long silence after Roanna spoke. Even if Sam knew what to say, Roanna's words stunned him like a punch to the gut. Sam wanted to tell her he knew how she felt, that he'd lost a parent too, but the coldness with which she recounted the story made him hesitate. Bad luck had taken his father from him. There was a distinct wrongness, a helplessness that came with that. The grief was crippling at times, but ultimately, there was nothing for Sam to avenge. His only act of honoring his father wasn't to make sure that he hadn't died in vain, but that he hadn't *lived* in vain. Sam honored his dad by remembering him and by allowing his lessons to still guide him. Roanna's situation was different. She'd seen the thing that had stolen her parents from her. It lived. And if it lived, then it could be stopped. Sam got the impression that Roanna couldn't focus on her parents' life because their death was left unresolved.

He felt sorry for Roanna. It had taken Sam a lot of counseling and a lot of support to cope with his dad's death, and he still felt lost. He seriously doubted Roanna had received similar support. Maybe when the Eldest Tree asked him to help his new friends, it wasn't just talking about helping them with what they wanted, but with what they needed.

Sam could've said that he was sorry for what happened, but the extended silence did that well enough. He decided instead to change the topic. "Forgive me asking, Roanna, but I actually don't know what a Scorcher is."

"You really *aren't* from around here." Roanna gave a quiet chuckle that told Sam the change of topic was appreciated. He heard her walk over to his nest. She sat down next to his bed, finding a gap in the roots that served as a natural chair. "Never thought I'd be teaching anyone about aether class structure. Sparker, Blazer, Scorcher, Inferno, Eternal. They're your basic levels of aether possession. I don't profess to know what each level can or can't do. You'd need an actual scholar for that. Most folks like me are born Sparkers and stay Sparkers. Taxes make sure of it. You have your successful merchants and knighted soldiers; they're the Blazers. That's what I am now—amazingly enough—after I ate that mottled truffle, but if I use it up or someone uses their aether to destroy mine, I would drop back down to a Sparker quick as a wink. Scorchers are your named warriors, noblemen, and princes. I haven't met too many of them, but they're the ones that can do simple hybridizations and grafting."

"They can do what now?"

"Have you seen anyone with animal features, or a body part made from stone or metal or something?"

Sam immediately thought of Reynold's cat eye and Gurn's wooden hand. "The two goons that took my backpack, actually."

"There you have it. It requires a bit of coin, but they would have gone to a black-market Scorcher to get the work done. In most cases it's to fix some injury, but other times it's an enhancement. Rumors talk about the emperor's soldiers getting upgraded with metal skin or eagle eyes. I've even heard that in wealthy cities people change themselves for fashion. Sounds crazy. Anyway, after Scorchers, you can count the rest on your fingers and toes: kings and queens and maybe some of the emperor's right-hand men are the Infernos. There's only one Eternal. That's the emperor."

"What about the Eldest Tree? Where would that fit?"

"Huh," Roanna said, scratching her head. "You know, I guess I hadn't considered non-humans before. It seems impossible that anyone or anything would have as much aether as the cursed emperor, but if what Willow says is true—if the Eldest Tree has access to all the forest's aether—I suppose it could be another Eternal."

There was so much about this world that Sam didn't know. It was the first time in his life he wished he could actually take a class on something. Avalon history, aether class structure, aether power theory, creatures of Avalon. A world of information to learn and he wouldn't find any of it online. That was an unsettling thought. His entire life, any answer he wanted was only a few keystrokes away. His grandparents were always going on about how things were before the Internet, how if you wanted to figure something out, you actually had to put some effort into it. Whether it was "what actor was in that movie," "where was the closest bowling alley," or "how to jump-start your car battery," you used to have to talk to people, look stuff up in books, or just be out of luck. Sounded exhausting.

"Hello, weary travelers," a voice called from the darkness, making Sam jump. Cornelius was back.

"It is you who looks the weariest," Sam replied with the predetermined phrase. If Sam and Roanna were in any kind of trouble, his line was supposed to be "weary enough, old friend."

"What is that?" the cowboy insisted, pointing to Gideon's tent. Sam could hardly see, it was so dark. Night vision was apparently among the list of characteristics Cornelius could enhance with aether. Sam was dreading this question. He thought about having Gideon camp farther away from their group and "stumble" on them once Cornelius got back, but Sam knew the cowboy wouldn't be so easily fooled. Plus, Sam needed Cornelius's trust. An odd goal, considering Gideon was here only because Sam expressly broke Cornelius's most explicit instruction.

"That," Sam paused, rising from his bed of leaves and grass, "is the tent of one Gideon Vanduker, rare-object seeker extraordinaire."

"What is it doing here?" Cornelius responded flatly.

"It's actually a funny story." Sam recounted the events of the day, making sure to emphasize how unique of an opportunity it was for them to come across a man with the exact skills they needed.

The cowboy stood in silence. Even without saying anything, or without Sam able to make out his facial features, there was no mistaking what Cornelius was thinking. It was along the lines of "I trusted you with something simple and now you've made things complicated." It was a phrase he had heard his mother say once or twice.

"Roh?" the cowboy asked, his entire question implicit with just her name.

"He could be useful," Roanna responded.

"So could a lightning storm in a fist fight."

"That doesn't even make any sense," Roanna shot back.

Even a world away from his mother, here Sam was again—in the eye of the hurricane. With his mom, he knew exactly what he needed to do to weather the storm, but Cornelius would be a new puzzle to solve. Sam honestly didn't want to make him mad. After all, the cowboy was only in this mess because Sam had come storming into his card game demanding help. Cornelius had never complained once about the circumstances being unfair or him not wanting or deserving this situation. Whatever it was that kept Cornelius with the group, Sam hoped to Merlin that it wasn't in short supply. Hopefully the old cowboy would come around after Gideon found the backpack.

Cornelius walked past the two and sat next to a tree. The trailing stench of alcohol was as strong as Sam had ever smelled on a man.

"Cornelius," Roanna said, almost like a mother getting ready to scold her child. "Well, at least you made a time of it, didn't you? You reek enough to have drunken all the barrels in Hagzarad."

"Do I sound drunk to you, Roh?" Cornelius challenged, his voice steady as stone.

"Well...no, but what does that prove?"

"It proves that I've burned through all my aether stores ensuring that when I *do* drink, I don't get drunk. How else do you think you get information in a town like that? Get everyone full as a tick and they start to talk, all the while I still maintain my good wits."

Sam leaned over to Roanna to whisper, "That's actually a pretty good idea."

Roanna snorted. "So, what did all your drinking get us, if I may ask?"

Cornelius grunted as he wiggled into a more comfortable position. "It got us a start. The pack *did* come to town, so I reckon Sam's techno-magic thingamajig was correct on that account. The emperor's men weren't far behind, however. They followed the rumors about a strange drainer boy and came back here looking for any signs. They left empty-handed."

"So the pack is gone?" Sam's heart sank.

"Don't reckon I said that. Just said that the emperor's men couldn't find nothing. Thing of it is, they hardly ever do when they come to Hagzarad. They don't take kindly to lawmen around these parts. I shared a whiskey or two with an off-duty guard who let slip the pack got picked up by the Guild Lord of Hagzarad himself, Lord Borinder Besselink."

"Is that a good thing or a bad thing?" Sam wished the cowboy would just get to the point. *Can we get the blasted bag or not?*

"Well," the cowboy said, spitting on the ground. "It's a bit like finding out that your lost coin purse is in the belly of a volcanic death worm."

"So...that's bad."

"Sure, but at least you know where your coin purse is. Borinder is not to be trifled with. He's a Scorcher who's renowned for being as shrewd as a fox, and for knowing everything there is to know about what goes on in Hagzarad. The good news is, there's only one thing Borinder likes more than making a profit, and that's spiting the emperor. If he knew the emperor wanted something, that would be reason enough to keep it from him."

"So you're saying that maybe Borinder would help us?" Sam asked, a bit of hope returning. "I mean, if the emperor is after me, wouldn't Borinder want to help us?"

"It's possible." Sam saw Cornelius's silhouette tip his hat forward over his face. "It's also quite possible that he'd just kill us."

21

JEWELRY STORE

The plan took all morning to devise. It wasn't that it was all that complicated, but it was risky. It also didn't take long to realize that Sam's gamble at picking up Gideon had immediately paid off. It turned out that Lord Borinder Besselink had a penchant for the rare and exotic and had actually dealt directly with Gideon on a few occasions. It didn't give them a direct path to the Guild Lord—only those who impressed his steward gained an audience—but it did give them a better understanding of what they were dealing with.

Stealing the backpack straight up was out of the question. You didn't rise to the top of a place like Hagzarad by being easily duped, and you didn't *maintain* your place by being an easy target. Borinder—with his genius-level intellect—operated from inside a fortress in the center of the city. His stronghold featured tall outer walls, multiple locked doors, a single flight of stairs leading to and from his office, and a few dozen guards scattered throughout. You were either let in, or you had sufficient strength to force your way in…and to this day, no one had ever forced their way in.

By mid-morning they arrived at Hagzarad, and it was unlike

any place Sam had ever seen. From the warnings that Cornelius gave, Sam was expecting the place to look like Mordor during an orc riot. If anything, however, Sam found that he actually preferred it to Ogland. Where Ogland was depressing, subdued, and stinky, Hagzarad was alive, busy, and…well it was still stinky. Everywhere Sam looked, the place was teeming with life. Some of that life was cordial, with people laughing or passionately haggling over a vendor's wares; and some of that life was not so cordial, with fist fights and brandished weapons at almost every corner. As they followed Gideon down one of the town's many winding cobblestone paths, Sam heard a screaming match coming from inside a primitive roadside post office. Seconds later, a man crashed through the front window, followed by a flock of escaping messenger pigeons. Sam could understand if this was some kind of seedy tavern late at night, but this was a post office. *What kind of person gets thrown out of a post office?*

Even more distinct than the constant noise and commotion of the town was the fact that aether was out on open display. Waterwheels, wheat grinders, and blacksmith hammers all moved and operated on their own, as if worked by a team of invisible ghosts. Animals, ranging from razor-teethed weasels to large bear-faced cats, were led around on leashes as if they were no more than common household dogs. Enormous beasts of burden lumbered dumbly down the streets, their backs stacked precariously high with goods. Even though it felt more alive, Sam still had no doubt that this was not a place to navigate alone.

They had all come into town this time, even Willow. In fact, when Gideon first saw Willow, he *insisted* they bring her to town. Apparently, the more unique and eccentric the group, the more likely they were to gain an audience with Borinder. Having a Nartareen would be unique enough, but Willow—from what Sam had seen—was a one-of-a-kind Nartareen. That had to be worth extra bonus points. Milla was the only part of the group that didn't come. There were other large beasts in town, but a gorilla-horse was quite uncommon and they didn't want to attract anyone's attention outside of Borinder's.

After winding through the streets for a quarter hour, they stopped in front of an unassuming shop door. A sign reading "Truchot's Fine Jewelry" hung above the entrance, while a small brass bell with a dangling string was mounted on the wall to the side. Gideon grabbed the string and gave the bell four distinct rings. They waited half a minute with no response.

"Maybe they're not in," Sam said.

"They're in," Gideon said, looking at his distorted reflection in the bell and adjusting his leather cap.

After another full minute, Sam heard footsteps from inside. The door opened and they were met by a smartly dressed middle-aged man with neatly styled, prematurely gray hair.

"May I help you?" the man queried, his voice as smooth and cold as a sheet of ice.

"Name's Gideon Vanduker, proprietor of the finest traveling establishment for the sale of exotics and rarities, here to seek audience with Lord Borinder." Gideon removed his skullcap and goggles and gave a sweeping bow.

"I recognize you," the gray-haired man said, voice still devoid of interest or emotion.

"I have had previous dealings of merchandise and trade with the good Lord Borinder Besselink."

The man pressed his thin lips together and cast glances at the rest of the group. "And who are they?"

"I speak on their behalf, my good steward," Gideon said, his confidence and air of salesmanship never faltering.

"Flip back your hood." The gray-haired man pointed at Willow.

Willow removed her hood as instructed and looked up. "Hello, unfriendly man."

"Get it inside," the man said, holding the door open and quickly shuffling the group into the store.

They entered a large room adorned with richly colored

pedestals and display cases, each containing glittering necklaces, rings, and other jewelry. With the unrelenting commotion outside, the elegant, luxurious interior of the store was almost laughably out of place. Sam looked back at the front door and was surprised to see it had no special locks or bolts. Borinder's reputation was apparently enough to keep out any unwanted visitors.

The gray-haired man walked behind a counter at the back of the store and waited for the group to congregate. He placed his hands on the countertop and Sam couldn't help but gawk. Each of the man's fingers on his right hand was made of a different precious stone: ruby, emerald, sapphire, and diamond. His thumb was polished gold. "You may call me Haydn. What else do you have to show me, besides the Nartareen?"

"Well, Mr. Haydn, may I introduce one Mr. Philbert McGibbons, worker of enigmatic magics and budding collector of otherworldly oddities," Gideon said, throwing open his arms and stepping back for Sam to approach the counter.

Haydn had all the expressiveness of a corpse as he waited for Sam.

"I have objects that you have not seen, and I am led to believe that you have objects that you have only recently seen, but do not know yet what they are." Sam had the utmost confidence in his ability to improvise, but he had memorized this line, trying to channel his inner Gideon. He spoke in an extra thick accent for good measure.

The claim coaxed a hint of an eyebrow twitch from the steward, which Sam figured was the equivalent of a normal person wetting their pants with excitement. "And where are these objects I have never seen?"

Sam held up his phone.

"And what does it do?" Haydn asked, unimpressed.

Sam tapped his screen twice. An image of Haydn was projected onto the nearby wall. Sam tapped his phone again and played back the video he'd just recorded.

The steward's eyes went wide. Sam couldn't resist a small smile. One of the simplest and oldest features of any smartphone, and to these people it was stranger than Sam seeing someone with fingers made of sparkly stones.

"You and you, come with me," Haydn said, pointing to Sam and Willow. "Everyone else must remain here."

"Uh, my good sir," Gideon started before being silenced by a look from Haydn.

"These two only, or no one goes at all." Haydn's emotionless demeanor shifted slightly from apathetic to menacing.

Sam's pulse quickened. He needed the whole group. How was he supposed to barter with Borinder without Gideon? If things went belly up—and they often did—he'd need Cornelius and Roanna to grab the backpack and make a getaway. He liked Willow, but she was like a fish out of water when she was away from the forest. Sam would be on his own to make this work, and if he didn't, Borinder could slit his throat before Cornelius or Roanna ever knew anything was amiss. Sam shot a nervous glance at Cornelius, who only returned a short, reassuring nod.

Haydn turned from the counter to face the unadorned, wood-paneled wall behind him. He reached up and pressed one of the panels, springing open a small hidden door. Ten small holes, arranged in a star pattern, adorned the surface underneath. He reached into his vest pocket and withdrew a key, which he inserted into each keyhole, twisting it different directions at each hole. When he was done, Sam heard a soft *CLICK* and a portion of the wall gave way, revealing a secret passage.

"This way," Haydn said to Sam and Willow, before turning to the others. "Remain here."

"How long will you be?" Roanna asked Haydn as the three entered the corridor.

"I'll leave that answer up to Lord Besselink," Haydn replied, grabbing the door. "But if we're not back by nightfall, I wouldn't bother waiting any longer."

22

BORINDER BESSELINK

Sam followed Haydn through a dimly lit corridor for several hundred yards before finally reaching another door. The door, like the last one, had a pattern of keyholes into which Haydn worked his key before pushing the door open. They entered a room constructed of solid stone blocks with ornate wooden furniture and an imposing spiral staircase. For all appearances, it looked like they were in a castle. Haydn stood at the base of the stairs and gestured for Sam and Willow to follow. As Sam started his climb, he wondered how many people had ascended these same stairs, but never came back down. Did they have any idea as they followed Haydn up to Borinder's office that these steps would be their last…that their time was up?

What was Sam going to do if Borinder wasn't swayed by his arguments and offerings? He racked his brain for a backup plan, but there were too many unknowns. They reached the top of the stairs and Haydn knocked on a large wooden door before pushing it open and walking into the room beyond. Sam and Willow followed.

To say that Borinder Besselink had a taste for the exotic was the understatement of the decade. The vast room was more museum than office, with objects mounted on every square inch of the two-story walls or in huge glass display cases. Swords, axes, bows, and other weapons that Sam couldn't even identify were on his left, each designed with unique shapes and materials. To his right was a section of curious geared contraptions that looked like a cross between medieval torture devices and Leonardo Da Vinci machines. There were maps, scrolls, statues, strange animal skeletons, and paintings. Sam paused at a parchment securely kept behind a pane of thick glass. It was old, ancient even, with frayed edges and fading text. Sam was no historian, but he would've bet his lunch money that it was Egyptian.

"Please do not touch anything," Haydn told Willow in hushed tones.

Sam looked over to see Willow tentatively reaching for a golden cup. If the place was curious to Sam, Willow was probably on the brink of exploding with wonderment.

"I am sorry, unfriendly man," Willow whispered back. "I have never seen things like this."

Sam took a closer look at the golden cup and noticed that it was actually a trophy with an inscription across the face. *Borinder Besselink - 75th Annual South Avalon Arithmetic Champion.*

"Lord Besselink," Haydn called, ignoring Willow's response, "I have with me two individuals that may be of interest to you."

Borinder Besselink stood next to a small cage at the far end of the room. In his palm sat a mouse-sized monkey, greedily nibbling on a nut that it held in both hands. The Guild Lord took his time gently placing the tiny creature back into its cage before closing the small wire-framed door. He had an average build, bald except for a fringe of white hair on his temples, and wore a pair of simple trousers and a button-up tunic with the sleeves rolled up to his elbows. From appearances alone, Sam would've pegged Haydn as the Guild Lord, and Borinder as the steward, if it wasn't for the man's eyes. Even from a distance Sam could tell they weren't human.

They were sharper, more predatory, like some kind wolf or eagle.

"Come," Borinder said, gesturing to a pair of seats in front of a large desk, which was completely bare except for a bowl of yellow and orange fruit that Sam didn't recognize. Sam and Willow made their way to the desk and sat down. Haydn stopped a few paces behind them and remained standing.

"May I introduce Mr. Philbert McGibbons, supposed worker of enigmatic magics and budding collector of otherworldly oddities," Haydn announced, repeating Gideon's introduction of Sam, "and his Nartareen companion."

"That's quite the title," Borinder said, walking to the other side of the desk to take a seat on an enormous chair covered with zebra-striped snake skin. "But titles intrigue me less than a boy who travels with a Nartareen, and manages to find his way to my office. And so you have my attention."

Sam swallowed awkwardly. There was nothing malicious in the way Borinder spoke. If anything, Sam would say the man's tone was more warm than threatening, but Sam knew that was probably intentional. He couldn't afford to get lulled to sleep here, or he might never wake up.

"I believe you have something that belongs to me," Sam said, struggling to steady his voice.

Borinder raised both eyebrows with a look of both surprise and amusement. "Is that so? I own many things, as you can see. I am genuinely curious as to which of them do you lay claim."

"A black backpack," Sam said, rallying his retreating nerve.

Borinder cocked his head slightly to one side. "And you're sure that I have this pack of yours?"

"I don't think Haydn would've let me up here if you didn't."

"Clever boy," Borinder said, nodding his head, "I suppose he wouldn't have. And how am I to know that this bag of which you speak is actually yours?"

"Because I can tell you what's inside and I can show you what those items do. And I'll wager anything I own that you don't know the answer to either of those questions." Sam stared at Borinder's keen eagle eyes. This wasn't some inquisitive museum curator. He had all of this crazy stuff because in a place like Hagzarad—a secret place for secret trade—it showed that you ruled the roost. If an item was unique, then only the top dog would get it. This room and its contents were the crown on Borinder's bald head. His taste for the exotic was a thirst for power. So here Sam was, claiming to have something, some knowledge, that no one else in Avalon had. Borinder would be drawn in like a moth to a Coleman lantern. Sam had the man's attention, now he just needed to play his cards right.

Borinder nodded to Haydn, who walked over to a large painting of a warrior riding a monstrous feral pig. The steward pulled one side of the frame, swinging it open to reveal a concealed compartment. He reached inside, withdrew Rinni's backpack, and deposited it on the desk.

"Fortune favors the bold, young McGibbons," Borinder said, reaching into his desk and removing an ornate dagger with a bone-white handle and obsidian-black blade. "Accidents befall the careless, however. I propose a test to determine which of the two you are."

Sam's eyes remained fixed on the exotic dagger. "Okay," he rasped, his throat dry as sand.

"I remove an item," Borinder said, taking a yellow fruit from the bowl on his desk and paring it with his dagger, "you tell me what it is, show me what it does, and if you're right, you can keep the item. Get five right and you can leave with the whole pack."

"And if I get one wrong?"

"Then you lose the item." Borinder stabbed a slice of the fruit and ate it off his dagger point. "And you lose a finger."

23
THE TEST

"Friend Sam," Willow leaned over to Sam's ear, whispering loudly, "this does not seem like a very good test."

"Thank you, Willow." Despite the impending threat, Sam figured this should be as easy as naming off his school supplies...that is, of course, unless Rinni had some gadget stashed in the pack that Sam didn't know about. "And if I refuse the test?"

"Then I'll be forced to assume that the pack isn't yours, and you lied to get in here for other purposes." Borinder's warm demeanor hadn't changed, but the context turned him from welcoming to nefarious. "I suggest you submit to the test."

Sam didn't see any way out of this but to go forward. He needed to gather whatever wits he had and commit. "Looks like I'm game."

"Wonderful," Borinder said, unzipping the pack. "First, I must mention that this stitched-in mechanism for opening and closing this pack is quite curious. It could have interesting applications."

"It's called a zipper. Does that count as my first?"

Borinder laughed. "I'm almost tempted to give that to you

just for having the pluck to ask the question. And how would I know you didn't just make that up on the spot?"

"Because I'm the only person in Avalon that has one on my pants, so I can pee without undoing my belt."

Borinder chuckled. "Interesting application indeed. Let us begin." Borinder reached into the bag and pulled out a hand-sized quadcopter.

"That is a Raptor Ultra XE Stealth Drone. Articulating night vision supreme-definition camera. It has auto-evade functionality, over fifty voice-recognized patrol commands, and performs stunts, just for kicks. There's also another one just like it in the bag."

Borinder's facial expression didn't change, but Sam could imagine the man didn't like hearing words he didn't understand, especially coming from a kid. Sam wasn't exactly sure the drone had *fifty* voice-recognized patrol commands, but sounding like you knew what you were talking about on details that couldn't be fact-checked was a large part of trying to convince someone you were an expert.

"Show me," Borinder said.

"With pleasure." Sam reached over and grabbed the drone from the desk. He turned the unit over, flipped the on/off switch, and pulled out his phone.

"Now what's that?" Borinder asked.

Sam looked to Borinder, as if surprised to be interrupted. "Oh, this? If I tell you, does it count as one?"

Borinder pressed his lips together. Sam was probably pressing his luck a bit, but at this point he had no choice but to go big. "Yes."

"This is my techno-oracle, Heinrich. A magical being that only I can control. It will allow me to link to other techno-magical devices and control them, as you will now see."

Sam tapped his phone and opened his *Drone Command* app. Another few taps and the drone's four blades whirred to life, smoothly lifting it from the desk's surface to about two feet in the air. "Explore," Sam said as the drone sped away. Without any additional guidance, the device skirted along the walls and ceiling in a precise switchback pattern, changing elevation with each lap of the room. When it was finished, it returned to the exact spot where it had taken off. Sam grabbed the drone, flipped it over, and turned it off.

"I believe that's *two* points for me," Sam said, holding up a pair of fingers.

Borinder raised a wary eyebrow, but didn't protest. He reached into the bag again and withdrew a small black box. "Next."

Sam leaned in, inspecting the box. All of Rinni's stuff had the same black tactical motif, so it was hard to tell at times what was what until you opened it up. "This is what we call a micro-ear or a bug. I'll need Haydn to help demonstrate this."

Borinder motioned for his steward to come over. "What do you have in mind?"

"I just need to place this on his jacket," Sam said. He reached up and placed a small pencil-eraser-sized dot on the underside of Haydn's lapel. From the man's facial expression, one would've thought Sam had dog poo on his hands. The steward was obviously uncomfortable with anyone touching his immaculate suit.

"What now?" Haydn asked blandly.

"Go outside of the room, well outside of earshot, and say something that we could never guess."

Haydn looked to Borinder, who gave a slight nod, before walking to the far side of the room and out the door. Sam placed his cell on the desk and waited. Half a minute later, Haydn's voice came over the phone.

"Sariah saw seven shells of splendid shine slip softly in surrounding sand."

"What does that mean?" Willow asked.

"It means," Sam said, looking at Borinder, "that this is my pack and I know what's in it."

"That doesn't seem like that's what it means, friend Sam."

Borinder stared back at Sam, his face unreadable. Sam would win this test, but would Borinder keep his word? Even if Sam proved all these objects were his, he was giving away his advantage by demonstrating to the Guild Lord how all of these worked. With the mystery dispelled, and the true power of these objects revealed, would Borinder allow such treasures to leave his possession? It's not like Sam had much of a choice other than to play along. Before he could think on it further, Haydn returned. Sam retrieved the listening bug and placed it back in the black case.

"That's three."

Sam smiled as Borinder removed the next object. Of all the things Sam thought he'd see pulled from Rinni's bag, an unopened can of Dr. Cola was not one of them. Not that it didn't make sense, however. Rinni lived and died by the stuff, but his parents had strictly forbidden him to drink any type of caffeinated beverage. Sam knew Rinni had a few secret stashes, but had no clue he kept a backup can in his tactical bag.

"Who is Dr. Cola?" Borinder asked.

Sam almost burst out laughing. His nerves mixed with the absurdity of hearing that question from one of the most dangerous men he'd ever met was almost too much to bear. "Dr. Cola is, quite simply, a genius. Heralded by many for having invented the world's most perfect beverage. Do you have any cups?"

Borinder again motioned to Haydn, who went to a display case and brought back two jewel-encrusted goblets and placed them on the desk. Sam slowly cracked open the soda can, careful not to have the stuff explode in Borinder's face. He poured a swig in each cup.

"You first," Borinder said, his expression never changing.

"With pleasure." Sam grabbed his cup and paused. How many people can say they drank Dr. Cola from a jeweled goblet? The awesomeness of the moment almost made him forget the impending danger…almost. He threw back the soda and placed his goblet back on the table. "This cup nearly doesn't match the majesty of the drink."

Borinder grabbed his goblet and peered into it a moment before tipping it back and drinking its contents. His eyes grew wide. "My stars," he said, the look of surprise lingering. "Haydn, you must try this."

His steward went to a nearby cabinet and withdrew a standard drinking glass. Sam poured him a swig and emptied the rest into Borinder's goblet. The two men drank, exhaling in satisfaction when done. Haydn let out a small burp and tried to quickly conceal it by coughing several times.

"Was I wrong?"

"Haydn," Borinder said, holding out the empty can of soda, "find a place for this…of *prominence*. I demand an audience with this Dr. Cola."

"Give me the pack and I'll see what I can do." Sam had no idea how he was going to fulfill this particular promise, but it was unexpected leverage and he'd be remiss if he didn't press the advantage.

Borinder breathed deep, seeming to regain his composure. "Last one. Then you'll have your pack fair and square." He reached into the bag for the last time and withdrew a palm-sized black rectangular tablet, about the size of Sam's phone, except several times thicker. This object was the main reason Sam had sought out the backpack in the first place: the secondary tracker.

Sam breathed a sigh of relief. He'd be able to finish the test. No curveballs. He grabbed the tracker and pressed the "on" button, unable to suppress a smirk. "This is an auxiliary GPS tracking system capable of providing…" Sam trailed off as he noticed the screen hadn't turned on. He pressed the "on" button again and still nothing happened. Sam's stomach dropped.

"Something the matter?" Borinder asked, a hint of menace finally noticeable.

"No, nothing's wrong. Just give me a sec." Sam held the

power button down, praying it would illuminate the screen. Still nothing happened. "It appears it's out of batteries. There should be a portable charger just inside—"

Borinder grabbed the bag and moved it out of Sam's reach. "Letting you fish around in the bag wasn't part of the test, young McGibbons. I believe you owe me something." Borinder picked up his knife.

Sam gulped, his panic rising. "Wait a minute. It's just out of power. It's out of...energy. I just need to give it more energy. I showed you all those other things. This pack is obviously mine. You can't say that it's not."

"The rules of the test were clear, fair, and agreed to, if you recall," Borinder said, grabbing another piece of fruit and slicing it in two. "You've earned your four objects and four of your fingers. Last I checked, you still had five on each hand."

"You can't be serious," Sam said, his heart hammering in his chest. "There's got to be something else you want. Anything."

Borinder made a show of stopping to think. "Well...there is one other thing. I typically never stray from the rules, as I am a man of word, but given the unique items you've shown me today, I am willing to grant an exception."

"Tell me. Whatever. Let's hear it." Sam was panicking too much; he was quickly losing any advantage he had before.

"Leave the Nartareen with me."

"What do you mean?" Sam said, looking at Willow then back at Borinder.

"Leave me the Nartareen and you can leave with your pack and all of your fingers. She is as rare a specimen as they come."

"Willow's not mine to trade. She's my friend, not my pet," Sam snapped. No bag of drones and gear was worth giving up his friend...but then again, without that bag of drones and gear, he would never find his other friend, a friend he'd known since he was four years old. His confidence faltered.

"Ownership is a fickle thing, Mr. McGibbons," Borinder mused. "Who decides what we can own? The man himself?

When an item becomes lost, when does the understanding of ownership become severed? I own many creatures and yet they had no say in the matter. I own them because I both want to own them and I have the power to enforce what I want. Someone can tell me otherwise, but do you think it would change anything? Ownership is nothing more than an agreement, and agreements are determined by those with the power to enforce them. So what will it be? Your finger, your friend, or your bag? You may keep any two."

"I would lose the finger, friend Sam," Willow said, nodding confidently.

Sam didn't know what to do. He could feel lines of sweat running from his armpits down his sides. Time was running out, but this wasn't a decision he could ever make. There had to be another way, another solution.

"Time's up," Borinder said, motioning to Haydn, who moved toward Willow.

"Don't you *touch* her," Sam yelled, springing from his seat to stand between Willow and the steward. "I swear you'll regret it."

Haydn gave a humorless smirk before advancing. He reached for Sam and caught hold of his arm. Before he could push Sam out of the way, Sam grabbed Haydn's shoulder with his free hand, felt the presence of the steward's aether, and drained it. Sam gasped at the cold shock rushing from his head down and out the soles of his feet. Haydn screamed and jolted backwards as if he'd just touched a live wire. The steward's five jeweled fingers detached from his right hand and thudded to the floor. Sam felt his phone buzz with an explosion of incoming text messages.

"My aether," Haydn cried, staring at his fingerless hand in shock. "It's…gone. It's all gone."

"Don't you *touch* her," Sam repeated, this time as the aggressor.

A smile split Borinder's face as he greedily rubbed his hands together. "Now *that's* something you don't see every day. Looks like someone lost their fingers after all, eh? I finally see why the emperor's goons were so keen on finding you."

"Keep your distance or you're next," Sam threatened, holding his empty palm out as if he could project his draining ability.

"Oh, I'll keep my distance, but I could have a dozen armed men in here before you'd make it to the door. And they don't need aether to make your hand look like Haydn's. So what'll it be?"

Sam strained to think. What motivated Borinder? It was his pride, his quest to be the best. How could Sam use that against him? How could he get the Guild Lord to agree to something that was secretly in Sam's favor? Sam had no leverage whatsoever. He desperately looked around the room and then he saw it: the large golden trophy.

"How about this?" Sam started experimentally. "We have a test of wits. A test of arithmetic. You win, and you can keep the whole pack, even the objects that I won. You lose, and I leave with the pack, Willow, and all ten digits."

Borinder raised an eyebrow. "Arithmetic, is it? Put a bit more skin in the game—say, a finger's worth—and you have yourself an amended deal, although I warn you, you will not win."

"If you're so confident, then why don't you put more of *your* skin in the game?"

Borinder shook his head, seemingly amused at Sam's boldness. "If you win, then you can have any object in this room." Sam had never heard an individual say a phrase with more confidence.

"Friend Sam," Willow said, tapping Sam on the arm. "I know you are not stupid, but this idea is stupid."

"Don't worry, Willow. You're speaking to the Techno Wizard."

24
ARITHMETIC

"Are you ready?" Borinder asked, steepling his fingers.

"I was born ready, Mr. Besselink." Sam loved to improvise, but pulling off an entire prank on the fly was pushing it. He tried not to think of the stakes and just focus on what he needed to do. He pretended to jostle his ear and slyly inserted his earpiece.

Borinder smiled. "We start with multiplication of two-digit numbers and move on to three-digit numbers. If you last that long, we can work backwards with division. First one to give an incorrect answer loses."

"Now, I must warn you," Sam said, holding up a finger. "My arithmetic powers are based in techno-magic and are received through revelation. The process may be foreign to you, but it cannot be bested."

Borinder scoffed. "We'll see about that. Begin."

"Forty-six times seventy-seven?" Sam asked.

"Three thousand, five hundred and forty-two," Borinder recited, as if he already had the answer memorized. "Thirty-three times eighty-eight."

"Yo, Heinrich," Sam said, throwing his hands out as if in

supplication, "what *is* thirty-three times eighty-eight? It is two thousand, nine hundred and four." Sam repeated the numbers back as he communicated with his phone through his earpiece. It was all Sam could do not to smile. If only his math teacher could see him now. He was horrible at arithmetic, and here he was trying to convince a bona fide genius that he received answers to math problems through a higher power.

"Let's get this moving along, shall we?" Sam asked. "Seven hundred and ninety-six times three hundred and thirty-three."

Borinder paused, and looked to the ceiling. "Two hundred and sixty-five thousand, and sixty-eight." This man was incredible. If Sam wasn't doing this to save Willow and his fingers, he may have felt bad for cheating. "Five hundred and sixty-four times nine hundred and seventy-seven."

Sam asked Heinrich again before reciting the exact answer. "Five hundred and fifty-one thousand, and twenty-eight. I'm growing weary of simple questions. What is sixty-four million, four hundred thirty-four thousand, six hundred and three, divided by ninety-two thousand, two hundred and twenty-two? With up to four decimals."

Borinder laughed. "What kind of absurdity is this?"

"Can't answer it?" Sam probed. "A bit too much for you?"

"The answer can be solved, but is a bit outside the realms for a mental arithmetic challenge, young Mr. McGibbons."

"For you, perhaps." Sam gave a small shrug. He turned and walked over to examine a nearby display of knives. "But not for me. What's so special about these blades? Before I pick my item, I will need to know a bit about its history if you would be so kind."

"Asking a silly question doesn't crown you the victor," Borinder said, his patience finally starting to wear thin.

"Ask any silly question you would like. I, for one, will not shy away. Multiplication, division, square root. It's all the same. My power knows few limits."

"All right then. What is the square root of seven billion, four hundred and thirty-three million, seven hundred and twenty-nine thousand, and four?" Borinder asked, somehow making a large number sound like a threat.

"Yo, Heinrich," Sam threw his head back and looked to the heavens. "What is the square root of seven billion, four hundred and thirty-three million, seven hundred and twenty-nine thousand, and four? It is eighty-six thousand, two hundred and nineteen...point zero, seven, five, six.

Borinder pulled out his desk drawer and removed a large leather-bound book and charcoal pencil. He threw open the book and began furiously scribbling. After close to a minute he froze, as if some witch had just turned him to stone. He looked up at Sam, face a blend of amazement, anger, and confusion. "*How* is that possible?"

Sam laced his fingers together and placed his hands on his chest. He could feel his heart slamming against his ribs in both celebration and relief. "You fell victim to one of the classic blunders. Never go in against a techno wizard when fingers are on the line. Any recommendations for a prize?"

Sam read the latest batch of text messages as he and Willow followed Haydn back through the tunnel to the jewelry store. Just more of the same. The most noteworthy thing was Rinni had moved up to fourth place on the global leaderboard in *Warcraft of Empires*. The days when Sam worried about things like video games felt a lifetime ago. He gave Rinni a quick update of what happened and sent his mom a more filtered version of the same. There was no mistaking the connection between a large release of aether and opening a portal through to Earth. Sam didn't know the particulars of how he would get back home, but he was at least starting to understand how things worked.

By the time they finally got back to the jewelry store, they'd been upstairs for almost three hours. When Haydn pushed the secret door open, Sam found Cornelius, Gideon, and Roanna right where he'd left them. Their faces blossomed from haggard to ecstatic as Sam and Willow entered the room.

"Sam!" Roanna squealed, her face lighting up.

Seeing Roanna's expression caused unfamiliar emotions to stir around in Sam's chest. He didn't know what they were exactly, but he liked them.

"Thanks for waiting. Sorry it took so long. Had to get a bit creative," Sam said.

Cornelius tipped his hat and gave Sam a wink. "Not sure how you fared so well, but I'm mighty glad you did. That's some fine work, Sam. I see you managed to get your pack, but what else you got there?"

"What, this?" Sam asked, brandishing a leather belt and holster. He reached for the holster and removed a black-barreled handgun. "It's a Colt Model 1873, more commonly known as a 'Peacemaker.'" Sam couldn't believe his eyes when he saw the gun on a shelf next to a broken clock. He'd never so much as *held* a real gun in his entire life, but he *had* wielded his fair share playing video games. *Call of the West* was his first-person shooter of choice two summers ago, and the Peacemaker was one of his favorite guns.

"An object of truly unique design," Gideon said, craning his neck to see, his eyes as wide as dinner plates. "Absolutely remarkable."

"But what *is* it?" asked Roanna.

"It's a weapon. A very powerful weapon if we can somehow manage to make the ammo. I figure we'd need some extremely talented metal workers and my oracle to make some. I'm almost positive it once belonged to your great-great grandfather." Sam turned to Cornelius and held out the belt and gun for him to take. "It's my fault you lost your pipe. I figured I owe you."

Cornelius slowly walked over to Sam and reverently took the belt, holster, and gun. He fastened the belt around his waist and turned the gun over in his hands, inspecting it. "You're a class act, kid. Well and truly. Many thanks."

"Save your thanks for when we can manage to get it working. For now, it's just a really cool fashion accessory."

"So now that you have the backpack," Roanna said, "does it have what we need?"

"Not here," Sam said, looking back at Haydn, who still stood near the secret passageway. "Pleasure doing business with you, Haydn."

"Please leave," Haydn said, hiding his fingerless hand behind his back.

"My pleasure."

"Goodbye, unfriendly man," Willow said, waving as if she hadn't a care in the world.

25
TRACKER

It was evening by the time the group made it back to their camp. Willow walked up to Milla and scratched the beast under the chin. Willow was the only one that treated the gorilla-horse with any measure of affection. Whether the Nartareen actually cared for Milla or just shared a special bond with all animals, Sam didn't know.

"Don't intend to be boorish," Gideon said, clearing his throat, "but I have fulfilled the measure of my commitment."

"Oh yes, of course," Sam said, raising a finger. He went to his stash of belongings and rummaged around until he found Milla's knocked-out tooth. "Payment in full, Mr. Gideon, as promised. Couldn't have done it without you."

Gideon took the tooth and pulled out a small magnifying glass from somewhere in his leather coat and examined the object like a jeweler would a diamond. He paused a moment and held the tooth to his nose, sniffing several times, quite *unlike* a jeweler would a diamond. Satisfied, he pocketed his prize. "The pleasure was all mine, Mr. McGibbons, or should I call you Sam? I'm a bit perplexed now."

Sam stared at Gideon, not sure at first what he was talking

about. Then it dawned on him. He'd first introduced himself to Gideon as Philbert McGibbons, then kept the persona going the entire time in Hagzarad until Roanna yelled his name. Haydn had heard that too. Playing a prank under a fake persona was one thing, but keeping it up indefinitely was asking for trouble.

Sam shrugged his shoulders and dropped his accent. "Sorry about that. Didn't know if you were a friendly at first. I wish you all the best in your travels."

"A truly impressive feat...you besting Borinder," Gideon said, nodding. "I believe you may be the first in very long time to have that honor."

"Well, you know," Sam said, coolly dusting off his shoulders. "All in a day's work for the Techno Wizard."

"I can't envisage him being all that pleased."

"Mad at himself, maybe. It wasn't like I broke any of his rules. I just played them better. To the victor go the spoils."

"Very impressive indeed. Say, you wouldn't happen to be about to use more of your techno-magic with anything in that pack of yours, would ya?" Gideon asked with the curious look of a seven-year-old asking to stay up late and watch TV with the adults.

For someone whose life revolved around traveling to the far ends of Avalon to collect and sell exotic items, seeing Sam's gear had to feel like winning the lottery. Having someone with Gideon's knowledge and experience on the team would be extremely useful, not to mention just plain cool. Gideon wasn't forced into this merry band like the others, so he would most likely need a different incentive to stick around. Maybe Sam could use Gideon's curiosity to his advantage.

"As a matter of fact, I am." Sam reached inside the pack and withdrew the tracker as well as a cord and power brick. The whole group gathered around as he hooked the gear together and turned on the tracker. His nervousness rose as the screen came to life.

"What are we looking at?" Gideon asked as images and maps flashed across the screen of the tracker.

"This is a tracker. It should tell me where my friend is, as long as he is within a hundred miles or so." Sam worked his way through the prompts until finally clicking on the *find nearby devices* button. "Please, please, please," he muttered.

After thinking for a moment, the tracker dinged and displayed a map with two markers. One for Sam's position and one for Lawrence's. They'd found him. The tracker map indicated he was seventy miles away in the town of Wanaka. That was, of course, traveling on New Zealand roads to a New Zealand town. Sam would need to ask the others what the path was here in Avalon. Regardless, the tracker had found Lawrence. It was a miracle. Sam let out a long breath.

"Did it find him?" Roanna asked.

"It found the location of some techno-magical gear he was wearing, yes. As long as he's still got it with him, we should be able to find him."

"Where's he at?" Cornelius prodded.

"Here," Sam said, swiping his fingers on the map and zooming in on Lawrence's beacon. "Anything important in this location?"

"Why, that's Trellston, my boy," Gideon said, as if Sam had just asked where his own nose was. "One of the largest cities in all of the South Isle."

"Geography was never my forte. What's the most direct route there?"

Gideon looked from Sam to the rest of the group, a look of confusion and disbelief written across his face. "You're *going* there?"

"Is there anything wrong with that?" Sam asked.

"After the emperor squashed the rebellion in Grahl, his men went to Trellston. The city is quelled."

"Quelled? What does that mean? Is Lawrence in danger?"

"Quelled means they just had an uprising, kid," Cornelius

said, his look suddenly distant, "and that uprising was just put down."

An uprising. Sam knew the term. He'd actually played a video game by the very same name based on the American Revolutionary War. In Trellston's case, however, it didn't look like the common man succeeded in overthrowing their oppressive overlords.

"I swapped some of me wares with a Trellstonian merchant on the road just five or six days ago," Gideon said with that look that all people have when telling juicy gossip. "The noblemen who ruled the city were fed up with the emperor's rising taxes. They didn't have the power to resist their ruler outright, so they came up with clever stratagems and schemes to keep their aether. The emperor had spies, however, and caught on to their swindles and ruses, so he sent the Collector to take back the overdue aether taxes…plus a little interest, which in this case was the heads of the five ruling noblemen."

"The Collector," Roanna breathed, as if muttering some ancient curse.

"What's the Collector?" Sam asked. He saw the surprise on Gideon's face and realized how much of an idiot he must look to the man. "I've lived a very isolated life, okay? Learned all my techno-magic from some monks…in a, uh, monastery."

"The Collector is an Inferno-class scoundrel. Can't be more than a dozen or so Infernos in existence, and five of them serve the emperor," Gideon explained. "Stories say that unlike the emperor, the Collector rose up from nothing. Left the ingot fields to become a knight he did, then a named warrior, and now he commands one of the emperor's armies of Enhanced soldiers. He always wears black, ghoulish armor, but rumors speak of steel skin, animal claws, and fangs underneath. He should be a hero for the commoner, but I assure you he's quite the opposite. Never been bested in battle, they say. He rides the skies on the back of a monstrous mutation, a giant crocodilian bat they call the Screecher."

"Wow," Sam said, "sounds hardcore. I might regret asking this, but why exactly do they call him the Collector?"

"Some erroneously believe that the name comes from his role as the emperor's tax collector," Gideon responded, "but he had the name before he was in the business of tracking down aether ingots."

"So what's the real reason?" Sam asked.

Gideon swallowed hard before continuing. "He likes to take mementos from his most noteworthy victims and prey. Broken weapons, pieces of armor, family heirlooms…body parts. He makes examples out of his strongest enemies, displaying his collection as it dangles from the saddle of his Screecher. He made quite a name for himself as a…" Gideon trailed off as he stole a glance at Cornelius.

"A what?" Sam asked, looking around at the group.

"A cowboy killer." Cornelius absently kicked a small rock.

"Oh."

"Cowboys are an exotic breed, Sam," Cornelius added. "That puts us at the top of his hunting list, and although I don't like to admit it, the big nasty cur also seems to have found quite a bit of success in knocking us off."

A cowboy killer? Sam couldn't even imagine it. Cornelius seemed as tough as iron. What kind of man was capable of hunting cowboys for sport?

"So you're telling me that this maniac is in Trellston right now, with an army of the emperor's men?" Sam asked, turning his thoughts from Cornelius to Lawrence.

"Last I heard," Gideon added. "If they feel they snuffed out all sparks of rebellion, perhaps they've already drawn back their forces, although after a quelling, the emperor will station a number of his men there indefinitely."

"We need to find a way into that city." Sam felt like he was going to vomit. He tried to breathe in through his nose and out through his mouth. The odds that Lawrence wasn't in serious danger in that town were next to nothing, and the risk of going there just to look for him was gigantic. Sam couldn't go but he couldn't *not* go. "What's the quickest route to get there? Can we cut through the forest?"

"Whoa there, partner," Cornelius said, raising a hand. "Running headlong into a big city infested with the emperor's men is not the most prudent form of action at this time, I reckon."

"Then what is?" Sam challenged. "We're stuck, Cornelius. There's no going back and this is the way forward. The Eldest Tree said to rescue my friend, not bury him, so I know he's still got to be alive. I won't leave Lawrence. I'll go alone if that's what it takes."

"I admire your spirit, kid, but hastiness won't get your friend back in this situation. It'll get your skull dangling by a rope from the Screecher's saddle."

Sam couldn't believe his ears. He didn't think Cornelius was afraid of anyone or anything, and yet here the cowboy was already conceding defeat. It was a sobering reminder that Sam had still only seen a fraction of this strange world and its dangers.

"I'll go with you," Roanna said, straightening and walking to Sam's side. Sam was glad to have Roanna's backing, but he knew deep down that she only gave it because Sam could drain aether. He was the tool she needed to defeat the emperor. The Eldest Tree had even said as much. She "already had the means to overthrow the emperor" and she was told not to lose it. Because of this, Sam got the feeling that Roanna—despite her original misgivings about him—would follow him to the ends of the Earth. But what happened if it turned out that the Eldest Tree wasn't talking about Sam at all? Sam knew the answer to that question. Roanna wouldn't so much as follow him with her eyes, let alone into some quelled city.

"If you are voyaging to Trellston, then I must truly take my leave of this party. I do apologize," Gideon said, busying himself with gathering his gear. "I wish you all the best in locating this friend of yours."

"What if I offered you this?" Sam asked, reaching into his pack and pulling out a black LED flashlight.

Gideon stopped packing and scuttled over to Sam. He withdrew his magnifying glass again and inspected the strange object. "What does it do?"

"It's a flashlight. It creates a very bright beam of light at the touch of your finger." Sam demonstrated, by toggling the light on and off, shining the beam, which was visible in the evening shade of the forest. "At nighttime, this one light can shine out for miles. It's charged by your movement, so it will never lose its power. We could really use your knowhow."

"A moment, if you would?" Cornelius asked, motioning with his head for Sam to step aside and talk.

Sam walked over to Cornelius and leaned in to whisper. "What's up?"

Cornelius briefly looked skyward before guessing at Sam's meaning. "You sure you want to drag Gideon further into this?"

"What do you mean?" Sam replied. "I'm paying him with one of the rarest objects in all of Avalon. It's not like I'm forcing him to go."

"And it ain't like we've ever explained to him that we're a merry little band currently being hunted by the emperor either. He don't know the risk that he's signing up for."

"Well, I'll just tell him then," Sam said simply. "I think he'd just about give up his left leg for this flashlight."

"You sure you want to do this, partner? Roh and me are in this thing 'cause there wasn't any other way around it. Gideon would only be in it for his own profit. It could work…for a bit. When profits and payments can come from elsewhere, loyalties tend to be a bit fickle. You follow me?"

"Gideon's already proven to be helpful," Sam said, a bit surprised that Cornelius would be questioning Gideon's loyalty.

"I think if he wanted to turn us in for profit, he would've done it by now."

"Sam, he doesn't even know who we are yet. What would he have turned us in for?"

"Huh," Sam said, contemplating. "Regardless. I have the same gut feeling I had when I first saw him in the woods. He's too helpful to just let slip away. He pulled through before, and I think he'll pull through again. We need all the help we can get, don't we? We're going to have to roll the dice if we want to pull this off."

Cornelius pressed his lips together. "So you think I'll be swayed by a gambling analogy, is that it?"

"Worked on Roanna." Sam shrugged.

Cornelius stole a glance at Gideon, who was busy showing Willow a swirling wind chime he'd removed from his merchant pack. The cowboy turned back and looked at Sam, shaking his head. "I don't like it, Sam. I don't like this whole ordeal, but if you're dead set on going, I'll back your play. I'm not familiar with the town, but I've got an old friend there that's long overdue for a visit. If Gideon can get us inside the walls, then I reckon she might be able to help us…if she's still alive."

"Let's hope we both have friends still alive in that city."

26
DÉJÀ VU

To Sam's relief, Gideon didn't seem that put off after learning that Sam, Cornelius, Roanna, and Willow were all currently wanted by the emperor. If they were ever caught, Gideon could always claim ignorance of the group's true motives and say that he was hired on simply as a guide. Payment of one LED flashlight would be made in full upon reaching Trellston and locating Lawrence, or at the very least his earpiece.

Although Gideon was their guide to towns, cultures, and current events, it was Willow, yet again, who led the way. According to Sam's Earth map, the most direct way lay south along the edge of Lake Wakatipu, east past Queenstown, north up Cardona Pass, and finally to Wanaka. The most common and direct route on Gideon's Avalon map wasn't all that different, except for the names, of course: Lake Vista, Yallington, Starp's Pass, and finally, Trellston. It was also *not* the way that they were going to go, as the risk of being discovered by the emperor's men was too great on the common roads. Their route would take them north, up a river valley, over a high mountain saddle, and down another river valley, before arriving on the opposite side of the mountain range that divided any direct path from Hagzarad to Trellston.

Sam plotted the path on his global trekking app. Distance: seventy-three point two miles. Elevation climb to the saddle—which was covered in snow on his satellite image: three thousand, nine hundred and forty-two feet. Sam's legs hurt just looking at the map. Maybe he could just send Lawrence a super sincere "best of luck" card.

After Cornelius ducked back into town for some final supplies, the group began their trek north. The constant mountainous traveling, although taxing, did have its perks. As Sam's conditioning improved, he found he could better enjoy the breathtaking scenery with its scores of drastic peaks and waterfalls. For several stretches during the day, Sam would dismount from Milla and walk alongside Cornelius, who still had hardly touched the beast since he punched it in the mouth and it threw him against a tree.

Although Willow led the way, she had never been this far north or east, which—as far as Sam could tell—just meant that she had to stop more frequently to talk to the trees. Sightings of large and unfamiliar footprints pressed into the dirt and snow were a constant reminder to the group to never let their guard down. On the night of the third day, Sam sent his drones to patrol the night sky. The infrared cameras revealed a forest littered with the glowing red heat signatures of wild animals, some of which appeared much larger than Sam himself.

The nights grew steadily colder as they climbed higher into the mountains, and Sam thanked heaven—and not for the first time—that they'd placidated Milla. The shaggy black monster could've used a good bath or two, but Sam's nose could tolerate the smell better than his body could tolerate the cold, and so he found himself snuggling with the gorilla-horse at night like she was the family dog. It was a far cry from their first encounter. Not too unlike how things were turning out with Roanna...well, he wasn't exactly snuggling with her on cold nights, and *she* smelled quite pleasant, but it was strange how their relationship had changed. She had softened considerably toward Sam, which was fantastic, but he still needed to know why. He couldn't just accept it at face value, however much ignorance was oftentimes bliss. He needed to talk to her.

On the night of the sixth day, they arrived at the highest elevation and halfway mark of the trek. Half-moon Saddle loomed large to the east, carving the night horizon in a sweeping crescent. Sam waited until Gideon and Cornelius's snores filled the night air in Avalon's most discordant duet.

"Roanna," Sam hissed, feeling a bit of déjà vu. He'd made sure to pick a sleeping spot just on the other side of Milla's arms from her. He sat up and tried again. "Roanna, if you're awake, I need to talk to you."

"Are you going to be making a habit of this?" Roanna whispered back.

"Sorry, I just wanted to wait until the others were asleep."

"What is it? Is everything okay?" Roanna asked, sitting up.

"I need to ask you a question." Sam tried to keep his cool, but felt no less nervous than when he talked to Borinder.

"What is it?"

"I need to know why you're nicer to me now." Sam held his breath. Would she laugh? Would she get mad? Would she stop being nice now that he'd pointed it out?

Roanna let out a small sigh. "I guess I owe you a bit of an apology. Sam, I was not happy that you barged into my life. You messed things up for me. You know that, don't you?"

"Uh, yes," Sam said, not really sure how this was an apology.

"I had my life built and you bumbled your way in and smashed it all to pieces. I wasn't happy about that, Sam. But a strange thing happened."

"And what was that?" Sam asked cautiously.

"When I built my life in Ogland, I didn't have the right pieces left to make what I *really* wanted for myself. It took you breaking things apart to free up the pieces I needed. I never would've removed those pieces on my own; they were safely put where I thought I wanted them. But now I'm glad that it happened. Does that make any sense?"

"Yeah, it does," Sam said. "My dad used to tell me 'you don't know what you're working with until you take it apart and put it back together.' His way of telling me you could salvage something from your failures, I guess."

"Your dad sounds like a very wise man."

"He was the best."

"Was?" Roanna asked.

"He...died a few years ago." It took Sam three months to say that phrase without crying and nearly a year without his voice quavering. It still wasn't easy to say. It always seemed to echo in a hollowness that refused to fill in.

"Oh, Sam. I'm so sorry," Roanna said. "I didn't know."

"It's okay. He didn't die a heroic death or anything. He just...fell asleep at the wrong time, but he was still *my* hero, my best friend really. Wanting the pieces to go back and fit like they used to only makes it hurt worse; I've accepted that. Thinking about him at all hurts—honestly—but the best memories are worth the hurt."

"Some part of us stays broken forever, I suppose."

"Maybe. But you can repurpose the broken bits, like you said." Sam took a deep breath before asking his next question, as if he needed the extra air to explore uncharted conversational waters. "Roanna, do you only want me around so you can use me to avenge your parents?"

Roanna paused long enough for Sam to know that no matter what she said next, the answer was partially yes. "How do you want me to answer that question?"

"Uh...with honesty."

"Sam, I've waited a very long time for just a sliver of a chance to set things right. Now with you here, we've got a chance to do more than that. We can set things right for all of

Avalon. I think that's the reason why we met, the reason why we're currently cuddled up next to an equine-ape in the mountains, and it would be reason enough for me to want you to stay. But no, it's not the *only* reason."

"No?" Sam asked, his hope rising.

"I also really like to see you get startled by Willow."

Sam laughed quietly. "I'm glad I could help."

"Goodnight, Sam," Roanna said, her shape in the darkness disappearing back behind Milla's arms.

"Goodnight, Roanna," Sam said.

27

THE CORPSEMAN

Four days after cresting the Half-moon Saddle, the city of Trellston came into view. Built on a mountainous island on the east side of Lake Alexandra, Trellston was by far the most impressive manmade thing Sam had seen in Avalon. Every square inch of the island was taken up with houses, towers, and other buildings, while a great wall confined the base of the island, which Gideon said fortified against seasonally rising water. Several long, stone bridges spanned the gap from the city to the eastern and northern shores. Atop it all, stood what looked to be a fairytale castle, its half-dozen white stone spires jutting skyward.

"That's incredible," Sam said, taking in the view of the city some ten miles out. He knew their path would be longer still, as he doubted they'd use any of the traditional means to access the city.

"It is indeed, my boy," Gideon replied, taking out his spyglass. The small telescope, as Gideon explained, was equipped with rare omnipitum lenses, which allowed the user a near limitless zoom, depending on the amount of aether infused. "Trellston, the Jewel of the South Isle."

"See anything curious?" Cornelius asked, spitting on the ground.

Gideon paused a moment, scanning the city and the dozens of large boats anchored around it. He clicked his tongue in disapproval. "Those ships are flying the emperor's symbol. The Collector's men are still here…a whole host of them."

"And the Collector himself?" Sam asked, his stomach sinking.

Gideon continued to survey the horizon. "Hard to say."

"He's still there," Cornelius said, chewing at the corners of his mustache.

"What makes you so certain?" Roanna asked.

"If there's that many dadgum men still there after all this time, then it means that they ain't yet found what they came for. If they ain't done with their business, then the Collector sure as snot ain't done with his."

Sam gulped. He pulled out his tracker and checked again. Now that he saw the city, Lawrence's dot looked to be right where the castle was. He'd prayed this entire trek that they would come to Trellston, find the emperor's men gone, waltz into the city nice and easy, and find Lawrence under the watchful care of some kind old grandma. Not knowing for sure where Lawrence was, or what he'd gotten himself into, was both nerve-racking and comforting, depending on which direction Sam's imagination went. This was the first concrete sign that Lawrence was, in fact, in very grave danger.

"So how do we get in?" Sam asked.

"You still desire to proceed?" Gideon asked, handing the spyglass up to Roanna, who was sitting on Milla's back. It wouldn't work for Cornelius or Sam, as neither of them had the ability to infuse aether into anything.

"Yes," Roanna said, stealing the word from Sam's mouth. "If it was going to be easy, we wouldn't have needed you to help us. Time to earn that flashlight, traveler."

As Sam had guessed, their passage to Trellston wouldn't be through the front gates. Although both the wall and lake restricted many of their options, it did not eliminate them. As it turned out, sneaking into a heavily fortified city had little to do with complex schemes and more to do with one's willingness to be unpredictable, like stow away on a barge full of corpses and coffins, for example.

Real estate was at a premium on the island, so there was hardly room to house the living, let alone the dead. Every dead body for the past fifty-four years was ferried from the island to a cemetery west of Trellston by the same man, Matthias Abromite: the Corpseman. Sam only knew two other things about the man: he owed Gideon a favor, and he was scheduled to meet the group tonight at a small cove on the south side of the cemetery. Earlier that day, Gideon went to the main lakeside village to make his contacts and seek out the Corpseman, as well as ask after Cornelius's old friend, Jezerelle Wilter. He returned several hours later with news that he had found a way into Trellston.

A lifetime of pranks had forced Sam to wait in plenty of strange spots over the years, but a graveyard was never one of them. A quarter-moon shone briefly in the night sky, peering through a break in the clouds and illuminating the cemetery in an eerie spectral gray. All the willpower in the world couldn't suppress the chill that ran up Sam's back. Sam, Cornelius, Gideon, and Roanna hid among the headstones, while Milla, as usual, was back in the trees.

"Hey," Sam whispered, not really sure why he was whispering other than it felt like the right thing to do in a cemetery. "Where's Willow?"

"What do you need, friend Sam?" Willow asked, appearing at Sam's side.

Sam gasped, his startled scream choking in his throat. "Gal dang it, Willow! Would you *stop* that?"

"I am sorry, friend Sam," Willow whispered. "You are easily spooked."

"We're in a *graveyard*, Willow. I have an excuse this time. Doesn't this freak you out a little bit?"

Willow tilted her head at looked at Sam curiously. "Why would I be afraid of a dead human that is buried under the dirt, friend Sam? I fear the mean humans who are alive and above the dirt."

"How very…logical of you, Willow." Sam shivered again. "I'm sure Nartareen graveyards are just full of chirping birds and happy flowers."

"That is correct." Willow nodded her head.

"Wait, they are?"

"Silly, friend Sam." Willow giggled. "You have been to our burial place: the flowers surrounding the Eldest Tree."

"Those flowers mark the graves of dead Nartareen?" Sam asked.

"The flowers are what's *left* of a Nartareen who has passed on. Before a Nartareen dies, they give up a death seed. When planted, a unique and beautiful flower grows. I have many friends whose flowers I visit. The roots draw in much aether. Many humans would want such a seed. Another reason we Nartareen stay out of sight."

"No kidding? So will you—" Sam's follow-up question was cut off by the faint sound of a distant bell ringing in from the open water. Cornelius put a finger to his lips, signaling for silence, as the entire group ducked down. The bell continued to ring, growing louder and clearer as they waited. After a minute, a small light appeared on the water, illuminating a lazily moving barge. A figure stood at the stern, steering the craft with a single long oar, only pausing to occasionally ring the bell. As the barge grew closer, an old man's voice carried to shore, singing to the rhythm of the bell.

The Corpseman comes when you are gone
   His barge by duty it is drawn
   Hey ho, hey ho, his barge by duty it is drawn
   He comes to take what you have left
   A body of a soul bereft
   Hey ho, hey ho, a body of a soul bereft
   To put it in its resting place
   A spot to which the soul could trace
   Its worth may rot, but not debase
   'Cause you have gone to Aether's grace
   'Cause you have gone to Aether's grace
   Hey ho, hey ho, 'cause you have gone to Aether's grace

After hearing the song several times, Sam watched as the barge landed at a small wooden dock on the water's edge. The Corpseman removed his lantern, held it high, and swung it back and forth three times before putting it back on its hook.

"That's the signal," Gideon said, standing up and leading the way down to the dock. The lanky traveler looked odd without his enormous pack of goods on his back. He'd buried his supplies earlier in the evening in an empty grave for safe-keeping, as the road ahead required them to travel light.

"Hullo, noble traveler," the Corpseman said, calling out to Gideon and sounding every bit a pirate.

"It has been ages, stalwart Matthias," Gideon replied, walking up to the old man and shaking his hand. "How have you fared?"

"Business has never been better." The old man let out a cackle. "Can't bury 'em fast enough during a quelling."

"Ye-e-es," Gideon drew out the word, unsure how to respond to the morbid comment. "These are my party."

The Corpseman grabbed his lantern and hobbled over to

Cornelius, Sam, Roanna, and Willow, looking each of them up and down like a drill sergeant performing uniform inspection.

"This one won't do," he said, waving his lantern at Willow. "Emperor's soldiers are checking under every hood. It wouldn't last a minute."

"Wait," Sam said, approaching the Corpseman. "There has to be some way for her to come."

"It is okay, friend Sam," Willow said, placing a hand on Sam's shoulder. "What creepy Matthias has said is most likely true. I will stay and take care of Milla."

Sam knew that there might be complications with bringing Willow along, but he still didn't like leaving her behind. "Here," Sam said, reaching into his backpack to pull out a spare earpiece. "Put this in your ear. Just press this button and it will allow us to talk over great distances."

"You are sharing your techno-magic with me?" Willow asked, her eyes wide.

"There's no one I can think of more deserving."

Willow threw open her branchy arms and wrapped them around Sam's neck, crushing him in an embrace. "This is a kingly gift, friend Sam. Despite your soft legs and jumpiness, I believe I have love for you."

"Uh, thank you, Willow," Sam mumbled as he struggled for air. Willow might be a little girl in stature, but her size belied her strength. Without another word, Willow released Sam and walked off the dock back toward the graveyard.

"Odd creature, that one," the Corpseman said, turning his head to look at the moon. "Time is short, my new friends. Time is short. Can't say I've had too many guests actually *walk* aboard my vessel. Usually my company is much more…grim."

One by one, Roanna, Gideon, and Sam boarded the barge while Cornelius remained standing at the dock's edge.

"You okay there, cowboy?" Sam asked. "You allergic to coffins or something?"

"Ain't nothing to do with the coffins. I don't like the water."

"You serious?" Sam replied.

"You can't punch it, fight it, or run from it. It just swallows you up and that's that. Plus, I can't swim."

Sam couldn't believe it. The cowboy had a weakness after all. Sam didn't quite know how to wrap his mind around the fact that water didn't bug Sam in the slightest, but had Cornelius stopping in his tracks.

"You gonna stand there or get on?" Roanna pressed.

Cornelius held his breath as he took two reluctant steps forward and landed on the barge. When they were all on board, the Corpseman pushed off the dock. He picked up his long oar and took his place at the back of the barge. Polished wooden caskets occupied most of the available space, their smooth surfaces reflecting the flickering light of the Corpseman's single lantern.

"So where will you take us, exactly?" Roanna asked. "Do you have access to an unwatched port?"

"That I do not, young miss. Unwatched ports have the tendency of being noticed, and those that are watched often-times go unobserved. We head straight for the main docks, dearie."

"I don't understand," Roanna replied. "What's the plan then? Are we posing as your usual crew or something?"

The Corpseman tilted his head back in hysterical laughter. "In a manner of speaking."

The group exchanged confused glances as the Corpseman continued to laugh, never ceasing his slow, methodical paddling. As they rounded the edge of the cove and turned northeast, Trellston exploded into view.

"It's beautiful," Sam caught himself saying. The mountainous island-city appeared to float in space, its lights perfectly reflected in the still surface of the dark water.

"Like the soft pale face of a maiden recently deceased," the Corpseman mused.

Sam wasn't sure if he meant that Trellston looked beautiful

on the outside, but was dead on the inside, or if a corpse was just actually something the man found beautiful. The Corpseman cleared his throat and began to sing again. The sooner Sam could get off this barge, the better.

After fifteen minutes, the Corpseman reached over to his bell and gave it four distinct rings: two long and two short. They waited, the soft gliding of water against the barge the only sound. He repeated the pattern several more times before an answering bell sounded in the distance.

"Take your places. Your accommodation awaits ya," the Corpseman said with a chuckle, gesturing to a line of four caskets.

"Wait," Sam said, paling. "You want us to climb *inside* one of those things?"

The Corpseman rubbed his chin. "Well, I got paid all upfront to smuggle ya here. If the emperor's men catch ya, they will most likely kill ya and I will get paid *again* for bringing what's left of ya back off the island, so I'm not even sure that I *do* want ya to climb inside now that I think about it. *You* definitely want to climb inside, though. That I can say for sure… unless ya paid me to ferry ya over here to die. In that case, stay outside."

Sam inched toward a casket and froze. He closed his eyes. The last time he stood next to one of these, it was his father's. His throat suddenly went dry and he struggled to swallow. He remembered his mother gently taking his shaking hand from the lid of his father's casket. When you crashed at eighty miles an hour, the casket stayed closed. How could that happen? How could someone so wonderful be turned off like a light switch? How could they be here and then not? Where did his father *go*? His personality, who he was, it was all just…gone. Reducing the greatest person he'd ever known to a collection of "remains" in a closed casket cheapened his father in a way that permanently unsettled Sam. His breathing quickened, but before he lost himself in the moment, he felt the strength and warmth of his mother's grip.

"Sam," a voice whispered in his ear. He looked over to see Roanna, then down at her hand clasping his. "Sam, it's okay."

Sam nodded his head, then wiped at his eyes with his free hand. He grabbed the lid to the casket and flipped it open.

"No, not there," the Corpseman said, shutting the lid. He bent down and slid open a hidden crawl space at the base of the casket just tall enough for someone to lie down. "Under here. They check the coffins."

Sam steeled himself before letting go of Roanna's hand and lying flat on the barge deck to wiggle into the cramped compartment. He took a shallow breath and coughed. It smelled like a combination of his grandma's basement and the school's chemistry lab.

"Don't worry," the Corpseman called down. "Might smell a bit corpsey down there, but there's plenty of air for our little trip."

Before he closed the compartment, Sam leaned his head out. "And what if they *do* check down here?"

"Then at least you got your coffin picked out." The Corpseman cackled as he slid the compartment door closed, sending the space into blackness.

28
POKER FACE

Sam kept his eyes closed and took shallow breaths. He wasn't claustrophobic, but this experience had a decent shot at changing that. He slid his hand into his jacket pocket and managed to withdraw his earpiece. He stuck it in his ear and whispered to Heinrich to play some music. Desensitized from the outside world, Sam actually fell asleep. He awoke to the sound of ringing bells and felt the barge come to a halt. There was muffled conversation accented with the Corpseman's signature cackle. After a few more minutes, Sam felt the casket move. He held his breath. Was he discovered? He tensed every muscle in his body, forcing himself to stay still. The casket jerked up into the air and swung to the side before being placed back down. A few moments later, the casket lurched forward and began bumping up and down. They were on the move, but there was no telling in whose custody.

After listening to three more songs, the movement stopped and the hidden compartment door slid open. Sam braced himself and squinted at the faint light outside.

"Arise forth, me lovely stowaways," the Corpseman announced.

Sam had never been so happy to hear the deranged man's voice. He shimmied out from his hiding place and stood up, stretching his cramped muscles and stiff joints. Judging by the dozens of caskets stacked around them, Sam guessed they were in the Corpseman's dimly lit warehouse. The rest of the crew crawled out from their spots and stood up. Sam checked his phone. It was 4:45 a.m.

"Where we at?" Cornelius asked, slicking his gray hair back and putting on his hat.

"Not in any *grave* danger if that's what you're worried about," the Corpseman laughed. He turned to see Sam yawn. "Dead tired, I presume?"

Sam rubbed his eyes. "Just never been a *mourning* person."

The Corpseman paused before tilting his head and exploding in laughter. "Took me a moment, it did!"

"Please don't encourage him," Roanna said, rolling her eyes.

"We should be on the southwest end of the island, not far from where we need to go," Gideon said, finally answering Cornelius's question. "We appreciate your services this day, fine Corpseman. We shall take our leave. This way."

The group exited through a door in the back of the warehouse and into a dark alleyway. Gideon pulled out his map, which Sam illuminated with his cell phone flashlight. Gideon stopped a moment, marveling at the device and the apparent nonchalance with which Sam used it.

"You certain you know how to find Jezerelle?" Cornelius asked, looking over the map. The cowboy hadn't spoken much of his old friend. All Sam knew was that she was their only source of help in Trellston and most likely their only hope of staying out of trouble and finding Lawrence.

"Yes, as certain as one can be," Gideon replied. "I am not unfamiliar with this city, as you know, and my contacts from shore knew of her work. A seamstress of some renown, I am told. As I mentioned previously, she's not far. It's late enough that the early risers should be out and about, so we should not draw too much suspicion from any of the emperor's men. On that note, I would suggest removing your hat."

Cornelius looked up at his hat and grumbled as he took it off and stashed it in his pack. Sam didn't know what they would've done without Gideon. Sam knew that there was a risk taking him on, but was glad he'd gone with his gut and convinced the others.

They exited the alley and followed Gideon as he made his way toward the meeting spot. Trellston's clean streets and taller buildings hinted at a town more ordered and prosperous than Ogland or Hagzarad, but Sam still couldn't shake the feeling that something was...off. Ogland was dirty, and Hagzarad chaotic, but even in the early hours of the day, Trellston felt like it moved artificially. It didn't take long to understand why. The Collector's men were everywhere. Soldiers in black and red armor stood at street corners and doorways, a visible presence of the recent quelling. True to the rumor, Sam caught glimpses of metal and stone grafted skin on some of the Collector's men. Others had animal hybridizations: claws for fingers, snouted mouths with sharp teeth, and even tails. The Collector had an army of monsters. There was no way someone as bumbling and out of place as Lawrence wouldn't have been picked up. Sam's nervous urgency stirred in his stomach like a hive of angry hornets.

The group casually steered clear of the soldiers and eventually found their way down another alley, not unlike the one they had exited by the Corpseman's warehouse.

Gideon checked his map again and nodded. "We have arrived."

The traveler approached a small wooden door and knocked three times. The door opened and the group was quickly ushered into a dark, windowless room by a shadowed figure. A single lantern burned at the far end of the space, backlighting the silhouette of an enormous man. Sam had never seen someone so large in his entire life. At first, he thought the shadow was some trick, a cardboard cutout or something, until it raised its huge arm and made a gesture with its hand. On cue, lanterns lit all around the room, revealing some two-dozen people, bows drawn, all aiming their arrows toward the center of the room.

"What's going on?" Sam asked, frantically looking around the room, his mind racing. Was this a trap? Had Gideon been given bad information?

"Thank you for coming," the massive figured boomed. His voice sounded like it came straight from a subwoofer. "Just as you promised, Mr. Gideon. Thank you."

Sam's heart stopped as he saw Gideon separate from the crew, casually walking over to the hulking man to shake his hand. "A man of my word," Gideon said.

"A man of your word?" Roanna yelled. Sam was still too stunned to even speak. "We trusted you!"

"A decision that profited you greatly," Gideon replied, "until I could profit more greatly."

"Your grammar stinks!" Roanna shouted.

Sam looked to Cornelius, who wore his ever-present poker face. "What are we going to do?"

"Hold tight," Cornelius said softly.

"I'll be taking that light flasher now," Gideon said, holding out his hand. "As well as the rest of what's in that pack."

"It's called a flashlight, you backstabbing dimwit," Sam said, unslinging his backpack and gripping it defensively.

"Come now, Sam," Gideon said, shaking his head. "What was it you said? To the victor go the spoils? I don't want to see any of you hurt, honestly. You're decent folk. But I will have that pack, and that Peacemaker pistol of yours, Cornelius, while I think of it. Hand them over, please."

There was no way out. Even if Cornelius could somehow fight his way through this, Sam would be a human pincushion before he took two steps. All the trouble and risks they had to go through to get this backpack from Borinder, and here he was handing it over. The thought made him want to puke.

Cornelius drew his pistol from its holster and tossed it at Gideon. Sam looked to Cornelius, who motioned with his head for Sam to do the same. Sam groaned and held out his backpack. "Very little of this will work if you're not a techno wizard. You know that, right? You might as well throw it in the garbage."

Gideon stepped forward, a self-satisfied smirk on his face. Cornelius had tried to warn Sam. He'd tried to tell him that people like Gideon weren't to be trusted. Sam had been so naive. What did he know about how the world worked? He was just a kid. He was just a—

THWACK. The giant reached forward and clubbed Gideon on the top of the head. The traveler fell to the ground like a marionette getting its strings cut. Sam hurriedly glanced around, not sure what was happening, and saw the archers lower their bows.

"Addi gives her regards," the huge man said, looking at Cornelius.

"Addi, who's Addi?" Roanna asked. "I thought we were here to meet Jezerelle."

"That's what I told our friend here," Cornelius said, walking over to Gideon's motionless body and retrieving his pistol.

"You suspected him all along," Sam said, still not entirely sure what was happening.

"This ain't my first time in the saddle here, partner. I sent a carrier pigeon to Addi when I went back into Hagzarad for supplies. Told her we were en route and that someone would be coming to the shore village asking after a certain Jezerelle Wilter. I needed to see if ol' Gideon here would stay true, so I had Addi feed information to try and buy the traveler's loyalty and turn us in. Offered him more than the emperor's bounty so his greed actually kept him from just turning us into a random guard. It would appear that Gideon here took the deal."

"That's genius," Sam said, relief washing over him.

"That's just common horse sense, kid. Comes with age, and age comes with a lot of mistakes. Always keep a card or two up your sleeve."

"I'm sorry I pushed you to trust Gideon. This never would've happened if I wasn't so stupid."

Cornelius gave Sam a look that seemed to say "you honestly think you pushed me into anything?" He pulled out his cowboy hat from his pack and put it on. "Look, Sam. You were right. We *did* need Gideon to get here. You did good, but yeah, you were kind of stupid."

Sam gave a short laugh. He looked back at the last few weeks in a completely different light. Here Sam was thinking that he was calling the shots and that Cornelius was just going with the flow. The gambling cowboy had been wearing his poker face for weeks, never letting on about a thing. Sam got that same sinking feeling he had when he was four years old and finally realized the video game controller his dad kept giving him didn't actually have any batteries inside. His dad had just given it to Sam so he'd stop bugging him, and so Sam could feel like he was playing too.

"So, this Addi," Roanna probed, "she seems pretty well connected for a seamstress."

"She's not a seamstress," Cornelius said, bending down and picking through Gideon's pack for any valuables. "She's a blacksmith."

"And?" Roanna said.

"And she's also the leader of the Trellston Mavericks."

29

OLD FRIENDS

Sam, Cornelius, and Roanna were blindfolded before being taken to see Addi. Between the caskets and this, Sam figured they were making a bit of a habit of being carted around Trellston with their eyes closed, which, as long as they were in trustworthy hands, was okay. It was, however, very difficult to tell whose hands were trustworthy. The only people he figured he could trust at this point were Cornelius, Roanna, and Willow. Anybody else would now be treated with extreme caution. Sam would make sure of it.

Sam shivered as the temperature abruptly dropped. Their footsteps echoed as they walked steadily downhill through what Sam figured was a network of caves or underground tunnels. After a quarter of an hour, the blindfolds were removed and Sam's suspicions were validated. He glanced around at scores of stalagmites and stalactites sprouting from the floor and ceiling. A few dozen people sat at tables or stood around wall charts and maps, all engaged in various discussions. A middle-aged woman with black hair pulled back in a bun stood next to the largest of the tables. Her sleeves were rolled up, revealing uncharacteristically muscled forearms.

"Addi Gleason, it's been a long time," Cornelius said, holding out his arms.

"Cornelius Thompson," the woman said, walking up to Cornelius and slapping him hard across the face, "the Fourth."

Cornelius slowly brought his head back straight, working his jaw open and closed. "I reckon I probably deserved that."

"You deserved a lot more than that, you obstinate jackass," Addi said, before wrapping her arms around him and kissing his freshly slapped cheek. "So good to see you."

"Roanna, Sam, may I introduce Miss Addi Gleason, an old friend of mine and owner of one heck of an open-hand slap."

"Don't worry," Addi said, flashing a warm smile. "Salutatory slaps are reserved solely for Cornelius."

Sam and Roanna stepped forward and shook her hand. Sam felt like she could crush his hand like a trash compactor.

"Pleasure," Sam said, nodding.

"Is this the one?" Addi asked Cornelius, gesturing to Roanna.

"That's her."

"You'll have to show me sometime what you can do with aether, my dear," Addi told Roanna. "Cornelius tells me impressive things."

"I'd be happy to," Roanna said, beaming.

Sam got the distinct impression that Roanna looked at Addi and saw herself, or at least what Roanna could one day become. She'd finally met someone—a woman no less—who was in charge of a bona-fide group of Mavericks, and Sam doubted she was going to be shy about pitching in and showing what she could do.

"I heard of the quelling and feared the worst," Cornelius said, chewing at his mustache. "How much were you involved?"

"Please sit," Addi said, motioning to the chairs at the table before taking a seat herself. She snapped her fingers and someone brought over a pitcher of water with some cups. Sam took his cup and drank greedily. The water had a hint of berry flavor, which was nice, but it could've been toilet water for all Sam cared. He couldn't even remember the last time he'd had a drink. "We were heavily involved, but the Collector's men don't know it. When we learned that the ruling noblemen were evading the aether tax, I arranged to launder their unpaid ingots. The emperor has many eyes and ears, however, and eventually he discovered that the figures weren't adding up. The Collector showed up, killed the ruling noblemen, and a riot ensued. It got ugly for a while, Neal. Hadn't seen it like that since Drindleton. I had the Mavericks keep a low profile. The time wasn't right to engage. It wasn't on our terms."

"I don't doubt it for a second, Addi," Cornelius reassured her. "I reckon that dodgasted Collector hasn't found a single ingot yet, has he?"

Addi gave a knowing smile. "No, he hasn't."

"How much we talking?" Cornelius asked, taking a swig of water. "Two or three thousand?"

"About ninety-seven hundred ingots."

Cornelius choked on his drink and broke out into a coughing fit. "Aether's gourd, Addi. You're lucky the emperor himself isn't here. Now what do you reckon you're gonna do with ten thousand ingots?"

"Fight," Roanna interjected absently, before turning to Cornelius. "They're going to fight."

Addi nodded her head and Cornelius slowly let out a breath. Everyone at the table exchanged glances, their expressions conveying more than words could. Cornelius hadn't come here to join a rebellion; neither had Sam for that matter. They came to rescue Lawrence and that was it. Sam didn't understand the history between Addi and Cornelius, but he'd be willing to bet his phone that they were close and had most likely fought together up north.

"We could use you, Neal," Addi said, her eyes pleading.

Cornelius cleared his throat and avoided Addi's stare. "We

came here to rescue a boy—Sam's friend—that's all. You know I can't get involved."

"No, I know you *can* get involved. It's *you* who doesn't know." Addi's tone took on a sharp edge. She turned to Sam. "Now who's this friend of whom you…who is this boy?"

Sam froze. Had he done something wrong? He suddenly felt like he'd just loudly passed gas at a funeral.

"He's Sam," Cornelius stated.

"You know what I'm asking, cowboy," Addi pressed. "That's opal berry water you're drinking there. I originally assumed he'd just used it up, but this 'Sam' still has absolutely no aether signature."

Sam slowly put down his cup as if he'd been caught stealing it. He didn't even know it was possible to sense how much aether someone had. This woman was obviously on a different aether level than anyone he'd previously met, except maybe Borinder.

"I don't want you getting any ideas now, you hear me," Cornelius said, holding up his hands. "This boy is just here to find his friend and make his way back home, not lead a suicide charge in some war against the Collector."

Addi's jaw dropped and her eyes went wide. "This is *him*, the Void. I'd heard rumors, but never thought…how did you find him?"

"He is just here for a friend," Cornelius repeated, seeing where Addi's mind was going.

"This is the opportunity we've been waiting for our entire lives, Neal," Addi said, rising from her seat. "We have some very talented aetherologists up north that could help make sense of it all. You realize what this could mean? This is the start of the next line of drainers."

"I don't think you're hearing me, darling," Cornelius stressed. "I didn't bring the boy here for breeding stock. He's a kid and he needs to go back to where he came from. I don't care if he lays eggs made of infused aether ingot, he ain't sticking around here any longer than absolutely necessary."

Addi stared at Cornelius, her expression carrying a lifetime of prior arguments. There was a long pause before she cleared her throat and sat back down. "Fine. I will see what I can do to locate this friend of yours, but first you tell me *everything*, Neal. I know you well enough to know that you wouldn't come to me for something simple. I need to know the risks involved."

"Well, the thing is," Cornelius said, removing his hat and scratching his head, "we don't need help finding the kid, per se."

Addi furrowed her brow. "Then what do you need my help for?"

"We need help rescuing him. He's in Trellston castle," Cornelius admitted.

"Trellston castle?" Addi raised both eyebrows. "And before I send my men into the Collector's stronghold for a complete stranger, may I ask how you know he's in the castle?"

"Call it a hunch."

Addi let out a short laugh. "No. If you can't trust *me*, then I can't help *you*."

Cornelius hesitated.

"I'm a techno wizard," Sam interjected. He couldn't take it any longer. Every second they wasted was another second that Lawrence was in danger. Sam got the impression that Addi and Cornelius could go back and forth for days.

"You're a what?" Addi turned toward Sam.

"I'm more than just a Void; I'm a techno wizard. It's easier if I just show you." Sam took out his phone and a few gadgets from his pack for a quick demonstration. Addi sat mystified as Sam flew the drone around the cave, projected video onto the wall, and showed her a game of *Angry Birds Unlimited*. Finally, he took out his tracker and showed Lawrence's marker on a satellite image of Trellston island, except in his image there was no Trellston city, just rocks and green grass. Sam gave the lady blacksmith a few moments for everything to sink in.

"Where did you come from?" Addi studied Sam like he had just stepped off an alien spaceship.

Sam looked over to Cornelius, who nodded for him to continue. "Same place as the cowboys and the musketeers. I don't really know how to explain it. It's a world connected to yours, but it's not yours."

"How did you get here, then?" Addi asked, her face a mix of skepticism and curiosity.

Sam shrugged. "Not quite sure, honestly. Has something to do with an earthquake in my world and a lot of aether in yours."

Addi stroked her chin for a while before continuing. "Can these techno-powers of yours be learned?"

Sam wasn't sure how best to answer this question. He didn't want to lie, but telling the absolute truth would be dangerous. If others knew they could take Sam's powers for themselves, they probably would. Sam had explained his way out of enough situations to know when the moment called for a "politician's response," or so his father had called it. You don't lie; you just answer a different question than the one that was asked.

"I'm the only one with the power to control the oracle," Sam said.

"That's a shame." Addi's expression fell. She turned her attention to a map of Trellston hanging on the wall, then back to the tracker. "The marker on your techno-magic map matches up with Trellston Castle. If your powers are accurate, then your friend is there."

"But can you help us?" Sam pressed.

"On a typical day, my men could smuggle a pack of rabid wolfrats through the front gate, but since the quelling, things are more…difficult. We've been carefully planning and placing resources around the city for months now, in preparation for our retaliation. We've managed to avoid the Collector's detection, but our cover is thin. Attempting a rescue inside the castle now would put this whole operation at risk. I'm sorry, but most of my men have their hands tied, and it's my responsibility to make sure they don't get their *necks* tied. Do you understand?"

"So you're not going to help us?" Sam couldn't believe what he was hearing. Everything they had risked to get here and now they were being turned away at the door like some unwanted beggar. They were so close, and yet Sam felt further from finding his friend than ever. There had to be something he could do.

"Addi, we can't just turn around, darling." Cornelius held out his hands in placation.

"Look, you can stay here, but I can't—"

"I'll join your fight," Sam blurted. All the eyes in the room turned in his direction. Sam swallowed hard. "You help me rescue my friend and I'll use my Void and techno-magic powers to help you fight the Collector."

Cornelius shook his head and let out a groan while Roanna smiled at Sam with a look of appreciation he felt like he'd waited for his entire life.

"Is that right?" Addi mused.

Sam briefly closed his eyes and took a deep breath. "Yes. And heck, if my guess is right, then once we get Lawrence back you'll have *two* Voids."

"What?" Addi cocked her head.

"Lawrence, my friend," Sam repeated, "I'm almost certain he'd be a Void like me."

Addi turned quickly to Cornelius. "The Collector has had a *Void* this whole time and you weren't going to tell me?"

"It ain't like he's out leading the Collector's men, Addi," Cornelius said. "He's a boy."

"You know as well as I do that the emperor would find a way to use that power, whether the boy is complicit or not. We need an immediate change in plans." Addi turned back to Sam. "Looks like you're getting your friend back."

Sam didn't know whether to be excited, grateful, terrified, or just sick to his stomach. He was glad to have the help, but it was clear that Addi thought of Sam and Lawrence as tools first, people second. It had taken him a long time to get over that particular doubt with Roanna and here it was resurfacing in earnest. His allies were accommodating thus far, but what would happen if he refused to aid them or if they saw Lawrence as a bigger threat than an asset? Would they simply let him walk away? Sam doubted it.

Before they could continue the conversation further, a man walked up to Addi and whispered in her ear. Addi thanked the man with a nod, dismissing him.

"It appears we're about to receive word from the Collector," Addi told the group as she stood from her chair.

"From the Collector? What do you mean?" Roanna asked.

"Come with me," Addi beckoned. "You'll want to hear this."

The group followed Addi out of the cavern, down a corridor, and into another much smaller room with walls draped in heavy tapestries.

"What's that?" Sam pointed at a large metal funnel coming from the ceiling.

"The ruling body of Trellston gives messages and announcements to the people from a balcony on the castle," Addi explained. "They speak into what's known as an 'echo-stone.' It's a rare material mined out of these very mountains centuries ago. Infused with aether, it greatly amplifies any nearby sound. Multiple stones linked with very thin copper rod can carry and reproduce the message all over town. There's nothing like it in all the South Isle."

"Aether speakers," Sam said, staring at the ceiling. "Cool stuff."

Addi gave Sam a funny look before continuing. "We tapped into the nearest echo-stone and funneled it down here. The tapestries are to absorb the echo. They say whoever speaks from the main stone speaks for the city. I'll give you one guess who that is now."

"The Collector," Roanna breathed.

"Attention, citizens of Trellston. Attention citizens of Trellston," a tinny voice came from the metal funnel. "The emperor's Tax Collector has an important message."

After a brief pause, the Collector spoke.

"Citizens of Trellston," the Collector's gruff baritone sounded from the ceiling. Sam didn't know if it was an effect of the echo-stone, but the voice had an eerie, distorted quality. "Your stolen aether remains in the hands of criminals. Despite his displeasure, the emperor has chosen to increase his goodwill toward the suffering of this city. The reward for information on the whereabouts of the aether has increased to four hundred gold marks. The offer will expire in three days; after that, a different type of incentive will be in force. I would hope one among you is wise enough to earn the emperor's generosity while it is still extended. Three days."

Cornelius let out a slow whistle. "Four hundred gold marks. I think *I'd* turn you in for that."

Addi slugged him in the arm. "We'll have to be extra vigilant. That's four times what the reward was yesterday. I trust my Mavericks, but everyone's loyalty has a price. We've got three days to find Sam's friend and plan our next steps."

Sam swallowed hard, not sure if he wanted to ask his next question. "What's the Collector going to do if he doesn't get the aether in three days?"

"He begins killing again."

30

NIGHT VISION

"Are you certain we couldn't go through one of the service entrances in the back?" Addi asked one of her advisors—an older, stringy-haired gentleman named Vendrin—as she pointed to a spot on a large map of the castle. The rest of the group sat around the main table poring over piles of drawings and sketches, each depicting some aspect of the city and castle.

"I'm afraid not, Madam Addi. It's not a primary entrance, but they know that, and the guard was bolstered considerably. Last week, we risked sneaking in a letter that way to one of our men on the inside. Almost got caught. Couldn't imagine trying to sneak in an entire person."

"So you can't go in any of the main entrances," Cornelius said, leaning back in his chair with his boots propped up on the table. "You can't go in the back door. We've talked over trying to scale the walls. That's out. We definitely ain't *invited* in. I'd call this a genuine pickle."

Sam put down his map of the castle's main front courtyard and cast his eyes around the room. "What about these caverns?"

"What about them?" Addi asked.

"There's no way to come up from underneath the place? Tunnel our way up from the closest cave or something?"

"Not in three days there ain't," Cornelius said.

"Plus," Addi added, "it wouldn't be a cavern you were digging from. It'd be the sewer."

"A sewer?" Sam repeated in astonishment, rifling through the papers on the desk. "That's perfect, isn't it? Why didn't anyone mention this earlier?"

"I forget you're not from around here," Addi replied.

"What?" Sam put the papers down and looked around the table. No one seemed to share his enthusiasm. "What's wrong with the sewers?"

"It's overrun with cave mongrels," Addi said, as if that settled any further argument.

"And that's bad, I'm assuming?" Sam shrugged.

"Yes," Cornelius said flatly, "that's bad."

"Three centuries ago, Trellston had a monarchy," Addi began. "The King of Trellston, like the emperor now, fed off the aether of the people. His power grew and he eventually gained the ability to mutate animal species. Some have used that power for the benefit of mankind. The king, however, sought to create an army of monsters to defend his kingdom and conquer the others."

"And he kept his monsters in the sewer?" Sam asked.

"Not exactly. The king may have had an impressive quantity of aether, but he was not skilled in its use. His blundering attempts to make obedient and ferocious monsters ended up being nothing more than aetherical torture. He carelessly disposed of his failed experiments down the city's sewer. Some survived. They adapted, they bred, and they multiplied in their isolation. No one goes into the sewers."

"We can't clear the sewers out or trap them or sneak past them or something?" Sam asked.

"We wouldn't be the first to try," Addi said, shaking her head, "or the first to die trying. Folks even tried capturing one of the beasts to placidate it, but the mongrels' aether returns as soon as it's drained. It may be some artifact of their mutated state, no one knows, no one understands why. They spend much of their life dormant, so sneaking by unnoticed would be the best plan, except for two main hurdles."

"Let's hear them," Sam said, trying to sound as positive as possible.

"It's pitch-black and they're attracted to any source of light. Bump into one? You're dead. Take a lantern so you don't bump into one? You're also dead. So unless you have a way of seeing in the dark without any light, we need to forget about the sewers and move on." Addi turned back to Vendrin, obviously considering the conversation over. "What are our best options for passing on a message to our contacts on the inside? Have we fully explored how they could—"

"I have one," Sam interrupted.

Addi stopped and turned to Sam, her annoyance thinly veiled. "You have one what?"

Sam unzipped his pack and rummaged through it before removing his HUD specs and holding them up into the air. "I have a way of seeing in the dark."

Sleep did not come easily for Sam. Haunting visions of mutated sewer mongrels made his dreams an unwelcome refuge. The irony was that the thing had been *his* idea. Sam, the strange, inexperienced newcomer, had a plan to achieve the impossible, and he was on the hook for executing that plan. The others tried to convince him it was foolish—which it was—but there was no other way to rescue his friend. If Sam didn't take this risk, he left Lawrence to the Collector. Sam couldn't have that on his conscience.

When morning finally came, he felt more exhausted than rested. Although he was hungry, his meal of eggs and oats went largely untouched. Before he knew it, he was staring at the slime-coated metal gate that barred the entrance to the sewers. Addi, Roanna, Cornelius, and the giant man, Jerg, had come to see Sam off.

"Here, take these," Sam said, reaching into his pack and removing two earpieces. He hoped Roanna and Cornelius didn't notice his hand shaking as he handed over the devices. "I should be able to talk to you from just about anywhere with these. Just stick them in your ear like mine. I can turn them on and off with my oracle."

Roanna took the communicator and put it in her ear. She anxiously wrung the bottom of her shirt. "Sam."

"Yes?" He looked her in the eyes and his heart skipped a beat. How could she still have that effect on him?

"Please be careful."

"You know me."

"That's why I'm reminding you," Roanna replied.

Sam looked to Cornelius, who just gave a fatherly nod of approval.

"Ready," Sam told the group as he donned his HUD specs. He tapped his phone screen and the cutting-edge glasses came to life. He selected the IR and night vision overlay to give him the most detailed information of where the mongrels were.

On Sam's command, Jerg reached into his jacket and pulled out a ring of keys like some kind of hulking medieval janitor. The keys jingled as the man's beefy fingers flipped through his collection before settling on one. Jerg stuck the key in the lock and twisted, liberating the mechanism from the heavy iron gate. He grabbed one of the metal bars and jerked hard, opening the way to the sewers beyond.

"I'm coming with," Cornelius said, making his way over to Sam.

Sam gave a thinly veiled sigh of relief. He wanted to do the heroic thing and tell Cornelius to stay. He wanted to object on principle, but the fact of the matter was that he was terrified, and he needed Cornelius desperately.

"Neal," Addi said, trying to control the strain in her voice, "could I talk to you for a moment?"

Cornelius acquiesced and followed Addi for about twenty paces before they stopped to have a hushed conversation. Sam knew he shouldn't, but he couldn't resist. He pulled out his phone, opened his communicator app, and activated Cornelius's earpiece.

"I don't understand this, Neal," Sam heard Addi say.

"What's there to understand? Kid's got the only plan that has a chance. Don't fault me for backing the best idea we got."

"It may be the best, but it still isn't good enough to not get you killed."

"There's always a chance we die, Addi, in everything we do."

"Yes, but there's usually a chance you'll live as well. Don't preach that fatalistic nonsense to me. Why are you even here to begin with?"

"Didn't you ask me to come?"

"Yes! As a matter of fact, I did…every month for the last five years, but that's not why you're here. You stroll into Trellston after all this time with some teenage Void on a suicide mission and expect me to act like everything's fine between us? That there's nothing we need to discuss?"

"There's nothing that happened up north that I feel like discussing, Addi."

"Nothing you feel like discussing? Your wife and son were murdered, for fracture's sake. She was my sister, Neal."

Sam's eyes went wide. Addi was Cornelius's sister-in-law? Roanna said that Cornelius came down south after the King of the Greenlands killed his partner, but Sam never once thought that that partner was the cowboy's wife. And Cornelius had a son? There was a long pause before either of them spoke.

"I reckon I don't need to be reminded of what I've lost in life, thank you kindly," Cornelius said.

"Well, you need to be reminded that the rest of us didn't take off down south after things went bad. While you were playing cards with drunkards in Ogland, the fight didn't stop for the rest of us. Your wife and son weren't the last people to die, Neal. We needed you."

"I couldn't. I'm sorry, Addi."

"If you couldn't help back then, then why do you help the boy now? Why march right back to the brink of war if you're so bent on never getting involved? Saving this boy won't bring Kolby back, Neal."

"You think I don't know that, Addi? I'm not trying to bring my son and wife back from the dead. I'm trying to let them die. I relive that moment every time I close my eyes. It's like they die all over again every…single…day. I don't want to see it anymore."

"And you think that helping Sam will end that?"

"I've got it on good authority that if I can keep Sam's mom from losing her boy, then it might help rebalance some things."

Good authority? Sam racked his brain to think of who Cornelius could be talking about. No one even knew Sam's mother existed. And who could even make that kind of promise…other than the Eldest Tree. That was it. Cornelius's peace wasn't "peace and quiet" while playing cards and smoking his pipe. It was peace from losing his wife and son. What had the Eldest Tree said again? Cornelius needed to stop someone from losing the thing that took his peace. He needed to stop a parent from losing their son.

"I don't understand this, Neal," Addi said, "but if a suicide mission is my only chance at bringing you back to the land of the living, then so be it. Please don't die."

"Never had it happen yet."

Sam looked over to see Addi give the cowboy a kiss on the cheek. Cornelius tipped his hat to Addi before coming over to

Sam's side. Sam now had one more reason to make it back home. He wanted that peace for Cornelius. He would never look at the grizzled cowboy the same way again.

Cornelius turned to Roanna and placed a hand on her shoulder. "He'll be fine. I'll make sure of it. You stay with Addi. Do what she says."

"I will," Roanna said.

"You ready?" Sam asked. Cornelius nodded.

Sam walked up to the gate and looked into the blackness beyond. Off in the distance, his infrared picked up a few rats scuttling in the darkness. He took a deep breath and instantly regretted it. He almost gagged on the humid, rotting stench. What had he gotten himself into? What if he never came back out? He paused.

"One second." Sam pulled out his phone again and penned a text.

Mom, I'm going after Lawrence. I may have found him. I've got the handsome cowboy looking out for me. I love you very much. I'm sorry I haven't made your life the easiest. You're a great mom. I love you.

He queued it up to send for whenever the phone got signal. Not exactly Shakespeare, but it would have to do for now. One more.

Rinni. Found Lawrence's earpiece signal. Need to go through a dark sewer full of mutated monsters to get there. Using the HUD specs to see my way through. Can't use a flashlight or it'll wake them and I'll be eaten. If you get another text, I made it. If you don't…I didn't.

31

INTO THE DARK

Sam pressed steadily forward in the darkness with Cornelius's hands resting on his shoulders. The cowboy had surprisingly good night vision, being able to enhance his eyesight with an infusion of aether, but it wasn't perfect. Sam still needed to act as the seeing-eye dog. They came to their first intersection. He could read the maps well enough with his specs, but his anxiety had spurred him to memorize the entire journey over the last twenty-four hours. Left, left, right, middle, middle, right, right, left. If their info was correct, Sam and Cornelius would come out at a sewer grate in the castle cellar. Addi had sent a message to one of her contacts on the inside to meet them there.

Sam tried to move as silently as possible while they waded through the shin-deep sewage. It was all he could do to keep his balance, as each step squelched into a layer of something he knew wasn't mud. The miasma of thick, rotting air seemed as hard to press through as the muck at their feet. Sam drew in shallow breaths; whether it was a reaction from the stench or the fear, he didn't know.

They turned another corner and Sam froze. Fifteen steps

away, the infrared signature of a hunched shape glowed in the darkness like a hot coal in a heap of ash. Sam held his breath. The beast's shoulders rose and fell in a slow and steady rhythm. The guttural wheeze of the monster's breathing was the only noise in the stillness of the sewer.

Drawing on every ounce of courage he had, Sam willed his body forward. One small step after the other, they neared the sewer mongrel. The roughly humanoid shape sat against the wall, with its freakishly small head tilted forward, and abnormally long limbs wrapped around its knees. Long, boney spikes jutted from its back like the spines on a dinosaur. Sam gave the grotesque creature as wide a berth as possible, putting as much effort into praying that it wouldn't wake as he did into moving quietly around it. The small stretch of tunnel seemed to take hours, and by the time they'd rounded the corner, Sam felt like he'd run a marathon.

"Give me a moment," Sam breathed as he leaned against the slick sewer wall. Sam ran through the map in his head. They had gone through four intersections, which meant they were roughly halfway through, and had only seen one mongrel. He didn't know whether that was a good sign or a bad sign. Sam felt Cornelius pat him on the shoulder. It was time to get moving again. However much Sam didn't want to go forward, there was also no going back. He had never wanted anything more in his life than he wanted out of these sewers, and the only way out was forward.

Three more intersections and Sam could hear it before he saw it. The noise started low, like the rumble of distant thunder, but it was accented with strange wheezing squeals. They turned yet another corner and Sam had to throw both hands over his mouth to keep from screaming. Hundreds of glowing infrared signatures filled his entire view, the closest not three feet in front of him.

Sam hadn't found a mongrel nest; he'd stumbled upon the birthplace of all nightmares. The frames of ghoulish, orcish, and beastly creatures heaved up and down as they slept, their croaking snores the only sound echoing in the tunnel.

With his trembling hands still covering his mouth, he felt a tear drip onto his index finger and roll down his knuckles. He couldn't do this. One errant step and he'd be devoured. This real-life haunted house would be his end. He felt lightheaded. His knees started to shake, but before his body gave in, he felt a strong, reassuring hand grip his left shoulder.

Sam closed his eyes and breathed. He was back on family vacation in Zion's National Park, Utah. It was a bright and sunny day, the dry desert air hot against his skin. In his right hand, he held on to a heavy chain strung from post to post along the narrow ascent of Angel's Landing. Although he didn't look, he knew that a few feet to either side were sheer drops of a thousand feet.

"I...I don't think I can do this," Sam stuttered.

"Yes you can, Son," Sam's dad called out from behind him. "You've come this far; you can make it the rest of the way." Sam didn't dare turn his head to see exactly how far behind his father was.

How did he ever let his dad talk him into this? Sam hated heights. This was the worst thing he'd ever been talked into. Worse even than the time Rinni had tricked him into believing those wild mushrooms they found in Lawrence's backyard would give him special abilities if he ate them. Unless, of course, projectile vomiting was considered a super power.

"Dad, I *really* don't think I can do this," Sam repeated. He could feel the sweat on his fingers and palm against the metal chain, imagine his grasp slipping as he tripped on a rock and went sliding off the edge to his death. This wasn't some morbid trick of the mind. How easy would it be for that exact scenario to play itself out? He could actually die here.

"Son," his father said, gripping his shoulder, "look forward. One foot in front of the other. Hold on to the chain. Nothing else matters and nothing else can happen other than you getting to that summit."

"Okay," Sam muttered.

Sam never let go of the chain and his dad never let go of him until they made it to the top. Sam would never forget that view as long as he lived. Not just for the beauty of the scene or the grandeur of Zion Canyon, not even because he had stuck it out and earned that view. It was because he had done it with his dad, and his dad had confidence in his son beyond what his son had in himself. Sam learned he could face frightening things, crippling things, and move on. Distractions would always be there, on the left and on the right. But that's not where Sam was looking anymore. He was looking forward.

The scene faded from his mind and he was back in the dank, soupy sewer. He knew the monsters were mere feet to his left, right, and overhead, but he continued to move forward. He knew that one slip, one trip, one sneeze, one anything would result in a very violent and horrific end, yet he continued to move forward. Step by step, he wove his way through the gauntlet of sleeping creatures, until at last, his infrared field was empty. Instead of standing atop a majestic mountain peak, he merely stood at another intersection in a sewer, but the view was no less rewarding. They took a left and continued on another hundred yards before they saw a shaft of light coming from the ceiling. A single rope split the light, hanging down from an open sewer grate in what would be the castle's cellar. They'd made it.

32

LIBRARY

Sam wrapped the rope tightly around his hands and tugged twice before being hoisted from the sewers, through the open drain, and onto the cellar floor. Sam's ascent from the sewers couldn't have felt more glorious if he was escorted to heaven on the shoulders of winged angels. Never in his life would he have guessed that arriving in a cellar would be so profound. He lay on the cold stone ground and pressed his face against its dry surface as if the floor was a kiss from his mother.

"My stars, you made it," a concerned elderly voice said. "Are you in need of anything…other than a bath, of course?"

Sam rolled over onto his back, took off his HUD specs, and looked straight up into the wrinkled face of an old woman. "Just to stay here…and never go back."

"I would suppose so," she said, handing Sam a cup to drink. "I've lived in Trellston my entire life—no short duration if you can't tell—and I don't believe I've ever so much as heard of anyone coming *out* of the sewer. Not in any recognizable form, that is."

Sam sat up, took the cup and chugged it, noticing the

familiar taste of opal berry. He looked over to see two large men pulling on the rope until Cornelius emerged from the sewer.

"Mighty fine work there, Sam," Cornelius said, putting his hand on Sam's shoulder. "A lesser man would've lost himself in those tunnels…in more ways than one. That's mighty fine work."

Sam certainly didn't feel brave. He was just glad he hadn't pooped himself in fear, although after walking through all the sewer muck it was very hard to tell whether he actually had.

"I'm not sure how much Addison told you, but my name is LaRue Overly, head housemaid here at Trellston Castle. I'm also one of the Mavericks' top informants." The old lady winked as she flashed a kindly grin. "Now, can either of you tell me why I needed to fish you out of the sewer in the first place? The communication was left vague in case it was intercepted."

Sam's hope that Lawrence was being taken care of by a hospitable grandmother might not be too far off after all. "We're looking for a boy named Lawrence. He's supposed to be in the castle. A boy about my age. A bit rounder than me, blond hair."

"I can't say that I know a Lawrence," LaRue said, scrunching her face.

"There'd be a certain degree of hush-hush and special handling going on with this one, LaRue," Cornelius added.

LaRue's eyes went wide. "You know, there's not much that goes on in this castle that I don't at least catch wind of, but now that you mention the hush-hush, there is something peculiar going on over in the northeast wing, just past the castle library. Food gets delivered to the door, empty trays are brought back. No one is allowed in. No one comes out."

Sam and Cornelius exchanged glances. "Can you take us there?"

"After working here for fifty-some-odd years, there are very few places that I *can't* take you. But, the first place you're going is the bath. We won't get far at all with you two smelling like that."

Sam had never enjoyed a warm bath so much in his entire life. The water was scented with what smelled like a mix of lavender and cinnamon to help "leech out the stench," or so he was told. So great was the sewer funk that the water had to be drained and refilled three times before Sam got anywhere close to not smelling like a human skunk. A fresh set of clothes—trousers, tunic, vest, and boots—were laid out for him while his tactical pants and shirt were getting washed. He hadn't parted with his pack, however, and had taken out his tracker to test LaRue's theory that Lawrence might be in the northeast wing. The last known signal was dead-on.

He got dressed and waited a few minutes for Cornelius, who came out wearing a similar outfit. Even without his iconic hat and poncho, Cornelius still managed to look like a cowboy. The deep-set lines in his face, his classic handlebar mustache, and the unfazed look in his eyes screamed cowboy as much as any hat or set of spurs.

"What took you so long, cowboy?" Sam asked. "I had three baths and still had to wait here for ten minutes."

Cornelius held up four fingers and winked. "You ready to find your partner?"

"Never been readier."

They walked to a large wooden door and gave three knocks. A moment later the door opened and LaRue ushered them into the room beyond, which looked to be a maid's supply room.

"So how complicated is it going to be to get to the northeast wing? What kind of disguises will we need?" Sam asked.

LaRue turned and handed them each a broom. "This should do."

Sam took the broom and looked it up and down as if the old lady had just handed him a rubber chicken. "That's it?"

"As long as you're with me and look the part, no one will pay you so much as a second glance. You don't work somewhere for half a century without earning the trust of others."

"But you're deceiving them," Sam said flatly.

"You don't work somewhere for over a half a century without breaking a few rules. Leave your pack here. You can hide it in that barrel over there. Take only what you need."

However much it pained Sam to consciously leave the backpack, he knew LaRue was right. Plus, if this worked, then they would be back here to retrieve the pack. If it didn't work, then not having the pack would be the least of Sam's worries. He couldn't think of anything in particular that he'd need, but just like his dad had told him a hundred times on as many Saturdays, "take the whole toolbox because you never know what tool you might end up needing next." Knowing he'd curse not having some bit of tech, he reluctantly deposited his entire backpack in the barrel.

Just before he closed the lid, Sam caught sight of a metal funnel stuck into the top of one of the food-supply barrels. A smile crept over his face as an idea started blossoming in his prank-trained brain. He grabbed his backpack and rummaged through it before retrieving a small black case. Satisfied, he stashed his backpack and closed the lid.

"LaRue, I was wondering if you ever got close to the echo-stone. The one that the Collector spoke from the other day," Sam asked.

"There's only *one* echo-stone, Sam, no need to specify. And yes, if the need arose, I could get to it...briefly. Why do you ask?"

"I was wondering if you could place one of these on the underside of the stone. Somewhere where it wouldn't be noticed." Sam opened his case and withdrew a black dot about the size of a fingernail.

LaRue took the small dot and studied it. "I suppose I could. For what purpose, might I ask?"

"A backup plan."

She shrugged and passed the brooms to Cornelius and Sam before leading the way from the supply room.

After ascending a few dozen stairs, they left the castle basement and exited into the great hall. The room was enormous. Large ornate windows of stained glass were spaced along the walls between a dozen towering pillars of mottled gray stone. Under each window stood a statue of some prominent figure or warrior, crafted in lifelike detail. The ceiling, some fifty feet up, was a web of elaborate wooden trusswork, while an interlocking square pattern of black and gray tiles comprised the ground underfoot.

"This place would be a nightmare to mop," Sam said under his breath.

"You see the Great Hall of Trellston and your first impression is what it would be like to clean the floors?" LaRue said, shaking her head.

"Just trying to play the part," Sam said, holding up his broom.

From the Great Hall, they moved from lavish room to lavish room, passing guards, noblemen and women, and other servants, all without a second look in their direction. A few minutes later, they opened the door to a garage-sized supply pantry where LaRue instructed them to put an empty barrel onto a wooden handcart and wheel it from the room. Four or five parlors later, they arrived at the castle library.

Sam had never seen so many books in his entire life. He remembered hearing his dad talk about the days before the Internet and having to do research papers by looking through encyclopedias. Although laborious, there was something appealing about the idea of staying in the library late into the night, digging through book after book, like a wizard studying to find some arcane secret. It didn't appeal to him enough to ever actually do it, but it sounded pretty epic. The only library he'd ever been inside was his school library, and most of the books there were replaced by touchscreen tables and 3D printers.

Hundreds of thousands of books were meticulously stacked and ordered from floor to ceiling. Dozens of people sat hunched at long, wooden tables. Sam wondered what they would think if they knew that the content of every single one of these books, if scanned, could be stored on the device in Sam's pocket. Sam and Cornelius wheeled their cart through the labyrinth of shelves to a secluded door in the far corner of the library.

"Past this door is a long hallway," LaRue said. "At the end of the hallway is the door you're looking for. As discussed, there should only be one guard there."

"You ready, kid?" Cornelius asked.

"Ready as I'll ever be."

"Things are going to move fast once we commit to this thing," Cornelius added. "Be prepared to improvise. You know what to do."

Sam took several deep breaths. This was his zone. This was where Sam Shelton showed his quality. It was time for a good old-fashioned prank. It wasn't overly elaborate, but some of the most effective pranks weren't. Sam opened the door, broom in hand, and walked into the hallway beyond. As described, at the end of the corridor stood one lonely guard in light armor, long spear at the ready. Sam pretended not to notice him and made a show of busily sweeping the floors.

"You there," the guard called out.

Sam paid no heed as he began humming loudly.

"Hey," the guard repeated. "You're not allowed here, boy. Move along."

Sam finally looked up at the guard and made eye contact. He shrugged and then returned to sweeping the stone floor.

The guard huffed and left his post, walking sternly in Sam's direction. He caught up to Sam and grabbed him roughly by the arm. "Hey, you daft or deaf, boy? I said move along."

Sam jumped, as if the guard's sudden presence was a complete surprise. "I beg your pardon, sir," Sam said in his British accent.

"You beg my pardon? Get scarce, you twit." The guard pushed Sam toward the door.

"That any way to treat someone just following orders... trying to do his job?"

"Well, I've got my orders, and they're to keep noisy busybodies like yourself out of this hallway. Now get."

"My headmistress is right outside," Sam said, jabbing a thumb toward the door. "I suggest you take it up with her. She told me specifically that this hallway was to be cleaned at all costs." Sam's nerves tightened. He needed to make the guard leave the hallway.

"I don't care what she told you. Scram." The guard wrung his hands on the shaft of his spear, obviously growing weary of this exchange.

This guard wasn't going to leave. Sam would need to ratchet this up a notch. He was hoping the guard would simply walk outside to see what this was all about, but that would be too easy. He steeled himself for plan B.

"There's only one person I take orders from," Sam said defiantly, "if you want me gone, I'm afraid you'll have to do it yourself."

Sam winced as the guard's vise grip clamped on his arm. The guard strode to the door, half dragging Sam the last ten feet. Just before they got to the door, Sam voided the man's aether.

"Gah!" The guard dropped his spear and clutched at his chest as if he was having a heart attack.

Sam pushed the guard backwards, opened the door, and ran out of the hallway.

"You worthless little twit," the guard yelled, chasing Sam through the door. "How did you manage—"

Cornelius's brass-knuckled fist abruptly ended the guard's protest. With LaRue standing watch, they quickly removed the soldier's armor for Cornelius to wear. The guard was a few inches shorter and considerably more rotund than the cowboy, but they would have to make do. With Cornelius dressed, they took the unconscious guard, put him in the barrel, and secured the lid, leaving an unstoppered hole for air.

"You ready to get your friend?" Cornelius asked, turning to Sam.

Sam paused, looking in the direction of the long hallway. "Ready as I'll ever be."

33

FRIENDS LOST

Sam and Cornelius stood at the door at the end of the hallway. They had no idea what they would find in the next room. It could be Lawrence held hostage by the emperor's men or held in a prison cell. It could just be the earpiece. It could even be the Collector himself. Whatever it was, they were only one door away from finding out whether everything they had done—bartering with Borinder at Hagzarad, trekking over a mountain pass, smuggling themselves in coffins, and trudging through a nightmarish sewer—was worth it.

Cornelius grabbed the handle and slowly pushed the door open. The hinges made a slight creak as they entered the room. Instead of finding a jail cell or medieval torture chamber, they found a cozy den, complete with a roaring fire, overstuffed chair, shelves of books, and large table full of an impressive array of food. The place looked remarkably similar to the introductory scene in *Masterpiece Theater*, an old British drama series that Sam's mom watched on occasion. In one of the chairs, chowing down a roast chicken leg was none other than Lawrence.

"Sam?" Lawrence said with his mouth full. "You're here."

"Lawrence." Sam did his best to suppress an elated scream.

He cautiously stole a glance around the room, but found no one else. He ran over to his friend and gave him a hug. "Dude, you have no idea what I've been through to find you. Why haven't you been wearing your earpiece? I've been trying to get in touch with you forever, man."

"Dude," Lawrence said, "you sound like my mother. So I'm supposed to keep that thing in my ear twenty-four-seven now? Those things are annoying."

"So is trying to track you down. It's been a long day. We got to get rolling."

"You're going? But you just got here," Lawrence said, reaching for a thick slice of buttered bread. "We need to catch up. You seen Rinni at all?"

"Not *me* going, *we're* going." Sam made a gesture, first at just him and Cornelius and then including Lawrence.

"Dude, slow down. You hungry? They don't have fast-food type stuff, but I basically get anything I ask for as long as they know what I'm talking about."

"Am I *hungry*?" Sam shook his head as if trying to free his brain from the stupidity of the question…although he *was* hungry. "Dude, we're here to break you out, not have a dinner date. Way too much to explain, but we have to move now if we want a chance at this."

"Break me out?" Lawrence laughed, taking a bite of his bread. "What are you talking about, man?"

"I'm talking about the Collector and his men, who could be here at any moment. The moment they find us, we're dead. We got to hurry."

"Dead?" Lawrence laughed again. "I think you're being a touch dramatic, don't you? Does it look like we're in danger? They treat me like a king ever since they found out I could destroy black magic. Hey…you wouldn't be able to do that too, would you? Dude, if you can destroy black magic, they are going to *love* you."

What was going on here? Sam looked to Cornelius then

back at his friend. Lawrence didn't know the truth. He didn't know what was actually going on in Avalon.

"Lawrence, I don't have time to explain, man. You're just going to have to trust me. This isn't what it seems. Bad things are going down and you don't want to be a part of them."

"Sam, I know. I was told *all* about that criminal group that stole all of that magic from the emperor. Believe it or not, that's actually why they brought me out here, so I can help. I can't just abandon them in the middle of all of this after how well they've treated me. Plus, they'd never find the stolen aether if I just bailed."

Sam couldn't believe what he was hearing. Lawrence was actually on the *emperor's* side in all of this. As usual, he was more moron than malicious, but the result was the same. How was Sam going to convince Lawrence to come with him before this situation turned ugly? "Lawrence, you're on the wrong side of this thing. The emperor is using you. He's done terrible things. He's killing people. He'll kill me, kill my friends."

"You can't be serious," Lawrence said, finally putting down his food. "For the first time in my life I'm useful, I have some valuable skill, and you want me to run out on the only people that have ever thought I was special? They told me someone might come to try and spin the truth, but I never thought in my wildest dreams that it would be you, Sam."

"Dude," Sam stressed, "you got to believe me. I can show you proof of everything, but we first have to make our way out of here."

Lawrence paused a long moment, his face frozen in concentration. "This is all because you're jealous, isn't it? Can't ever let stupid ol' Lawrence have the upper hand. He always has to be the butt of all your jokes. This Maverick gang stole from the government, Sam, and then killed a bunch of the emperor's men."

"Lawrence, you have this thing backwards."

"How do you know *you* don't have it backwards?" Lawrence

raised his voice, jabbing a finger in Sam's direction. "You know what that aether tax goes to? They use it to help struggling villages and protect the empire's borders."

"Protect the borders from *what*?" Sam challenged, almost laughing at the absurdity of the claim.

"I don't know. Monsters and stuff."

"Monsters and *stuff*? Are you hearing yourself? We're on an *island*, man. These monsters coming in from the sea? We're in flippin' New Zealand."

"New Zealand?" Lawrence laughed derisively. "Take a look around you, Sam. You know of any magical wizard-emperors in New Zealand? This is Avalon."

"Sam," Cornelius spoke quietly. "Not sure if this is what you had in mind, partner, but one way or another we need to vamoose."

"Lawrence," Sam gritted his teeth, trying with everything he had to stay calm, to get his friend to see clearly. "We…need…to…go. This will not go well for any of us."

"Well, it's going awesome for *me*—for once—so I guess you're wrong there. I'm not going anywhere."

Cornelius looked to Sam as if asking permission. "I could knock him out."

Sam knew the situation was dire when he was seriously considering the cowboy's offer of punching Lawrence in the head. Heavens knew the fool deserved it. Might even fix some things. How could Lawrence be seeing things so backwards? The emperor must have poisoned his mind, only shown him things that supported his argument. But wasn't that exactly what had happened with Sam and the Mavericks? He had only ever heard their side of the story and had never even thought to question it. The emperor was bad. The Collector was bad. The aether tax was bad. Sam seriously doubted Cornelius and Roanna were deceiving him, but then again, he had thought the same thing about Gideon. Maybe Cornelius and Roanna were completely convinced that they were doing the right things, but were actually causing more damage than good.

"You're with *them*, aren't you?" Lawrence insisted, a look of horror on his face. He stood up from the table and quickly moved to the wall, where he grabbed and tugged on a tasseled rope dangling from the ceiling. "This is for your own good, Sam."

Sam's mind swam. The clock was ticking, and he didn't know what to do. He wasn't even sure what the right thing *was* anymore. What if joining Lawrence was the right thing to do? He'd known him longer than he'd known everyone in Avalon combined. What was he supposed to do? The indecisiveness nearly tore him in two until—as with most unmade decisions—the choice was taken from him.

The doors burst open on every side and streams of soldiers filled the room. When they stopped, Sam and Cornelius stood surrounded by no less than twenty armored men. Most of the soldiers gripped black wooden clubs or chained whips while several others had handfuls of spiked wooden balls, which floated ominously above their open palms.

"Well…poop."

34

DINNER GUESTS

Sam looked around for any possible escape. The room had no windows and every door was clogged with at least three soldiers. There was no getting out.

"You summoned us, milord?" one of the soldiers asked Lawrence.

Lawrence leveled a glare at Sam before looking back to the soldier. "Could you please escort my guests to Captain Spitzer? I believe they've lost their way."

"What are you *doing*, Lawrence?" Sam pleaded, not understanding how his friend could be so careless, so misguided.

"I don't know what happened to you, but you need some help, Sam. Don't be so dramatic." Lawrence's smug look revealed just how much he was enjoying this. He loved calling the shots, but the role fit him like his dad's suit coat. Lawrence tried looking smart and important, but just ended up looking ridiculous.

"Don't be so dramatic? I'm currently surrounded by two dozen armed men. I apologize for my overreaction."

What was he going to do? Sam didn't know who this Captain Spitzer was, but he did know that a meeting with him would probably end up in a meeting with the Collector. Before Sam could think of a plan, Cornelius spun and uppercut the nearest solider in the chin. The cowboy snatched the man's club and threw it across the room, cracking another soldier in the head and knocking him out cold. Sam stood there, not knowing how to help or what to do. Cornelius was a whirlwind of speed, precision, and power. He weaved between soldiers to strike with his hands at joints and armor gaps. Some soldiers held to their weapons while others sent them airborne on bursts of aether.

"Get down," Cornelius yelled.

Sam dove behind a couch as the air was ripped with a maelstrom of flying clubs, wooden balls, and whipping chains. His ears were filled with the sounds of splintering wood, shattering ceramic, and clanging metal, but above it all were the screams. He peeked around the side of the couch to see Cornelius grab one of the soldiers and use him as a human shield against the vortex of flying debris. With a kick, Cornelius sent the table full of food skidding across the room to plow over three men like a charging bull. The cowboy made his way to the fireplace and grabbed an iron poker. The metal rod might as well have been Excalibur with how fast he dropped his enemies. Sam counted the remaining soldiers. As long as Cornelius's aether held, they actually might get out of this situation alive.

Just then, Lawrence popped out from behind a chair and Cornelius whirled toward the sudden movement.

"No, don't hurt him," Sam screamed.

Cornelius stopped short, freezing mid-swing. Lawrence took advantage of the hesitation and lunged at Cornelius, grabbing him by the leg.

"No!" Sam yelled, but this time in concern for Cornelius, who Sam knew would be completely drained of aether now.

The remaining guards fell on the aetherless cowboy, beating him repeatedly with their clubs until he was still. Sam rushed to Cornelius, but was grabbed by a pair of guards.

"Lawrence, I came to *help* you!" Sam yelled, tears filling his eyes.

"Your friend shouldn't have hit that guard," Lawrence said, his confidence replaced with a look of growing doubt. He looked uneasily at Sam and then at Cornelius, before being escorted out of the room by a pair of soldiers. It was the last thing Sam saw before a sharp crack on the head turned the world black.

Sam and a semiconscious Cornelius sat in two wooden chairs—hands tied behind their backs—in a cold, windowless room. Its cramped space and unadorned stone walls were the polar opposite of the cozy den that Cornelius and two dozen soldiers just obliterated. Soldiers stood in two corners of the room while an empty chair was placed opposite Sam and Cornelius.

The sound of a barking voice came from outside the room, growing louder as someone approached. The door burst open and a female soldier strode into the room and took the empty seat. Her long black hair was pulled back in a tight ponytail, making her hawkish facial features all the more prominent. A thick, faded scar bisected her cheek from her lip to her ear.

"I am Captain Spitzer," she said in a husky voice. "Why are you in my castle?"

Sam and Cornelius said nothing.

"What did you do with Sergeant Hill?" Captain Spitzer remained calm, but gave a glare that could make a rabid dog whimper.

"With *who*?" Sam asked indignantly, his anger over Lawrence's betrayal burning away any sense of fear or intimidation.

Captain Spitzer briefly clenched her jaw. "The soldier I had posted outside of Lawrence's door. He is missing."

"Sounds like a good question for Lawrence," Sam scoffed.

"I'm not sure you realize the situation you are in here, boy," Captain Spitzer said, scooting her chair closer. "Your family isn't here. Your friends aren't here. You are being held for trespassing in a city under the Collector's martial law and from this room, no one can hear you scream…no one that cares at least."

Sam struggled defiantly against his bonds. "Well, where is he, then? Where's this big, bad Collector? I'm sure he'll be *thrilled* to find out that your soldiers let two nobodies slip by to see his prized Lawrence, and that they demolished his room while Lawrence was still *inside*. If just one of those wooden balls had gone astray and cracked Lawrence in his fat head, he could have been killed. I'd be more than happy to explain that to the Collector. Oh Collector! Can you hear me?"

"Shut your mouth," Captain Spitzer hissed.

"Oh, I apologize, I thought no one that cared could hear me scream."

"Captain," said one of the guards, leaning into the room, "should I fetch him?"

"No, you twit," she snapped, looking around at all the soldiers in the room. "Any word of this leaks to the Collector and you'll be lucky to work for the scullery maid when I'm done with your demotions…if I'm still left to make your demotions. However much I would enjoy torturing these two for more information, we need to get rid of the evidence of our little mishap. Quickly and completely. The longer they hang around, the more likely this story slips out. You know what to do."

"Yes, Captain."

Captain Spitzer stood and left without saying another word.

Out of the corner of his eye, Sam saw two of the soldiers walk to the middle of the room and bend down to grab something on the floor.

"Blimey, these things are heavy," one of the soldiers said, shaking his hands. "Hey Barry, you got any aether left?"

"You got to be kidding me," grumbled one of the soldiers from the hallway as he came in to help.

"Sorry, mate, but these sewer covers weigh a ton."

Sam jerked his head around, twisting his chair a quarter turn in time to see a thick metal sewer cover float from its spot in the floor and fall with a loud clang a few feet away.

"No!" Sam screamed, realizing what Captain Spitzer meant by "disposing of the evidence quickly and completely." "You can't put us down there. I can't go back down there!"

"Go *back* there?" one of the soldiers laughed. "What's this kid going on about?"

Sam couldn't go back to the sewers. He didn't have his HUD specs. He didn't have his gear. Cornelius didn't have any aether. They would be completely blind. They'd be torn to shreds in minutes. Sam thrashed in his chair, trying madly to break free, to fend off the soldiers and prevent them from dropping him to his death. One of the soldiers backhanded Sam across the face. Sam's head jerked back and his vision swam. He felt the sensation of being lifted up. He came to just in time to see a pair of soldiers drop him down the sewer hole. Sam bit back a scream—knowing it would only draw the mongrels—as he plummeted ten feet before splashing into the fetid water below. Sam smashed his chair to pieces as he hit the floor and went sprawling into a layer of sewer muck. He rolled out of the way as Cornelius came crashing down moments later.

Sam heard laughter as the sewer cover was lifted over the circle of light from the opening overhead, eclipsing it until there was nothing left but darkness.

35

ALL IS LOST

Complete darkness. Everything about the environment reflected how Sam felt. He sat against the slimy sewer wall, Cornelius's head cradled in his lap to hold it above the foul water. The cowboy still hadn't regained consciousness. Sam let the tears freely run down his cheeks. This was all his doing. Thinking only of himself, he'd barged into Cornelius's life and led the man to his death. *Sam* may have deserved this for all his stupidity, but Cornelius didn't. The cowboy was only trying to protect Sam from hurting himself. Now they would never make it out. Sam's mom would lose the only person she had left, and Cornelius would never find his peace.

Was this really how his life would end? Betrayed, abandoned, trapped, and devoured. Even if he had a way out, he wasn't sure he could will his body to move. The loneliness crippled him as sure as two broken legs. How did it come to this, stuck back in the sewer with no gear? He'd known the second he stashed his pack in that barrel that he'd regret leaving it behind. He could always try to find the cellar opening, but fumbling around in a dark sewer wasn't the best of strategies, and without someone ready and waiting with the sewer lid off, he could walk directly underneath the place and never even know it was there.

He *did* still have his phone. It seemed like an oversight on the guards' part to not check his pockets, but why would they have even bothered? What could he possibly smuggle into the sewers that would make a lick of difference? He could have been hiding a submachine gun in his pant leg for all it mattered.

He could check his phone for signal, but the light might invite unwanted guests. Even if he did have signal, it wasn't like he could talk to anyone that could help him. Roanna didn't exactly have a cell phone number…but she did have an earpiece! Roanna, and Willow for that matter, had earpieces. Sam wore his so often that he forgot it was jammed into his ear. Taking a chance, he reached down and withdrew his phone—hiding the light of the screen with his shirt—and activated all the communicators.

"Can anyone hear me?" Sam whispered as quietly as he could. He waited a minute and repeated himself several times, each time risking a louder whisper. "Is anyone there?"

"Ooooh, friend Sam," Willow's voice came over the earpiece. "I am here. I have never ever not worn your techno-magical ear bug. I have planted it into my head. Are you doing well, Sam? Have you found your friend?"

The freshness of Willow's voice was like a breath of clean mountain air. "I did find my friend, but it didn't go well."

"Oh no, friend Sam," Willow gasped. "Are you okay? Why are you whispering?"

"Long story. My friend was deceived. He betrayed us, and Cornelius and I got thrown into the sewers."

"That seems like a *short* story."

"You got *what*?" Roanna's voice broke in over the channel.

"I don't have my glasses, Cornelius is drained and unconscious." Sam started to choke up. "I don't know what to do. We're trapped, Roanna."

"Stay there, I'll get a group together. We'll come get you," Roanna said, obviously doing her best to sound hopeful.

"No," Sam hissed. "Do *not* come in here. You'll be dead before you get within a mile of me and Cornelius. No one else will have to die because of me. I've seen these mongrels, Roanna. They're the stuff of nightmares. Promise me you won't come in here."

"Okay, I promise," Roanna said. "What do you want me to do?"

"Just...just don't stop talking," Sam said. "Tell me a story or something, but just don't stop talking. I don't want to be alone."

Roanna started slowly, not confident with fulfilling the odd request, but soon launched into the tale of Esmerelda Wanderfeet and her boat of bubbles that took her far beyond the shores of Avalon. The story was ridiculous and was obviously for kids, but Roanna's voice was like a dose of emotional morphine to an injured soldier dying on the battlefield.

Sam focused on the story and let the horrors of his situation temporarily fade to the background. He didn't know how long he'd listened to her speak when he heard Cornelius moan. The cowboy lifted his head off Sam's lap.

"Where in tarnation are—"

"Be quiet," Sam hushed. "We're back in the sewer. Lawrence drained you and you got pummeled pretty bad. I don't have my glasses. We're stuck."

"Well, good morning to you too," Cornelius whispered back.

"I'm so sorry, for everything," Sam said. He'd wanted to say it ever since things turned south with Lawrence. He could only imagine what Cornelius was thinking then, and what he must be thinking now. "It wasn't supposed to be like this."

Cornelius permitted himself a muted chuckle. "Such is life, kid."

"And death," Sam said flatly.

"I might feel it, but I ain't dead yet. Don't know about you.

Well, you've now lived long enough to be betrayed. Welcome to manhood."

"What are we supposed to do?" Sam said, praying that Cornelius would have a plan.

"Yes, we'll help any way we can," Roanna's voice came through the communicator.

"I do not believe I can help at all, friend Sam," Willow chimed in, "so I will sit here in the trees if that is alright."

There was a pause before Sam realized that Cornelius probably still had his earpiece in his pocket. "Cornelius, put your earpiece in. I've got Roanna on the communicator—"

Sam felt Cornelius's hand cover his mouth, while his other hand slowly pressed against Sam's chest, pushing him up against the wall. Sam's heart stopped before exploding into a frenzy. Was he being too loud? It took a few more seconds before Sam heard it. A far-off growling wheeze echoed down the sewer tunnels. Sam prayed for the creature to go another way, to turn down one of the dozens of passages and leave him and Cornelius alone. But the breathing only got louder, the rhythmic slosh of water more clear.

"What's going on? Are you still there? Sam? Cornelius?"

Sam didn't dare respond. If he could've stopped his heart until this thing passed by, he would've. It grew nearer and nearer, gurgling as it breathed. Just a few more feet and it would be upon them. Sam willed the beast to just continue walking past. The breathing continued, but the sloshing of water stopped. The monster was standing right in front of them. Sam held his breath and felt his entire body start to shake.

Sam heard a splash followed by a defeating screech. Cornelius screamed in pain and Sam sensed the cowboy go down.

"Run!" Cornelius managed to yell as he thrashed around with the mongrel in the darkness.

"Sam? Cornelius? What's happening?"

Sam didn't know what to do. The noise would surely draw

others. What good would running do with a horde of monsters closing in? With no weapon, no hope, and no alternative, Sam turned toward the sound of Cornelius's screams and lunged. His hands grabbed what felt like the slimy scales of a giant fish. He felt the presence of the mongrel's aether and pushed down to void it. As soon as Sam drained the monster's aether, it replenished. Like trying to bail out a leaking boat, every time Sam exerted himself to void the aether, more was there. He held his breath and pushed harder. The frigid shock of passing aether was like diving into an ice bath, but Sam didn't let go. His fear, his worry, his pain, his anger, it drove him forward, but more aether kept pouring in. To his left and right, he heard the splashing and squealing of approaching mongrels.

Sam couldn't give up, he couldn't give in. He had made mistakes. He had been selfish. He had even been an unfair friend to Lawrence over the years. He needed to help his friends, both old and new. He needed to set this right.

Sam tilted his head and screamed as the glacial coldness overwhelmed him. He collapsed and rolled off the creature into the water. His body was numb. His brain was numb. His very soul was numb. He strained to hear signs of approaching mongrels, but heard nothing. He would've thought his hearing had completely left him, if not for the Zelda treasure chest sound effect repeatedly emanating from his earpiece. Sam had just received a whole lot of text messages.

36

FAME

It took Sam five minutes to regain enough feeling in his body to even make an attempt to retrieve his phone. He slowly moved his arm over to his pocket and withdrew his cell, turning on its flashlight. The grotesque mongrel was motionless, except for the steady rise and fall of shallow breathing. The creature looked like some horrific cross between a human-sized rat and a piranha. Scores of comatose mongrels filled the long tunnel to either side. Sam looked to Cornelius. Large bite marks oozed red from his chest and shoulder.

"Cornelius," Sam called out, rushing to his side. Sam got a closer look at the wounds. He wasn't a doctor, but they looked deep. He grabbed at his own shirt and ripped off one of the sleeves, before pressing the pathetic bandage to Cornelius's wound. Cornelius moaned in pain. "You still with me, cowboy?"

"Dumfungled. Need…aether," Cornelius mumbled.

Even if his wounds were beyond standard medicine, Cornelius was a Leech. All he needed was enough aether and he could heal himself.

"Sam, Cornelius. Is that you?" Roanna asked over the communicator, her voice a mix of relief and concern.

"Yes, Roanna, it's me," Sam responded.

"What happened? Are you alright? I kept calling out but you didn't respond."

"I'm fine. Cornelius isn't. Had a little run-in with a mongrel. He needs aether now or I don't know how long he's going to last."

"Sam…I…" Roanna hesitated, obviously unsure of what to do. Sam had just had her promise to stay out of the sewer. Now he was requesting help.

"The mongrels are drained," Sam said.

"Which mongrels? The one that attacked Cornelius?"

Sam flashed his light up and down the tunnel. "I'm pretty sure all of them. It felt like I voided the whole blasted world of its aether. My head's still ringing. I swear the drain was going to kill me, but I held on."

"You held on to *one*? But how did you drain them all? I don't understand."

"They must be like a hive or something. I think they share aether somehow. I must've pulled the whole horde's aether through that one stupid mongrel. I don't know how it works, but I do know that Cornelius needs help and I can see about a hundred of these monsters passed out on the ground nearby."

Sam heard Roanna shout to a few people, re-explaining Sam's situation. After a bit of back and forth, she spoke again to Sam. "Hang tight, Sam. We're coming in after you."

Sam put his phone down with the light shining upward and went back to putting pressure on Cornelius's wounds. No matter how hard he pressed or what he tried, he couldn't stop the blood from seeping between his fingers.

After a few minutes, Cornelius mumbled something and Sam had to lean in close to hear.

"What's that, cowboy?"

"Is that you?" Cornelius muttered.

"Yeah, Cornelius, it's me. Help is on the way."

"I've missed you, son," the cowboy said weakly as his eyelids drooped shut. "How did you grow up so fast? Time never seems to stop...never when you need it to."

"Stay with me, man. Don't go to sleep. No time for sleep." Tears streamed from Sam's eyes as he shook Cornelius as hard as he dared. "Roanna, I need help. I'm losing him."

"We're in the tunnels now, Sam. We have a dozen parties looking. Hang on."

Each minute that passed felt like an eternity. Sam could feel Cornelius's blood coming out slower now and didn't know if that was a good sign or a bad sign.

"Cornelius, how we doing there, partner?" Sam jostled the cowboy's shoulder.

Cornelius didn't reply.

"Cornelius? Say something, man. Cornelius, please wake up. *Please.* You have to come back. You have to come back to find your peace, remember?" Sam choked on a sob as he felt himself start to break. "Why does this keep happening to me? I can't do this. I can't lose someone again. Please no."

Sam buried his face in Cornelius's blood-soaked chest and wept. He would rather wade through a hundred mongrel sewers than go down this path again. He could feel his old emotional scars tear open as he listened to the cowboy's raspy breathing begin to slow. Just as Sam accepted that his friend would die, a faint light appeared to his left, followed by echoed talking. Sam turned to see the light grow brighter, emanating from a nearby tunnel.

"Over here," Sam screamed as he waved his flashlight. "We're over here. Hurry."

The light grew brighter before a group of four Mavericks appeared in the tunnel and rushed to Sam's side.

"He's not responding. You got to do something."

"Open his mouth," one of them said, removing a small vial of liquid from her pocket. Sam did as he was told and propped open the cowboy's mouth. The woman poured in half of the small vial, waited, and then poured in the rest. For a moment, nothing happened, then Cornelius coughed several times before taking a gasping breath. The woman pulled out another vial and handed it to Cornelius, who drank the contents on his own this time. Within minutes of being at death's door, the cowboy was on his feet and casually chatting with the team of Mavericks. The transformation was mind-boggling.

"Hey, as much as I'd like to sit in the sewer having idle chit chat," Sam butted in, "I'd really like to get out of here now, if you wouldn't mind."

"Yes, of course," one of the men said. "Follow me."

As the group made its way back to the Mavericks' lair, Sam lost count of the foul mongrels strewn limply on the sewer floor. They must have all been coming for him. He was *that* close to an inescapable death. Before he left the tunnel, he told his rescuers of where he and Cornelius had stashed their gear. They would need a ladder and someone with enough aether to lift off the sewer cover, but it would only be a short distance to the barrel after that. Whether LaRue would be close by was anyone's guess. Sam wondered if the old maid had made it out okay, and if she was still unsuspected as a spy. If LaRue was clever enough to survive the last fifty years as a Maverick, however, then Sam figured she knew her way out of a pinch.

What had taken hours to make his way into the sewer only took minutes to go back out. Even though the mongrels were completely drained, the group still did their best to not disturb the monsters. Completely avoiding contact was impossible, though, as they actually had to climb over a number of huge, hippo-sized creatures. Sam almost cried when he finally saw the entrance to the Maverick caverns.

He exited the sewers into the arms of half a dozen people who checked him for any wounds before whisking him away for a warm bath, a change of clothes, a hot meal, and...another warm bath. As soon as Sam was feeling somewhat human again, he was immediately summoned to the main meeting room. It all seemed to be happening so fast. Didn't he deserve some time off or something after narrowly escaping a horde of sewer mongrels? Apparently Addi didn't want to wait very long for Sam to fulfill his end of the bargain.

Before entering the room, his phone buzzed. His texts! He'd forgotten all about them in the rush to get out of the sewers. Sam took out his phone and saw he had over seven hundred unread messages.

"Whoa, aren't I Mr. Popular." He opened his texts and noticed the vast majority were from numbers he didn't recognize. His number had gotten out, apparently.

Hey Quake Boy, give me a shout!

I saw your picture on the news. I think U R cute. My name is Macie McGuire. Send me a text back.

Dude, I have a bet with my friends. If you reply I'll get like 50 bucks. Hit me up.

This is Jonathan Boldt with Newsline National. Please text, call, or video-chat us back. We would like to do a story on the Quake Boy of Bozeman.

I don't know how you're doing this, but I'm gonna find out. You're a troll and you know it! I'll expose you for the fraud you really are! Your days are #'d Quake Boy!!

"Huh," Sam said, flipping through the messages. He filtered the messages for just his contacts.

Honey! Are you safe? Did you find Lawrence? Please be safe. You text me as soon as you find Lawrence. His parents are worried sick.

Dude, a sewer full of monsters?! How come I don't ever get to do anything cool like that? You better not lose my stuff again!! Jk. Seriously though, find Lawrence. I'm sure in a place like that he'll be stoked to see a familiar face.

Another message came through from an unknown sender and Sam changed the settings to file away everything that wasn't from one of his contacts. He checked his reception and noticed he still had three bars of signal. He clicked on Rinni's name and pressed the video button. Rinni's face appeared after two rings.

"Dude!" Rinni shouted, his pearl-white grin stretching from ear to ear. "You're alive. Where's Lawrence? Do you have Lawrence?"

Sam pressed his lips together and shook his head. He explained to Rinni everything that had happened, from when he first went into the sewer, to his meeting with LaRue, to the crazy battle in Lawrence's den, to being thrown back in the sewer.

"No way, man," Rinni said at the end. "Where do I even start?"

"I don't know. Everything's wrong. Nothing is going as planned. I don't know what to do. I should've been a better friend to Lawrence."

"I don't know," Rinni said, "going on a suicide mission through mongrel-infested sewers to rescue him seems like being a pretty good friend to me."

Sam sighed. "Yeah, but it's the day to day stuff, you know? What percentage of the jokes we told ended up on Lawrence?"

Rinni screwed up his face in thought, finally seeing where Sam was going. "Maybe nine out of ten. But how many times did he bring it upon *himself?* Seventy-five percent of the time? That means like ninety percent of twenty-five percent is our fault and uncalled for. So I'll admit that we went twenty-two-and-a-half percent overboard."

Sam gave Rinni a look. "Well, it seems that was enough for him to turn against me and almost get me killed."

"So now what?"

Sam looked at the door. He knew why he was summoned to the main meeting room. He'd promised Addi he would join her fight. "Now I have to go talk to the Mavericks about how they want to use me to fight the Collector. I'll keep you posted. Oh, one other thing I forgot to mention from a while back. When I met with Borinder, I saw what I thought looked like an ancient Egyptian scroll. Between that, Cornelius, talk of Musketeers, and a few other things, I'm thinking there's been more crossover between Earth and Avalon than we thought."

"Duh," Rinni said. "I don't think the name 'Avalon' coming from the Arthurian legend is a coincidence. Not to mention that everyone there speaks English and not some indecipherable Avalonish. I'm still looking for the connection, but so is half the Internet, so I'm sure something will turn up soon."

"Sweet. Keep me posted. Any dots you can start connecting might help me actually get out of here."

"Hey, you didn't happen to get a picture of that Egyptian stuff, by chance?"

"I wasn't on some school field trip, Rinni. Sorry if I didn't take more selfies to document the time I almost had a crazy guy amputate my fing—wait a sec." Sam stopped to think. "I had the drone explore his whole collection when I was showing off my techno-magical skills. I should have his whole collection on video."

"Techno-magical skills?" Rinni raised an eyebrow.

"Dude, don't judge me. I do what I have to do to survive this place."

"Alright, alright. Send me the file at least. Should be a gold mine of clues if this guy is half the collector of rare objects you say he is."

"Will do, but after I go to this meeting. I gotta run."

"Wait," Rinni called out. "Take me in there. Don't hang up if you don't have to. I want to see this."

Sam pursed his lips. To Rinni this was all a game. Part of

that bugged Sam, but another part of him wanted to lighten the mood. "Fine."

"Yes! You won't regret it."

"Uh-huh," Sam said, shaking his head. "Hold tight. I'm pocketing you for now, but will bring you out in a bit. Let's go find out how we're going to take down the Collector."

37

AN ARMY AND A GENERAL

Sam put his phone away and pushed open the door. Addi, Roanna, Cornelius, and a number of advisors sat around a large table, including the stringy-haired Vendrin and the mammoth Jerg.

"Sam!" Roanna jumped from her seat and ran to Sam, crushing him with a hug. "I'm so sorry about your friend."

After smelling sewer water for most of the past day, the scent of Roanna's hair was like the first breath of air after nearly drowning.

"Good to see you, Roanna. Thanks for sending help."

Roanna took a step back and regained her decorum, gesturing to an empty seat at the table. "Of course. Please, we have much to discuss."

Sam took a seat next to Cornelius, who leaned over and patted him on the shoulder.

"How many baths this time?" Cornelius whispered.

"Two," Sam whispered back.

Cornelius nodded his head and flashed three fingers.

"Welcome, Sam," Addi said. "I'm sorry to hear about your

friend, but am very impressed with your resourcefulness. It shows great promise. A promise that we hope will prove an advantage in the coming days."

"What do you need me to do?" Sam asked, trying his best to sound brave.

"We're not sure yet," Addi replied, leaning forward. "We have less than two days before the Collector starts killing again. The fact that he has a young Void—your friend—in his employ also adds an additional piece to the game board that we did not anticipate. If we take no action and don't deliver up the aether ingots, then the citizens of Trellston will—no doubt—partially blame us for the Collector's actions. Anyone with information on the Mavericks could turn on us in order to end the Collector's killing. If we give in and give back the aether, then we lose everything we stand for and will be punished for our defiance regardless."

"Doesn't sound like we have a lot of options," Sam said.

"Oh, there are plenty of options, Sam," Addi countered, "just not many good ones."

"Are you not preparing to actually fight the Collector and his men?" Sam asked. "I thought you wanted to fight and take back the city, force him out."

Addi glanced around at her advisors before continuing. "The Collector is powerful enough by himself, but don't forget the number of Enhanced he had under his command. In an urban war, he'll use those Enhanced soldiers with devastating effect. This is not the first city he's quelled, mind you. We'd need an army to defeat the Collector and we'd need a mastermind to command that army. The Mavericks have many resources, Sam, but here in Trellston an army and a general are not numbered among them. Our strengths lie elsewhere. We would be crushed in an open war with the Collector."

"Okay," Sam said, straining for a good idea. "Forgive me for asking—this *is* my first actual war-planning session after all—but what are we working towards here? What's our endgame?"

"The endgame," Roanna said, "is to turn back the Collector. Defeat him. Drive him out."

"So, forgetting about the army of Enhanced for a second, how do you defeat or drive back an Inferno-level evil mastermind?" Sam asked. "Do the Mavericks even have enough power to take on the Collector by *himself?*"

Addi looked around at the table. "It's hard to say, really. We don't know how much aether he has exactly. You can only detect those kinds of things with the right amount of aether at close proximity and we haven't been able to pull that off. Even if we don't have enough combined aether to overpower him, we might be able to exhaust him to a point where he might retreat. That may be a viable strategy, but again, we could run out of aether before he does."

"Unless," Sam said, raising a finger, "you can drain his aether without costing you any of yours. If a Void does it, for instance."

"That is our hope, yes," Addi said. There was no remorse on her face for asking this of Sam. In her mind, she was at war; risky moves were played. She'd helped Sam and now it was his turn to step up to the plate.

"So how do we do it?" Sam asked. "How do we get me close enough to drain him without getting me killed in the process? If what you say about his power is true, we won't be able to rush him. What we need is a trap." Sam looked down at the table and tapped a finger on his temple. He didn't know warfare, but his involvement in this war had nothing to do with swinging a sword. It was pulling a prank, a prank to drain the Collector's aether. *This* he could do.

"We have yet to devise any sort of trap that would likely succeed," Vendrin said, smoothing over his stringy hair and shuffling through his notes.

"You can turn anything into a trap with the right bait," Sam said, not looking up from the table.

"And I suppose *you* have this bait?" Vendrin rolled his eyes.

"As a matter of fact," Sam said, looking up, "I do."

"Well, let's hear it," Vendrin replied, his annoyance growing. "This isn't the time to leave us all in suspense."

"When I came here, Addi told me that there is one thing that represents control of the city, one thing that showed you were in charge."

"The echo-stone," Addi said. "You're suggesting we somehow get control of the echo-stone?"

"I'm not suggesting it. I've already done it." Sam had never received word from LaRue that she had successfully placed his remote speaker on the echo-stone like he'd asked, but last night he went to the tapestry room and sent a low-volume sound effect to the speaker from his phone. The old maid was true to her word. Telling LaRue to put the small speaker on the echo-stone was nothing more than playing a hunch, but now a plan was coming together.

"How is this possible?" Roanna asked.

"A bit of techno-magic is all. I took someone's advice to put another card up my sleeve." Sam nodded to Cornelius. "If we can get me near the echo-stone and then lure him back, I might have a chance to grab him."

"Allllright," Addi drew out the word, piecing together a plan of her own. "But how do we draw him out?"

"What other assets do we have?" Sam asked.

"We have a few," Addi said, rising from her seat and pacing the room. "We still have the aether. The idea was to split it up and give it back to the people of Trellston, but we recently discussed the option of using it to create a fighting force. We could pool it into a few individuals or spread it among the Mavericks. Aside from the aether, we also have you. And if we're lucky, we still might have the element of surprise. We're hoping the Collector still doesn't know you're here."

Sam laughed. "What do you mean? Not sure if Cornelius filled you in on our little adventure there, but we didn't exactly go unnoticed."

"Who other than Lawrence knows that you're a Void?" Addi asked.

Sam thought a moment. Lawrence never said anything to the soldiers about Sam being a Void, and Sam only drained the first guard in the hallway. What LaRue did with the man, Sam couldn't begin to guess. "Okay, I see your point, but how do you use me?"

"We do have one more advantage," Roanna said, "thanks to you and Cornelius."

"What's that?" Sam asked.

"We can infiltrate the castle from where they least expect it and catch them completely off guard. The Collector doesn't have the sewers well-guarded because they think they're *already* guarded by a horde of sewer mongrels," Roanna replied.

"We're sending a crew in shortly to clear out the beasts, which will allow us to move freely in the sewers," Addi said. "We also have one of the smaller creatures in our possession in the event the monsters somehow absorb enough naturally occurring aether to wake back up. If what you say is true and their aether is connected, then draining the one in captivity will drain them all."

Sam ran through Addi's last sentence multiple times in his head. If he drained one, he drained them all. Their aether was connected. "Wait!" Sam yelled, startling half the people at the table.

"What is it?" Addi asked.

"Don't get rid of the mongrels," Sam said, the wheels of his mind spinning into motion.

"What do you mean?" Addi responded.

"You said you needed two things to take on the Collector: an army and a general."

Cornelius laughed, connecting the dots where Sam was going. "Now there's an idea."

"What he going on about?" Vendrin asked, obviously upset to be out of the loop.

"Use your aether ingots and infuse the mongrels," Sam said. The room burst into a clamor before Addi silenced them. "They're plentiful, they're disposable, they'll make you wet your pants, and the Collector has no clue they'll be on our side. They're the perfect army."

"There are hundreds of them, maybe thousands," Vendrin said. "If they actually share aether then we can't divide their numbers and control them separately. They'll have to be infused and controlled by a single person. Who could do such a thing?"

"An aether prodigy." Sam smiled and turned to Roanna.

Roanna's green eyes went big, half from surprise and half from the hunger to give it a shot. Sam knew that she wanted nothing more in her entire life than to have the chance to poke the emperor straight in the eye. Commanding a surprise army of sewer mongrels against an unsuspecting Collector would do more than poke.

"Impossible," Vendrin said, throwing up his hands. "This is absurd."

"Let's give her a chance," Addi mused, clearly intrigued by the idea. "We'll start her out slow with the aether and see how many mongrels she can handle. With the Collector's strict curfew in place, there should be no innocent citizens on the streets either. This might actually work. What do you say, Roanna?"

"However I can help," Roanna said, trying to contain her excitement. "But even if I can control them, I'm no general. It will be chaos."

"Oh, Roanna's not the general. She's just the queen of the army," Sam said with a smirk.

"Then who's the general?" Addi asked, looking around the room.

Sam flashed a wide smile. "That, ladies and gentlemen, will also be provided via techno-magic, where a live aerial view of the city will be streamed from my drones to one of the greatest battle strategists of our time." Sam reached into his pocket and took out his phone, propping it up on the table. "May I introduce the current number-four ranked commander in the world in the *Warcraft of Empires*, Mr. Rinnivas Manikhantan."

38

FINAL PREPARATIONS

Sam was confident his plan was sound, but he was still shocked when Addi eventually backed his play. In the land of the blind, the man with one eye was king. And in the land of no plans, Sam's cobbled together mega-prank reigned supreme. On Addi's order, the Mavericks flew into a flurry of preparations. Roanna was immediately whisked off to begin the process of absorbing the aether cache and infusing the power into the mongrels. Sam's backpack and clothes—and Cornelius's hat and poncho—were retrieved and returned to their rightful owners. After a fitful sleep, Sam called Rinni back and went over every detail and contingency possible.

"Go over all the available gear one more time," Rinni said, paper and pen in hand. For a guy who loved tech as much as Rinni, Sam always found it weird that his best friend liked to go old school and plan out pranks by hand.

Sam picked up his phone and panned over the gear, which was laid out neatly on a table. "We want to use any of it?"

"You know, I don't think so. I think we have it right." Rinni nodded. "We won't need it all. Just the essentials. I don't want to get distracted with stuff that doesn't matter. Drones in the sky and action cams and earpieces on my heroes."

"Your *heroes*?"

"Uh, yeah. My strongest and most influential pieces on the field. We have Cornelius, the Berserker: max hit points, healing ability, enhanced speed, strength, and experience. I have Roanna, Queen of the Sewer Mongrels: she's…uh…well, Queen of the Sewer Mongrels. We've got Addi, a mid-level enchantress with advanced leadership skills. Then there's you: Sam, the Magic Assassin. We're pitted against a powerful Mage Knight who rides atop a dragon-bat Screecher, and commands an army of elemental cyborgs and crossbreeds. That sum it up?"

"Not bad," Sam mumbled. "But…the *Magic Assassin*?"

"What's wrong with 'Magic Assassin'?"

"Nothing, actually," Sam admitted. "It's actually pretty awesome. Way better than 'Quake Boy.' You up for this, man?"

"Who, me?" Rinni asked, acting insulted that Sam even asked the question. "I was born for this, dude. I know this might seem weird, but in a way, nothing feels more natural than planning this out with you. Just like planning an elaborate prank, you know?"

"Yeah, except this one involves commanding an army of sewer mutants against a mass-murdering tyrant with my life hanging in the balance."

"Minor nuances."

"Minor *nuances*?" Sam repeated, eyes wide. "You do realize that this isn't a game for me, right?"

"Dude, from what you tell me, you were almost killed like four or five times in the last month. You should be getting used to it by now."

"Huh," Sam said, thinking over Rinni's claim. There was Reynold and Gurn, the tavern brawl at the Cup of Rosemary, when they first encountered Milla, Borinder Besselink, two journeys through mongrel-infested sewers, and the fight in Lawrence's lair. "I actually count seven."

"See?" Rinni insisted. "You're an expert at this. Just keep doing what you've been doing. Seven for seven ain't luck, man. You've either got mad survival skills or some seriously territorial guardian angels."

"Let's hope they keep up the good work," Sam said, checking the time. "Hey, it's T-minus thirty. I'm going to go check on Roanna right quick. The signal was fading a bit, but since they dumped the aether into Roanna and then she dumped it into the mongrels, I've got four bars. I don't think we'll see any connection issues. See you in a bit."

Rinni nodded and Sam pocketed his phone. As soon as he was done talking to Rinni, the nervousness began to settle in. Getting thrown into danger was one thing. You had to react, think on your feet, but there wasn't the horrible, drawn-out anticipation of waiting for the thing.

Their timeline was crunched if they wanted to hit the Collector before he started executing innocent people. The Mavericks were well-equipped and well-connected, but even they had their limits. They had a decent plan, but they were rushed.

Doing his best to calm his nerves, Sam asked around for Roanna, who'd gone up on the surface to make some final preparations. Sam followed the main passage up and out of the caverns, ending in one of the many secret access-ways hidden throughout the city. This particular entrance came up in the basement of a large three-story home. After a brief search, Sam eventually found Roanna on the top floor overlooking the city's lights from the main bedroom balcony.

"Hey there," Sam called out. Roanna turned and Sam stopped in his tracks. Her hair was freshly done in a complex series of tight side braids. She had black makeup around her eyes that bordered more on war paint than anything else. Over her normal clothes she wore a bodice of crisscrossing dark leathers, accented with brilliant blue and green stones. More than all of this, there was something different about *her*. There was a radiance, an air of power, that didn't exist before. Whether an effect of her elevated aether or his ever-growing infatuation, Sam didn't know. Even though he was still trying to sort through all of his feelings about her, Sam was sure of one thing: he had never seen anyone look more epic than Roanna did at this moment.

"You going to be alright there, Sam?" she asked, raising her eyebrows.

"Uh...yeah." Sam swallowed awkwardly. "Just wanted to bring you a camera. It'll let Rinni see what you see. You could probably just clip it into your hair, actually." Sam drew closer and took his time clipping the camera to one of her side braids. "You, uh...look awesome, by the way."

Roanna favored him with a small smile. "The vest is a bit uncomfortable, but they tell me it's supposed to help me focus my aether. Something to do with the special stones. In my opinion, I think they just made that up to make me feel better."

Sam gave a short laugh. "Whatever works, I guess. How you holding up, by the way? You okay?"

"In many ways, never better." Roanna looked down at her hands as if she could see her newfound power pooled in her palms. "These creatures are different than anything I've controlled before, although I honestly haven't had all that much experience. They remind me a bit of a dollywag."

"Of a what?"

"A dollywag. It's a swarm insect. I used to catch them as a kid and placidate them for fun. The whole group of mongrels runs on one central thought, but each mongrel maintains a degree of limited independence by using neighboring mongrels as boundaries. It's hard to put into words."

"Sounds...complicated, but I'm not the prodigy in the room. I hear they got Cornelius all juiced up on aether too."

"Yes," Roanna said with a slight smile. "As long as I've

known him, I've wanted Cornelius to show all of Avalon what he is capable of. As a Leech, there is a limit to how much aether he can consume at once, but if he has an ample supply to heal his wounds and maintain his strength, the cowboy will be an army unto himself."

"Cornelius smash!" Sam said, doing his best Hulk impression.

"What?"

"Oh, nothing." Sam felt his phone alarm buzz. He took a deep breath. "Well, you ready?"

Roanna looked out over the night sky. The city's lights were almost as impressive as the stars above. "In a way, this is what I've wanted my entire life: the power and a chance to fight back. It's finally here. It feels…surreal. Whatever happens, I want to thank you, Sam. You can be reckless and stupid, but you're also brave and clever, and you've given me this opportunity."

"I suppose I'll take that as a compliment. I look forward to seeing what you can do, oh Queen of the Sewer Mongrels."

"I suppose I'll take *that* as a compliment. Stay safe, Sam," Roanna said as she reached out and put her hand on his arm, her touch awakening a swarm of butterflies in his stomach.

"Don't know if I can stay safe, but I'll do my best to stay alive."

Roanna nodded and Sam let her hand slide off his arm as he left the room.

"Ooh la la," Sam heard Rinni's voice over his earpiece. "Someone's in *love*."

"Oh, shut up," Sam said, kicking himself for not turning off his earpiece. He was just glad he didn't have Cornelius's activated, or he would never hear the end of it. "What would you know about it?"

"Don't know if I can stay safe," Rinni mocked in his best tough guy voice, "but I'll do my best to stay alive."

"You keep this up and I'll put a voice modifier on you that makes you sound like a fairy princess."

Final Preparations

Sam checked the time and made his way back down to the Maverick caves before reaching the main command room. Cornelius, Addi, and a dozen or so well-armed advisors stood around the meeting table, busily discussing and pointing at maps and diagrams of the town and castle.

"Not a moment too soon," Addi said, noticing Sam and waving him over to the table. "Are your techno-magic devices ready?"

Sam pulled his HUD specs out of his pocket and put them on. He took out his phone and activated all the earpieces before opening up the voice control settings on Rinni's channel. As satisfying as it would be to select something that made Rinni sound like an idiot, Sam needed his friend to seem like an unrivaled general, not a moron. The time for pranks had ended. Sam scrolled down the list of voice mods and selected one he thought Rinni would appreciate: Admiral Nuke Razeum, Rinni's favorite character from *Warcraft of Empires*. "Just say the word and I can send my drones airborne to get an aerial view of the city. Master Commander Rinni, are you ready?"

"I am as ready for war as a heart is to beat blood," Rinni's voice was seamlessly morphed into the deep, no-nonsense voice of Admiral Razeum. "There is no need to be ready for more when I never stopped in the first place."

"I'll take that as a yes." It took Sam every ounce of self-control to not roll his eyes. He knew Rinni wouldn't be able resist playing up the moment. The fate of the world could be hanging in the balance and Rinni still wouldn't pass up an opportunity to put on a show. "Addi, Roanna, Cornelius, speak back if you can all hear me over your earpieces."

They all replied with a "yes," and Sam saw their voice signatures scribble across the corner of his HUD. Sam tapped his phone twice, activating the action cameras and sending the drones into flight. Small video-feed windows from Roanna, Addi, and Cornelius popped up in the other corner of Sam's HUD. "You getting all of this, Commander Rinni?"

"Your techno-magical uplinks have provided me with the vision I will need to consume the enemy's forces as the mighty gold-scaled dragon of the Orient devours a farmer's sheep."

"Thank you for the analogy, Rinni," Sam replied flatly.

Cornelius made his way over to Sam. The cowboy's standard hat was complemented by an entire set of armor made from what looked like knobby crocodile skin.

"It's bona fide draggator hide," Cornelius said, holding out his arms to display his new armor. "I feel like a dadgum reptile jester, but this stuff will stop an arrow dead in its tracks. Going to be a lot of close-quarters fisticuffs in the next while. You're one brave hombre, Sam, but when things go south, and if we're not able to get you a clean grab at the Collector, I'm pulling you out of the fray."

"*When* things go south?" Sam repeated. "Don't you mean, *if* things go south?"

Cornelius laughed and patted Sam on the back. "Kid, I've never seen a plan *not* go south."

The image of a small ringing bell popped up on Sam's HUD. "That's the alarm," Sam said to the group, motioning for them to move to the tapestry-covered room with the echo-stone funnel.

Not fifteen seconds after everyone crammed in the room, a voice came over the metal funnel. "Attention, citizens of Trellston. Attention, citizens of Trellston. The emperor's Tax Collector has an important message to relay."

39
LIVE BAIT

"Citizens of Trellston." The Collector's ominous voice sounded from the echo-stone. "The emperor is disappointed that this city, always a valued and trusted part of the Avalon Empire, still refuses to pay its fair share. I take no pleasure in doing this. But the time has come to—"

"Now," Rinni's altered voice came over the earpieces.

A chorus of savage shrieks and growls filled the night air, cutting off the Collector's speech. Sam checked the drones' infrared feeds and saw a swarm of glowing mongrel dots flood onto the street. The few guards stationed on the street were quickly run down and consumed by the oncoming tide of mongrels. After another thirty seconds of virtually unimpeded progress, four sizable groups of dots—the Collector's Enhanced—came pouring out of buildings near the castle. The Collector's voice came over the echo-stone issuing counter-commands to soldiers all over the city.

"Here they come," Sam said over the communicator.

"Divert fifty mongrels to the alleyway coming up on the left." Rinni began issuing commands to Roanna. "Seventy-five break off from the rear and loop around the outermost road of the city until they reach the north side of the castle. Split the remaining group in half when your current road comes to a fork. Have the left group stop and the right group run as fast as they can until they come to a large courtyard."

Sam saw the mass of glowing dots break away from the main group in what seemed like random maneuvers, except Sam knew that every move Rinni made was part of some grander strategy. The question of whether Roanna would be able to control the beasts with sufficient accuracy and finesse seemed to be answered. Sam kept one eye on the chaos of swarming dots while he made his way back through the sewer, flanked in the front and back by two dozen armed Mavericks.

"Cornelius," Rinni said, not a hint of excitement or nervousness in his voice. He was in the zone. "There looks to be a group of about a dozen men heading into the castle from the east courtyard. I need these out of the way."

"On it," Cornelius said, the background from his video feed rushed by as the cowboy launched into an aether-aided sprint.

"And, Cornelius?" Rinni added.

"Yeah?" Cornelius breathed hard as he ran.

"Try to draw as much attention as possible."

"Yee haw!" Cornelius yelled as he knocked a heavy wooden door clean off its hinges with a stiff kick. The flying door carved through a group of soldiers who stood stunned at the cowboy's sudden entrance into the large foyer. Cornelius grabbed the nearest soldier by the leg and swung him around in circles like a doll before flinging him through a large decorative window with a crash. He bellowed like a madman as he took another soldier and tossed him twenty feet overhead straight into a crystal chandelier, which detached from the ceiling and exploded on the ground in thousands of glittering shards.

Cornelius was a blur, moving from soldier to soldier landing hard blows to the head and stomach with his studded brass knuckles. It was over before it even began. Cornelius panned around, revealing a dozen limp bodies littering the room.

"That," Rinni said, "is not a bad start. That got their attention. More soldiers closing in."

"Should we engage?" Addi's voice came over the line.

"Do *not* engage," Rinni commanded. "We need to set the hook deeper. We've got to get them fighting a two-front war. I need their forces fully divided before you come in from behind. I can hear the Collector's orders as he issues them from the echo-stone, so we'll stay one step ahead. Cornelius, keep going east. I'm having the mongrels congregate on the west side. I need you to draw as much of the enemy force to you as possible before I send in the backup and try to sneak Sam in. Don't push it too far. I still need you in fighting shape, but keep them flowing to you as long as you can."

"Will do," Cornelius said. Sam saw the cowboy grab a vial from inside his vest, unstop it, and down the contents.

Sam's escorts came to a halt underneath a sewer grate and quickly set up a ladder. The plan was to wait until Rinni gave the order to move. Sam checked his various video feeds. The mongrel army continued its frenzied clash with the Collector's soldiers west of the castle. The Collector issued more orders, but Rinni quickly countered, giving several audibles to Roanna to break off teams of mongrels to different locations around the city. How Rinni could divine any sort of order or strategy from the chaos was beyond Sam.

"Looks like the Collector and his Screecher haven't budged from the echo-stone," Sam said over the line. The comment was beyond obvious, but he felt helpless just sitting there while the rest of the group was already well into the battle.

"He needs to feel like he's losing control before he'll come down off his perch," Rinni replied. "I'm not sure that will happen until Addi and company move in."

Sam watched his drone feeds and saw a wave of soldiers chase after Cornelius as the cowboy dashed into a large open courtyard full of dozens of empty wagons and carriages. Cornelius grabbed a wagon wheel and tore it from its axle just as the first enemy group rounded the corner. The incoming soldiers sent a barrage of aether-driven spiked balls zipping through the air. Cornelius spun, letting the spikes thud harmlessly into the back of his draggator armor. The cowboy turned back around and hurled the wheel like a giant discus, slicing a path through the center of his attackers. Instead of pressing the advantage, Cornelius used his speed to evade the soldiers, quickly disappearing into the maze of parked wagons and carriages. Instantly, Cornelius changed from berserker to assassin, moving stealthily to pick off his enemies, one by one.

As the minutes wore on, more and more soldiers poured into the courtyard. "We're getting close here, Mr. Rinni," Cornelius whispered over his earpiece.

"Addi, arise from your place of hiding and press our enemies with the unyielding hand of exacting justice," Rinni commanded.

Sam watched as Addi's forces split into two and rushed to the backsides of the Collector's two forces already engaged with the mongrels and Cornelius. As designed, Addi's forces caught their foes completely unawares. Rinni was a genius. Almost every single one of the Collector's Enhanced was sandwiched between either the mongrels and the Mavericks, or Cornelius and the Mavericks. For the first time in the fight, Sam couldn't help but be optimistic about their chances.

Sam scanned his various video feeds. He watched the Collector swing onto the back of the Screecher and take to the air. "Brace yourselves. Looks like the Collector is on the move."

"Now, Sam," Rinni urged. "Make haste."

Sam's escorts used aether to lift off the heavy sewer grate before scrambling up the ladder with Sam in tow. They moved quickly through the castle, which seemed all but abandoned except for the muted yelling of distant battle echoing through the halls. Several times, a runner came back from scouting ahead and told the group to switch directions or momentarily stay put. Sam didn't know if his heart pounded more from running or the anticipation of being discovered. It was a familiar feeling, a rush that Sam had spent his entire youth manufacturing pranks to experience. The warring anxiety and exhilaration mixed together in an intoxicating wave of adrenaline that carried him forward.

After a few minutes, Sam's escorts stopped.

"We're here, sir." One of the escorts gestured to a large wooden door.

Sam looked around at his group then back to the door. He swallowed hard and slowly pushed the door open. The hinges gave a slow creak as Sam peeked out onto the sweeping balcony beyond. The balcony was empty, except for a few stone benches off to the sides and an oversized wooden podium at the far end, near the edge. Atop the podium, like some kind of ancient microphone, sat the echo-stone.

Sam scanned the area. He needed a place to hide for his plan to work, but the balcony offered little by way of cover.

"I'm losing so many," Roanna cut in, strain evident on her voice. "I can feel their connections drop off."

Sam watched his video feeds as the Collector and his dragon-like Screecher wreaked havoc on Roanna's mongrel army. Instead of fighting the mongrels hand-to-hand, the Collector stayed airborne, shredding the city's buildings with blasts of aether and raining the debris upon his enemies.

"Furthermost east group, fall back and regroup with the main force to the south. Northernmost group of thirty, loop back around...no, dang it. Scratch that. Stay put." Rinni scrambled to counteract the Collector's chaotic rampage. "Sam, I'm not sure how long we can hold out here."

Sam glanced desperately around the balcony for somewhere to take cover, for anywhere the Collector wouldn't notice him. "I need more time, man. There's nowhere to hide up here. It's not like I'm Willow and can just disappear into thin air."

"Friend Sam," Willow's voice came over the communicator. "Did you call my name?"

"Willow?" Sam hated to admit it, but he had completely forgotten about her. "No, I wasn't calling you. I don't really have time to talk right now."

"Oh," Willow said, sounding disappointed. "So you do not want my army of beasts that I have gathered over the last few days? I see. I will tell them to go back into the forest."

"Wait, what?" Sam and Rinni both said in unison.

"I knew you would need help, friend Sam, so I was busy gathering some friends. We are at the forest edge by the west bridge, but I will leave now."

"Willow," Sam squawked. "Why didn't you say anything before?"

"You were always so upset when I startled you. I did not want to startle you again until you called my name. I have waited here patiently for the last two days."

Sam slapped his face with his palm. "Willow, what *army* do you have exactly?"

"Oh, friend Sam, I have gathered all sorts of my friends. I have found dog-bears, wild cats, hawk-rats, vipers, a family of seven weasels, five marmots, a dozen very large squirrels, and two dugongs that are out in the harbor."

"You have two *dugongs*?" Sam asked. "Like the big manatee-walrus things?"

"Yes. I do not know if they will be of much help with the fighting. Dugongs are mild-mannered and these are extra nice dugongs. They actually just came to see rugged Cornelius."

"The two dugongs came to see Cornelius?" Sam repeated slowly.

"Hate to interrupt here," Roanna said, "but if there are reinforcements, I need them *now*."

"I forgive you for interrupting, pretty Roanna," Willow said. "I will still come to your aid if you need it. Friend Sam?"

"Yes, yes, please. As soon as you can get here. Where do you need her, Rinni?"

Rinni gave the commands and Sam watched his drone feed

as Milla burst from the tree line with Willow on her back. The gorilla-horse ran toward the gate protecting the western bridge and let out a manic roar that Sam could hear from halfway across the city. Instead of slamming against the heavy doors, Milla leapt into the air and grabbed the top of the stone wall. In a blink, she was on the other side, ripping soldiers from their posts and hurling them off the bridge into the lake below. Willow scrambled off her mount and experimented with the levers controlling the doors, until they eventually swung wide open. Milla roared again and out of the forest came a flood of beasts. Bear, cat, and dog-like creatures sprinted down the western bridge toward the city.

"Hang in there, Roanna," Sam tried his best to reassure her. "Help is on the way. Remember, the plan isn't to use the mongrels to defeat the Collector. They just need to buy me enough time to hide."

"Well, how much time do you need exactly?" Roanna shot back.

"More."

Sam looked around the balcony again. Even if Willow managed to buy Sam an hour, he wasn't sure he'd ever find a spot to hide. There simply wasn't any place to take cover. He probably could get his escorts to set something up, but the Collector wasn't stupid. He'd sniff out that trap from a mile away. Sam needed to find a hiding place with what was here, but how could he make something out of nothing?

Sam walked out on the balcony and approached the echo-stone. He looked around the podium. Still nothing. In frustration, he punched the side of the podium. "Dad gummit." He bit his lip in pain as he shook his fist. What did he think was going to happen? He was going to punch through it? Sam stopped. On a hunch, he took his other hand and rapped on the side of the podium with his knuckles.

"It's hollow," Sam muttered. "Hey, can one of you guys aether-lift this podium up in the air?"

Without a word, one of the escorts came over, touched the podium, and levitated it six feet in the air. As Sam suspected, the podium was hollow, like a giant overturned wooden cup.

"Perfect," Sam said. "Now put it on top of me."

"Beg your pardon, sir?" the escort said with a confused look.

"This is the only place I can hide. Drop it back down. I'm going to hide in the middle of that thing. You're going to have to pry off a panel or something so I can pop out and grab the Collector."

The escort hesitated, looking from Sam to the podium several times. Sam walked into place—trying his best to appear confident—and nodded to the escort, who reluctantly lowered the podium. The world went momentarily dark before the escort carefully pried off a small panel from the side of the podium, just big enough for Sam to squeeze through in a pinch. From Sam's side, not a trace of light could be seen when the panel was put back into place.

Sam heard the footsteps of his escorts as they left the balcony. This was it. He was on his own. The trap was set; he was the bait, and one of the most dangerous men in all of Avalon was the mark. All that was left was to ring the dinner bell.

THE COLLECTOR

Sam hunched down in the darkness and took slow, steady breaths, steeling himself for what came next. "Cowboy," Sam said, "how we hanging in?"

"Just dandy," Cornelius whispered. The cowboy lay in wait with his video feed completely still. Sam saw a flash of movement and heard two soldiers scream before Cornelius dove behind more cover. "I'm running low on aether, though, kid. If we want to make our move, it has to be soon. I need to hang on to enough…consarn it."

"What?" Sam asked. "What is it?"

Before Cornelius could respond, Sam heard the cry of the Collector's Screecher come from Cornelius's earpiece. Sam quickly redirected one of the drones to the courtyard for a better view. Sam watched in horror as the Collector hovered over the courtyard, extended his hand, and sent the wagons and carts hurling through the air as if thrown by the winds of a tornado.

Cornelius's video feed went dark, but Sam could see the cowboy's steady heartbeat signature scribble in the corner of his

HUD. Cornelius was somehow weathering the storm. After a few more seconds, the whirlwind of wreckage subsided.

The Collector turned his head from side to side, scanning the debris. "I heard rumors of a cowboy stirring up trouble in the area. I'm honored. There aren't many of you left. So which one are you? I know you're not Quigley Longshot or Earl Dustrider. I've broken those men." The Collector ran his hand over the various bone and weapon parts dangling from the saddle of his Screecher. "I've got quite the cowboy collection here, now that I think of it."

Sam saw Cornelius's pulse quicken.

"Don't listen to him, Cornelius. He's trying to draw you out," Sam urged, but heard nothing in reply.

"You couldn't be Cornelius Upriser, surely," the Collector continued. "I didn't have the pleasure of breaking that particular cowboy, but I know the man who did. Took his wife. Took his son. Took his…resolve. Robbing a man of those things will maim him far worse than simply taking his hand or his leg. I have to tip my hat to the Greenlands King. Cornelius the Broken or Cornelius the Deserter, perhaps, but surely not Cornelius Upriser."

Sam watched as Cornelius's pulse erupted. In a flash, the cowboy burst from the debris with a guttural roar. Shards of wood jutted from the back of his armor like the quills of some bizarre porcupine. Cornelius latched onto the Screecher's neck and began pounding the beast with his brass-knuckled fist and hammer. The Screecher screamed and recoiled, nearly throwing the Collector from the saddle as it beat its wings and retreated skyward. Sam tagged the drone to follow and watched as Cornelius used the saddle strap to climb underneath the beast and pummel it on the underbelly. The Screecher clawed at its chest, missing Cornelius by inches as it continued its awkward flight away from the city and over Lake Alexandra.

Sam needed to help, but what could he do? If Cornelius fell now, he would be dead. Not that the cowboy Leech couldn't survive a fall, it was that this particular cowboy Leech couldn't swim. It was time to draw the Collector back to the echo-stone.

Sam took a deep breath. "Addi, we need to get the Collector back to the echo-stone *now*. You ready?"

"Yes, I'm ready," Addi replied, the sounds of battle close behind her.

Sam tapped a few times on his phone. "You're patched into the echo-stone. Your next words will be heard across the entire city. Make them count." There was a short pause and then Addi spoke.

"Rise up!" Addi's voice sounded across all of Trellston. "To those whose anger and sense of justice has outstripped their fear, I tell you to rise up and free yourselves from the emperor's tyranny. Rise up and do not give ground quietly. The power has already shifted. We control the echo-stone. The tortured, neglected, and forgotten things of this empire have risen up together. We are here to tell the emperor that the missing aether was returned to his Collector, but not in ingots. It was wielded by the people, in the form of our choosing. We are strong and the emperor grows weak. Rise up!"

On cue, Sam switched his phone to music. Heavy metal music blasted from every echo-stone speaker on the island.

Sam turned his attention back to the Collector, who had finally righted himself in his saddle. The Inferno turned his head sharply back toward the direction of the music. Fed up with Cornelius, the Collector removed a long razored whip-chain from his hip and infused it with aether.

"Cornelius, watch out!" Sam yelled, not knowing what else to do.

Like some sinister mechanical serpent, the long-bladed chain snaked under the Screecher in search of Cornelius. With a burst of aether, it sprang to life, whipping wildly. The cowboy tried desperately to dodge the weapon, swinging on the base of the Screecher like a crazed monkey on a jungle gym. The razored chain lashed against Cornelius's armor before finding an unprotected spot on the cowboy's wrist. Sam watched helplessly as Cornelius let go and fell through the open air.

"He can't swim!" Sam yelled to no one in particular. No one else was watching. No one else saw what had happened.

"What's that?" Addi asked over the com.

"Cornelius fell from the Screecher," Sam said as the cowboy finally hit the water's surface. "He's way out in the lake. He'll never make it."

"Sam," Rinni broke in. "Stay focused, man. You've got like thirty seconds before the Collector is on top of you."

How could Sam stay focused? He'd just watched his friend plummet to his death. There were no boats within a mile and none at all under Maverick control. Cornelius couldn't swim. The cowboy was afraid of the water for that very reason. Sam's mind raced. He needed to help Cornelius, but there was nothing he could do. The distant shriek of the Screecher broke him from his thoughts.

"This is it, man," Rinni said. "Good luck, brother. Just stay away from his dragon-bat."

The Screecher. A horrific chill washed over Sam. "We didn't account for the Screecher," Sam breathed.

"What?" Rinni replied.

"Dude, we didn't account for the Screecher in our plan," Sam whispered, his anxiety rising to a fever pitch. "I grab the Collector, but what are we going to do about his Screecher? We've got my escorts to take away the Collector once I drain him, but that thing will tear them to shreds…after it tears *me* to shreds. How did we not account for the Screecher?"

"Uh," Rinni said, showing his first ever sign of indecision. "Dude, just stay there. Don't move. He'll come back up to check out the echo-stone, but will eventually have to go back down to take care of Willow's army."

"Yeah, okay, but how do we beat him *now*? He's going to go back down and slaughter our whole army. I *have* to drain him."

Sam didn't need to check his video feed to know that the

time to think about his next move was over. He could hear the pulsing beat of the Screecher's wings as it approached. The beast let out another shriek as it landed on the balcony. Sam held his breath and willed his body to remain as still as a statue. Sam could hear the creaking and jingling of the Collector's metal armor as he approached the podium. Sam could imagine the Collector's confusion at seeing the balcony empty and yet hearing the foreign rock music still pumping out around the city.

Heavy footfalls landed on the steps of the podium. What was Sam going to do? He had to make a decision. He could end this battle. He could deal the emperor a defeat he never saw coming, but it may cost Sam his life. If he remained hidden, he would survive the moment, but how many more people and creatures would suffer at the hands of the Collector because of Sam's cowardice?

"Sam," Roanna cut in. "Help is on the way. Hold on, Sam."

"Milla? Where are you going?" Willow's voice came over the channel.

Sam scanned his video feeds to try and understand what was going on. It took him a moment to see it, but there was Milla, climbing the castle wall like a mini King Kong scaling the Empire State Building. Willow had looked after the gorilla-horse all this time, but Roanna still had control of the beast. Milla let out a roar as she drew closer. The Screecher, sensing some approaching danger, answered with a blood-curdling scream of its own.

"Pretty Roanna," Willow said, her voice carrying a hint of reproach. "Do not hurt Milla. Do *not* hurt my Milla, pretty Roanna."

Sam grabbed his phone and zoomed the camera in on the balcony just in time to see Milla launch herself from the castle wall and race toward the Screecher.

"I'm sorry, Willow," Roanna said as Milla vaulted into the air and tackled the Collector's winged monster, sending both of them over the balcony's ledge. "Do it now, Sam!"

Cornelius hadn't cowered before the Collector and neither would Sam. Not trusting his courage to last, Sam burst from his hiding spot and blindly grasped in front of him. He felt a stab of pain on his hands as he latched onto the sharp metal armor. The arctic blast of aether almost threw him backward, but he somehow managed to hang on. He pulled harder, forcing himself to plunge deeper into the blinding chill. Both Sam and the Collector screamed, one for the desperation of victory and the other for the shock of defeat.

Regaining his composure, the Collector reached down, grabbed the front of Sam's shirt, and yanked him out of his hiding spot like a farmer plucking a carrot from the dirt. Sam dangled at the end of the Inferno's grasp before being brought down to within inches of the Collector's sinister helmet. Sam held on to the Collector's hand and felt the aether continue to drain. He heard voices from behind. The escorts must have finally come to help. Just as Sam thought they'd won, the Collector reared back and threw Sam across the courtyard. He slammed into the wall on the far side of the balcony, whacking his head on the hard stone. He rolled over; his eyesight blurred. A dark shape disappeared over the balcony's ledge as Sam's vision faded to black.

41

THE LIVING AND THE DEAD

Sam opened his eyes, awakening from a dreamless sleep. He lay on a bed staring at an off-white ceiling, wondering where he was, as if his eyes had somehow gained consciousness before his brain. His memory came back in disconnected images and moments. Roanna looking over a city, nightmarish fish-skinned monsters skulking in dark tunnels, Cornelius dropping from the sky, Milla jumping through the air at the Screecher, and…the Collector. The pieces to Sam's memory started to form into a coherent image. His head throbbed. Sam turned to see the elaborate trappings of a castle room. Cornelius sat on a chair by his bed.

"Cornelius," Sam said weakly. "Are we…dead?"

"Dead? Well, I ain't dead, though I can only speak for myself." Cornelius stood up and walked over to the bedside table, where he poured a cup of water and handed it to Sam. "How many times do I got to come back from the brink before you realize that it's a tall order to kill off *this* cowboy?"

Sam took the cup and drank. "I guess you've got a point."

"You did good, kid, real good. The Collector managed to

slip away—the rat. I reckon he's not all that happy, never having lost before. His men are captured, dead, or fled."

"I bet the Collector will think twice before provoking the wrath of Cornelius again." Sam gave a small laugh that died when he saw the cowboy's expression turn.

Cornelius took a deep breath, his eyes suddenly distant. "Every man's got to control his own darkness, Sam, especially one as black as mine. Shouldn't have let myself go like that. Giving in to that part of ya can get ya killed...or worse."

Sam swallowed hard. He didn't profess to know much about Cornelius's past; he only knew there was a great deal of pain there, and pain was something Sam *did* know. "But how...how are you *not* dead? I saw you fall into the lake. There was no one within a mile to rescue you."

"Funny story, actually." Cornelius's face visibly relaxed. "I hit the water and thought I was a goner. I flailed around as long as I could manage, but started going down. Then out of the blue come two big sea cow critters to save my drowning hide. Goofiest-looking guardian angels I ever saw, but I never look a gift horse in the mouth."

"The dugongs?" Sam couldn't help but laugh. "No kidding. Willow told me they had actually come to see you. Looks like they got their chance."

"I reckon they did."

"You can't make this stuff up. Hey, how long was I out?" Sam pressed his hands against his pounding head.

"Only a day. You seem to be making a habit of it."

"Tell me about it."

"What I *will* tell you about is that you're a hero, kid. Legend of the great Techno Wizard has already spread across this city. They got banners with the letters 'TW' flying from every rooftop in the city. Word will get back to the emperor of what happened here, no doubt."

Sam never wanted to be a symbol of the Mavericks' rebellion, but he was quickly learning that life was less about what you wanted and more about what was required. He'd been dealt a very difficult hand in a very high stakes game, but if anyone could help him play his cards, it was Cornelius.

"So what do we do now?" Sam asked. "If what you say is true, the emperor will be after us in no time. What are you and Addi going to do with the Mavericks?"

"What am *I* going to do? Nothing. Addi offered me a position as a Maverick general, but I turned it down. I told you before that I ain't getting involved."

"Not involved?" Sam chuckled. "It's a bit too late for that, don't you think? What are you going to do, just march back to Ogland and play cards?"

"Nah." Cornelius shook his head. "I reckon I'll stay on for just a bit more and make sure you stay out of trouble."

Sam smiled. "What, like a bodyguard?"

"More like a very capable chaperone, I figure."

"Fair enough. Hey, did you find Lawrence?"

The cowboy shook his head. "I'm afraid we did not. There were a few vessels that got away when the fighting started. We're rather confident that he was on one of those ships."

"What makes you say that?"

"Dugongs again, actually. I guess Willow can talk to the dadgum things. They said they saw a boy being hustled off the island."

"You might think I'm crazy, Cornelius, but I have to go after him. Even after all he did to us. I still have to save him."

"I know, kid," Cornelius said, walking over to Sam and patting him on the shoulder. "Trust me. I know."

"Thank you, Cornelius. For everything."

"Don't need no thanks. Just keep doing what you're doing." Cornelius walked to the door. "You got a visitor, kid."

"Sam!" Roanna yelled as she ran past Cornelius and into the room. "You're awake. Are you alright?"

Sam nodded to the cowboy before turning back to Roanna. Her war paint was washed off and her battle clothes were swapped for more practical trousers and a tunic. Her hair remained in tight braids. Sam's stomach predictably stirred.

"It's good to see you," Sam said.

"We did it." Roanna's face was hope personified. "What you did was incredibly brave, Sam."

"I couldn't have done it without you. I mean, I couldn't even have gotten up to the echo-stone without you, let alone been able to grab hold of the Collector. I would be toast right now if you hadn't sent Milla up there. That was the last thing I remember seeing, actually, Milla tackling the blasted Screecher. What happened in the end? Is Milla okay?"

Roanna's hopeful face turned sullen. "She didn't make it, Sam. When I sent Milla to save you, I sent her to her death."

"Oh no," Sam said under his breath. "How's Willow?"

"I don't think she'll ever forgive me."

"What makes you say that?"

"When she said 'you are not pretty Roanna. You are heartless Roanna. I will never forgive you for sending Milla to her death, not even if I outlive the Eldest Tree.'"

"Oh," Sam said, pursing his lips. "Yeah, that's not good."

"I don't regret doing it, although I do regret having to. I'd make the same choice a hundred times over if it meant the Collector's downfall. We're at war now, Sam. Lots of Willow's animals died. Many Mavericks died. Addi told us that any victory worth having comes at a cost."

"And is that what you believe?" Sam asked. Roanna was as independent-minded as they came, but Sam felt like ever since they came to Trellston, she seemed to be taking a lot of her cues from Addi.

"It is," Roanna said, looking as confident as ever.

Something about the way Roanna spoke didn't sit well with Sam. He hadn't wanted Milla to die, even if the animal would have torn Sam in two if it wasn't placidated. The morality of placidating animals was something he'd yet to take a side on. He knew where Willow stood. She would say that the animals and

Mavericks had died fighting a war they chose to fight. Milla hadn't decided to climb that castle and fall to her death. That choice was made *for* her, and wasn't that what they were fighting against in the first place? Wasn't this fight against the emperor about overthrowing a force that sought to control the people of Avalon and take away their freedom? But how could Sam be anything but grateful? That decision to sacrifice Milla had saved his life and defeated the Collector. "Some questions have no right answers, just different answers." It was another pearl of wisdom from his father that Sam had never appreciated more than in this moment.

What irked Sam even more than the moral quandary of Milla's death was Roanna's apparent indifference to the whole ordeal. He didn't think any less of her for it, however. He empathized with the pain of her past and understood her yearning to set things right. Roanna's decisiveness had saved Sam's life, but he feared that it also might one day end it. To Roanna, Milla was a tool that, regrettably, had to be sacrificed to achieve a grander goal. Sam knew how much Roanna wanted this all to work. Her initial interest in Sam was purely based on his usefulness. He was hopeful that Roanna now saw Sam as a person first, a useful tool second. He prayed that the day would never come—like it had for Milla—when his usefulness in the moment outweighed the value of his life.

"So what's next?" Sam asked, trying to shake away the difficult thoughts.

"We gather our forces and strike again." Roanna's face was resolute. "No telling how much aether the Collector has left, but he'll regroup. He'll be back. Word of his defeat will spread like wildfire and we need to fan the flames. We've won at Trellston and we need to win again and again and again."

"But where do we actually *go* from here?" Sam asked.

"Addi says if we want to have a chance at taking on the emperor, we'll need help from the strongest in all of Avalon."

"What does that mean, exactly?"

"It means that we'll need to unite the three strongest kingdoms in Avalon with the help of their leaders: Zienna Rose, Ruler of the Wildland Kingdom of Trotterian; Olen, Lord of the Volcanus Region; and High Queen Abrigail of the Greenlands. I'm told they all like the emperor about as much as we do."

"That's awesome," Sam said.

"Yes, it is, but I'm also told they like each other even less."

"That's not so awesome."

"No, it isn't." Roanna shook her head. "They're powerful, but thus far they haven't come out in open rebellion against the emperor. By themselves they would be crushed, but together, we may just have a fighting chance."

"And you think we can do it?"

"With the legendary Techno Wizard," Roanna arched an eyebrow, "I'd say just about anything is possible."

EPILOGUE

Sam's phone rang. He checked his reflection in his screen and smoothed his hair over before answering the call.

"Hey, Mom."

"Samwise!" Sam's mom yelped, tears already forming in her eyes. "You're alive. You're okay."

"Yeah, of course I am, Mom. Why wouldn't I be okay?"

"Why wouldn't you be okay?" Sam's mom repeated as if it were the most ridiculous question she'd ever been asked. "Well, for starters, you send cryptic texts that sound like some kind of last goodbye, then you don't return my messages, and the next time I see you is online in the middle of some war zone."

"You saw that?" Sam cringed.

"The whole *world* saw that, Samwise. Your friend Rinni, whom you have no issue contacting and explaining your plans to in detail by the way, decided to stream the video feed to the entire planet from your cameras and drone. I've had every news personality in existence contact me for an interview, all the while they know as much as I do, since my blessed portal-traveling son won't return my texts or calls."

Sam sat wide-eyed, taking the scolding. It seemed like such a weird thing to be reprimanded by your mother after pulling off something so objectively epic, but in truth, he *had* kind of left his mom out of the loop lately. Sam hated the eye of the hurricane.

"I'm sorry, Mom." Maybe it was the half-dozen near-death experiences, or the time he'd spent away from home, or the tough decisions he'd recently had to make, but Sam found himself actually meaning his apology, not just saying it to get her off his back. "You're right. I should've told you the truth. I know this can't be easy on you."

Sam's mom let out a sigh. "It's not easy. I'll give you that. I'm worried for you all the time. I don't understand what's going on. No one does. Some of the greatest minds on Earth are trying to figure out how this happened. There are no answers. I just want you to come home, Sam. I've already lost your father. I can't lose you."

Sam's mom wiped at her eyes. Sam had very rarely seen his mother cry. She'd always been a rock. Sam had, on occasion, heard her cry from the other room, but whenever she came out she was a monument of strength. She didn't do it because it was easy; she did it for her son. Sam had never appreciated his mom more than right now. It was as if he'd never really tallied the magnitude of her sacrifice until this moment, and the total was staggering.

"Don't worry, Mom," Sam said, fighting back tears of his own. "That handsome cowboy said he'll watch out for me."

Sam's mom laughed through the tears. "I'm glad to hear it. I love you, Sam."

"I love you too, Mom. The signal is still spotty, but I promise to keep you in the loop more."

"That will be nice."

"Gotta go." Sam waved to his mom and hung up the call. Before he could pocket his phone, Rinni was calling.

"The Techno Wizard lives," Rinni said, with a wide smile. "I feared the worst, dude. How do you feel?"

"Relieved and a bit like I got hit by a bus. Is there a word for that?"

"Victory."

"Yeah, well, I couldn't have done it without you, man. Who knew your mad video game skills would actually come in handy one day, huh?"

"Uh, I did," Rinni replied. "Dude, Sam. We're famous."

"Yeah, my mom told me." Sam shook his head. "You realize the trouble that got me into, right? She saw the whole thing."

"Sam." Rinni leveled an incredulous stare. "I don't think you're hearing me, man. We're *famous*. The whole world thinks you're some kind of superhero. Quake Boy has become the Techno Wizard. They're selling Techno Wizard T-shirts online. I even heard talk of a Netflix show already in development. People are reaching out from all over to help."

"Help?" Sam asked, raising his eyebrows. "How can anyone help?"

"Dude," Rinni said, eyes wide. "I've got everyone from medieval historians to modern-day engineers contacting me and posting YouTube videos they want us to see. Anything from instructions on how to help the Mavericks construct simple machines all the way to building advanced weaponry. One guy even claims he could bring Avalon to an Industrial Revolution level of technology in five years. That's like total steampunk gadgets and stuff. Oh, and I got like a hundred dudes who want to step you through how to manufacture bullets for Cornelius's pistol."

"Whoa," Sam nodded. "That's actually pretty awesome."

"Tell me about it. Master Commander Rinni can go into any forum on the entire Internet and I'm immediately treated like royalty. I got an email like five minutes ago inviting me to Comic Con. *Comic Con.* They want to give me an award, or trophy or something. This is like a dream come true, Sam."

"Nightmares are dreams too," Sam said. "You living the same dream where scary monsters and magical bad guys are trying to kill you at every turn? Here, let me go outside and slay a dragon so you can get nominated for an Oscar."

"Dude, *someone's* got to make the best of a bad situation."

Sam wasn't honestly mad. How could he be? Yet it was weird to hear that he was a worldwide celebrity when he wasn't even *in* the world. Sam had just won the lottery, but got paid in currency he couldn't spend anywhere.

"Well, live it up for the both of us, Mr. Celebrity," Sam said.

"Don't you worry about that. It's not all just sunshine and rainbows, Sam. Working on our brand doesn't happen by itself, you know?"

"Our *brand?*"

"Uh, yeah," Rinni raised both eyebrows, "over the last few days, the 'Techno Wizard and Commander' YouTube channel has the fourth most views of any channel online. I want us on top."

"The *fourth* most views?" Sam scrunched up his face. "The world's only known inter-dimensional traveler has an epic battle that liberates a city from an evil mage knight and we're only fourth? Who is possibly pulling in more viewers than that?"

"Well, let's see." Rinni held out his fingers to count them off. "We have the guy who records himself opening up chocolate eggs, the lady who unwraps Disney toys, and the forty-five-year-old dude who streams Digcraft 5000 tutorials."

"You're kidding me, right?"

"No, man, the egg guy had limited-edition Easter chocolates from 2020. That's stiff competition."

"We'll just have to up our game, apparently. I'll try doing it next time with one hand tied behind my back," Sam said, glancing at his signal strength. "Looks like we're about out of time. You got anything else?"

"Oh yeah, I can't believe I forgot to tell you."

"Forgot to tell me what?"

"Another piece to the puzzle. I put that drone footage of Borinder Besselink's collection on our channel and the Internet went crazy. I've had everyone from respected history professors to wacko conspiracy theorists reaching out to me for more information. They're trying to piece together the clues on the connection between Avalon and Earth."

"And?"

"There are lots of theories, but the one thing they agree on is that most of the items trace back to around the twelfth or thirteenth century. They think that's when a whole lot of people may have gotten transported over at once."

"Okay, but how does this help me?" Sam asked.

"Listen to this. The people in your world call it Avalon and speak English for a reason. I was messaging a professor from Oxford who says there was a big earthquake in Syria during the Crusades. It destroyed a British Crusader castle. Most records talk about the bodies not being found, but I don't think there were bodies *to* find."

"You think they all came over here?"

"All nine hundred of them."

"Interesting, but I still don't see how that helps me."

"It helps you," Rinni leaned in closer to the camera, "because that Oxford professor has an account from the thirteenth century that historians have always dismissed as a fairy tale."

"Which is?"

"A monk claiming to have been transported to and *returned* from a 'heavenly world of magic and snow-topped mountains.'"

Sam's face went slack. "Tell me everything you know."

ACKNOWLEDGMENTS

Although I began writing this book in October of 2016, the journey to publication began much earlier than that. Sometime in the fall of 2008, I got the crazy idea that I wanted to become an author. Why that fleeting thought stuck so completely to my bones, I'll never know. We had just moved to Texas to start my career in the energy industry and were up to our necks in dirty diapers. My plate was pretty full. The pull to develop my own world and tell my own story, however, was unrelenting. I hadn't taken an English class since high school, but writing was in my blood and telling stories was in my DNA. And so, not knowing where I was going, I set out to write a book.

Like many naive, self-assured, aspiring authors, I decided to cut my teeth on the most ambitious and epic idea I could devise. For years I tried to soak up everything I could and write whenever I had the chance. Through crippling injuries, family tragedies, international relocations, and life in general, I wrote. Because of a back injury, I would often write while lying down on the ground. I'm sure my wife could give you a more accurate estimate of how many times she found me asleep on the ground in some random corner of the house at some ridiculous hour of the night with my laptop splayed open on my chest, but it's in the hundreds. I listened to podcasts and audiobooks, attended writers retreats, watched online lectures, and gave up hobbies, all in the pursuit of writing.

After seven years, I had finished multiple drafts of a 200,000 word epic fantasy behemoth entitled *A Place Among Heroes*. Although the story remains unpublished, it was during those years that I refined my craft enough to where I could write *The Techno Wizard* books. I owe a huge debt to the folks who spent hours and hours beta reading early drafts of my fledgling attempt at my first novel.

In the very beginning there was Jordan Pomeroy, Drew Hausen, Jon Boldt, Eric Detton, James Van Duker, Steve Thayer and others who read my early drafts, brainstormed, and gave me encouragement and feedback.

In my Australia years, there was the unrivaled Scott Laidlaw, to whom I owe dearly for his surgically detailed review and edits, his willingness to always talk shop, his confidence in my ability, and the collector's edition Lord of the Rings Pez dispenser set (which remains unopened to this day). There was James Stevenson, for his interest in the story, revelatory insight, and being my main Aussie culture insider. My brother, James Thayer, for all the time he put into reading my draft and for all the time he spent trying to figure out how to get me his notes.

Special thanks to Alexander Verbeek and Alissa Leonard, who both took the time to beta read an experimental book when I split *A Place Among Heroes* into two. Much of their feedback was what sealed the deal and helped me make up my mind that I needed to try my hand at something else from scratch.

Thanks to Mrs. Goode's 2nd grade class in Sale, Australia, for being the first school group to listen to me talk about writing...*well* before I was published.

Without all of these people I couldn't have even attempted to write *Passage to Avalon*. It was one of the hardest decisions of my life to shelf *A Place Among Heroes*, but once I made up my mind and moved on to *Passage to Avalon*, I knew I had made the right decision.

I have many more folks to thank for help on *Passage to Avalon*. I'd first like to Annie Condon, Benson Thayer, James Thayer, and Clark Rowenson for their beta reads and helping me polish the story, highlight the cool stuff, and cut the lame stuff.

Thanks to my editor (Laurie Klaass), my pair of Italian artists (Carmine Pucci and RenflowerGrapx), my cover designer (Deranged Doctor Design), and my proofreader Claudette Cruz. These five professionals helped take my book to the next level, and I am forever grateful. If I couldn't make a book that I was confident could stand next to the books from the big publishers, then I didn't want to make a book. These folks helped make it happen.

I owe a lot to Frank Morin for his endless patience and timely advice on all things self-publishing. He was an absolute lifesaver.

Thanks to Katie Thompson's 5th grade class at Laurel Middle School, whose letters of encouragement kept me going through the tough times. Thanks for Matthew and Addi for their great questions.

Special thanks to authors Dan Wells, Amie Kaufman, and Brian Staveley who owed me nothing, but were always accessible and always took the time to give me advice when I asked.

Thanks to my "Street Team" for getting pumped about my book and helping create some buzz: Aaron Brewster, Kaylin Booker, CoDele Lurker, Ethan Luker, Jon Boldt, James Van Duker, John Wilson, Clark Rowenson, Naomi Cranston, Krystal DiPeri, Poppy Grout, Melinda Neist, and Helen Isitt.

Thanks to my sister, Katie Willson, for her keen insight on design and branding and helping me make the right professional decisions in bringing this story to the world.

Thanks to my kids, Abby, Owen, and Sienna, who always supported me and kept me going. I'm grateful for their numerous dinner table prayers of " please help dad to publish his book." They've always known how much this book meant to me. Special thanks to Abby for being *Passage to Avalon*'s biggest fan from day one, always pushing me to write more, demanding I write the next chapter so I could read it to her before she went to bed (pretty sure she just wanted to stay up late, but whatever), and for unwittingly providing the inspiration for Willow.

Thanks to my mom for her always honest, always loving feedback and for teaching me to murder my darlings and stop overwriting (I'm still working on it).

Thanks to my late father for his advice, his humor, his example, and for passing on the soul of a storyteller. I gave everything I had for nearly a decade to be able to stand by my dad in this life as a published author, and I missed it by five months. If not in this life, then surely in the next. If nothing else, writing this book was cathartic as I contemplated his impending passing and then brought solace after the fact.

Above all else, I would like to thank my wife, who was always supportive, never complained about my ridiculous goal, and who—more often than not—fell asleep alone while her husband was up creating other worlds.

I can't believe I finally, finally, finally made it.

STUDY GUIDE

1. In *Passage to Avalon*, the story starts out in the year 2032. The author imagines a world slightly different than the one we live in today (2018). Things like self-driving cars and mini-drones are more commonplace. How do *you* think the world will be different in 2032? 2072? 2102? Why?

2. During his adventures, Sam is betrayed by both new acquaintances and old friends. Did you guess that these betrayals would happen? What clues did you have? Should Sam have known better than to trust these people? Why or why not?

3. How did Sam change and grow as a person as a result of his adventures? What does he do or say as evidence of this change?

4. How did Roanna change and grow as a person as a result of her adventures? What does she do or say as evidence of this change?

5. Who was your favorite character in the story? Why? What do you want to see them do or accomplish?

6. Who was your least favorite character in the story? Why? What would you change about them?

7. What was your favorite part of the story? Why?

8. What part of the story surprised you the most?

9. Toward the end of the novel, Sam questions the morality of placidating animals. Do you think it would be okay to placidate animals? How is using aether to control animals different than the emperor using an aether tax to control the people of Avalon?

10. Many great stories follow similar structures, plot progressions, and patterns. The author outlined this book using the Seven Point Story Structure. Can you identify each of these points in the story?

   1. Inciting Incident — The event that kicks off the story.
   2. Plot Turn 1 — The point of no return. The Hero sets off on his/her adventure. No turning back!
   3. Pinch point 1 — Conflict is introduced or ramped up. The Hero gets a taste of the bad guys' power.
   4. Midpoint — The Hero moves from reactive to proactive. The Hero stops running and decides to fight back!
   5. Pinch point 2 — More conflict is introduced. By the end, the Hero is in his/her darkest moment and seems further from his/her goal than ever.
   6. Plot turn 2 — The Hero acquires the last thing he/she needs to achieve his/her goal.
   7. Resolution — The Hero succeeds…or doesn't!

GLOSSARY OF TERMS AND CHARACTERS - CONTAINS SPOILERS

- ADDI GLEASON: Accomplished blacksmith and leader of the Trellston Mavericks who fought with Cornelius in the battles of the north.
- AETHER: Magical force that radiates throughout all of Avalon.
- AVALON: Parallel world to Earth where aether permeates all living and non-living things.
- BLAZER: Aether tier above Sparker. Can placidate animals. Aether level common to lords, knights, businessmen, and local magistrates.
- BORINDER BESSELINK: Guild Lord of Hagzarad and collector of rare and unique items.
- THE COLLECTOR: Inferno-level enforcer for the emperor who specializes in quelling cities and retrieving missing aether tax. Rides atop a dragon-bat hybrid and collects mementos from his most notable victims. Has a penchant for hunting down cowboys.
- CORNELIUS THOMPSON IV: Leech and cowboy of the purest blood. Passive member of the Ogland

Mavericks who fled from the battles in the north to seek a quiet life of smoking his pipe and playing cards.
- DRAINER: One who can destroy aether without using aether of their own.
- ELDEST TREE: The oldest and most powerful of the Nartareen. Uses the collective aether of the Nartareen race to grant miracles to those she deems worthy.
- EMPEROR: Ruler of Avalon and only human to reach Eternal tier.
- ENHANCED: Soldiers of the Collector that have been granted enhanced characteristics through grafting and hybridization.
- EQUINE-APE: See GORILLA-HORSE
- ETERNAL: Highest tier of aether possession. Extent of abilities is largely unknown.
- GIDEON VANDUKER: A traveler and trader of rare and exotic goods.
- GORILLA-HORSE: Rhino-sized hybridized animal with gorilla-like facial features, long arms, clawed hands, and shaggy fur.
- GRAFTING: Process by which aether is used to augment a living thing with inanimate material.
- GURN: One of the first two thugs that Sam meets upon arriving in Avalon. Has a grafted wooden hand and a deep voice like a bullfrog.
- HAGZARAD: City at the northern tip of Lake Vista and home to the largest black market in the South Isle.
- HAYDN: Steward of Borinder Besselink. Has grafted fingers of precious stones.
- HYBRIDIZATION: Similar to grafting, it is the process by which aether is used to augment a living thing with parts from other living things. Extreme

hybridization is used to create new species of animals.
- INFERNO: Second highest tier of aether possession. Level reached by kings and queens, rulers of races, and the emperor's most powerful enforcers.
- JERG: Hulking member of the Trellston Mavericks.
- LaRUE OVERLY: Head housemaid at Trellston Castle and longstanding member of the Mavericks.
- LAWRENCE BRINTWORTH: King of worthless information, blown pranks, and one of Sam's best friends.
- LEAGUE OF COWBOYS: Group of cowboy Leeches descendant from the first cowboy who arrived in Avalon ~1870 A.D.
- LEECH: Aether level designation several generations removed from a Void. Is limited in the total amount of aether he/she is able to possess but has the unique ability to use aether on his/her own body, increasing speed, health, strength, etc. Cannot infuse aether into other objects.
- MATTHIAS ABROMITE: AKA the Corpseman. Undertaker who ferries the deceased from the island of Trellston to the city cemetery.
- MAVERICKS: Rebel group who opposes the emperor and his aether tax.
- MILLA: A gorilla-horse that joins Sam, Cornelius, Roanna, and Willow after being placidated.
- MONGREL: A distorted and grotesque creature that is the outcome of a failed species hybridization.
- MUSKTEER GUILD: Group descended from musketeers who came over to Avalon ~1650AD. Have all but lost their ability to drain aether.
- NARTAREEN: A dryad-like race of tree people who live in the forest and are lead by an Eldest Tree.

- OGLAND: Walled town east of the Sea Cliffs and south of the Vale of Edgemont.
- PLACIDATION: When an animal is drained of its natural aether and infused with the aether of another being for the purposes of controlling that animal. It is a practice of controversial morality.
- REYNOLD: One of the first two thugs that Sam meets upon arriving in Avalon. Has a grafted cat eye and has an unpleasantly squeaky voice.
- RINNIVAS MANIKHANTAN: Sam's best friend and technophile. He holds a fourth place standing on the worldwide leaderboard for the computer game *Warcraft of Empires*.
- ROANNA: Adolescent aether prodigy and member of the Ogland faction of the Mavericks.
- SAMWISE SHELTON: Prankster extraordinaire from Bozeman, MT who gets inexplicably transported to the land of Avalon during an earthquake. Later called the Techno Wizard for his power as a Void drainer and his control of his technological gear.
- SCORCHER: Tier of Aether possession above Blazer but below Inferno. Enables one to detect aether levels in other individuals by sight (within a certain distance). Has the ability to graft and hybridize. Typical level of Named warriors, Noblemen, Princes/Princesses.
- SCREECHER: The Collector's large, dragon-like creature famous for its terrifying scream.
- SPARKER: Lowest tier of aether possession. Typical level of farmers, peasants, and craftsmen.
- TRELLSTON: Beautiful island city on the east side of Lake Alexandra.
- VENDRIN: Member of the Trellston Mavericks and advisor to Addi Gleason.
- VOID: Completely without aether. Term is used to

describe those who are completely incompatible with aether to the point that they can drain limitless amounts by touch.
- WILLOW: A young member of the Nartareen race, she is a fascinated with humans and is the first in Avalon to befriend Sam.
- ZIPTALK APOLLO: Shatterproof, waterproof, shockproof, and solar-powered. It is the very latest in cell phone technology and Sam's birthday present from his mother.

THE EPIC ADVENTURE
CONTINUES IN BOOK TWO:

THE UNCHARTED LANDS

ABOUT THE AUTHOR

Mike Thayer is a proud father of three, lucky husband of one, passionate author, viral blogger, degreed engineer, decent impressionist, inept hunter, erstwhile jock, and nerd.

He has cast a ring on the slopes of Mt. Doom, eaten a feast at the Green Dragon Inn, cemented Excalibur in a sandstone block, tasted butter beer at Diagon Alley, built a secret door to his storage room, and written a fantasy novel. What else is left, really?

Website: www.TheTechnoWizardBooks.com
Blog: www. Mike-Thayer.com

youtube.com/Thaydawg
facebook.com/MikeThayerAuthor
instagram.com/MikeThayer

Made in the USA
Las Vegas, NV
23 July 2021